I too Hear the Drums

STORIES

PETA-GAYE NASH

2014

I TOO HEAR THE DRUMS

STORIES

by Peta-Gaye Nash

Published by: In Our Words, Inc.
inourwords.ca

Editor: Cheryl Antao-Xavier

Design: Shirley Aguinaldo

Cover Photo: © Aviron/Dreamstime.com

Library and Archives Canada Cataloguing in Publication

Nash, Peta-Gaye, author
I too hear the drums : stories / Peta-Gaye Nash. -- Revised edition.
ISBN 978-1-926926-44-5 (pbk.)
I. Title.
PS8627.A776I86 2014 C813'.6 C2014-907926-5

First Printing, September 2010
Second Edition, December 2014

0 1 2 3 4 5 6 7 8 9

For Dominique, Reine, Jade, Liam and Meadow
who mean everything

And for Wayne Brown, in memory

Acknowledgements

I would like to thank my publisher Cheryl Antao-Xavier. This book would not have been possible without her.

Thanks also to my creative and unique family members who are sources of inspiration – my grandmothers, mother, father, stepfather, sisters and all my aunts. They have rallied around me on this journey and celebrated my successes. Special thanks to my mother who sent me those first short story newspaper cut-outs that helped me to see that stories don't have to be novels; Rachel and Lindsay who have been supportive and have never stopped believing in me; and Reine and Jade who babysit to give me my "writing time."

Leeanne, thank you for your friendship.

Finally to my amazing husband, Dominique, because housework doesn't stop and meals don't get prepared on their own. A very special thank you for all you do.

Contents

1977

During the summer of 1977, my parents stopped talking to my Aunt Rita and Uncle Frank.

Aunt Rita and Uncle Frank were not my real aunt and uncle by blood, but in the way of our culture, close family, friends and even some acquaintances were called auntie this and uncle that. It would've been rude to call an adult by their first name, and too formal to call those we saw every Sunday dinner 'Mr. and Mrs. So and So.' Older adults, friends of my grandparents, or old Mrs. Eubanks next door, who wore deodorant under her neck because she had a double chin and sweated, were always 'Mr.' or 'Mrs.' It wasn't strange to me then, only now so, because my children, growing up in America, call all adults except their teachers, by their first name.

In 1977 my family migrated to America. Aunt Rita and Uncle Frank had gone on before us and migrated six months earlier. Before that, we saw them almost every Sunday. Either we went to their house, or they came to ours along with other couples. Sometimes we took trips to the country together and the proof is there, in old dusty yellowed photo albums of us all in a vaguely-remembered beach house with a pool, sitting on lounge chairs, smiling for the camera. Albums my parents never look at anymore.

I remember Sundays best. At our house, the adults arrived around 2 and chatted over drinks while our maids Doris and Cynthia sweated and quarrelled over the ham and roast beef, the baked sweet potato and marshmallows, the rice and peas, the plantain, and the green salad my mother insisted should accompany every meal. The lunch would be ready at 5 and we ate with our plates on our lap, except the younger children who sat at tray tables on the verandah.

By 8 or 9 o'clock the women would be begging their husbands to stop the drinking and go home because the children had school the next day. The men, laughing and getting louder, either ignored their wives or enjoined them in some flirtatious banter. My mother and Aunt Rita, school friends from high school since first form, tidied up and whispered conspiratorially about how Jenny McDonald got a little too tipsy and flirted with their husbands, how she sat a little too close for comfort and how they wished they didn't have to invite her but they had to since her husband Martin and my father were close friends.

Those were good times when everyone we knew lived nearby and families were huge because the mass migration had not yet begun. There was a sense of euphoria and up-and-comingness in the air. I knew it because my father bought a new car, a Mercedes Benz, and we moved from a small two-bedroom bungalow into a large sprawling four-bedroom house in Norbrook even though I was an only child and we didn't need the space. It was a line I'd heard my father's mother say to my mother each time she visited. "But my dear, you really don't need all this space."

Aunt Rita and Uncle Frank also bought a new car and moved from their small house in Mona to a large house in Stony Hill where, at night, I'd stand on their verandah mesmerized by the twinkling lights of Kingston.

"See that down there," Uncle Frank would say taking my hand. "That large black space, that's Kingston Harbour."

In retrospect, that time felt to me quite Gatsbyish. Of course I only know that now having read the book, but there was an air of decadence and wealth, where my parents' generation was carving out a new way, with their wild parties, disco-dancing and the club scene. They flaunted their new wealth extravagantly and to my grandparents, tastelessly. Men started to run around with each other's wives, something my grandmother insisted simply was not done in her generation. "Oh, there were the few rotten eggs," she'd say dismissively, but nothing compared to how it is now. "I don't like what's going on. Don't like how the world is going."

And then it seemed to me that it disappeared quite suddenly. There was talk of violence and of things changing. My father and Uncle Frank said the country was being ruined a little more every day. There was talk in hushed voices, of Communism and Castro, of guns coming from Cuba, of hard times and murder, and migration.

"Everyday somebody gone and so secretly," Aunt Rita said, "Who is going to be left here?"

"Nobody you'll want your daughter associating with," Uncle Frank warned my parents, nodding in my direction.

The air got heavy and tense and I sensed a pervading gloom.

"But of course it is that way," said my mother when I tried to articulate my feelings. "It's all doom and gloom around here. It's all downhill for Jamaica now."

People left in droves, what is now called the brain drain. It was decided we'd go too, my mother and father, Aunt Rita and Uncle Frank, their newborn daughter and I, to Florida, where my father and Uncle Frank would start a business. Almost every evening Aunt Rita and Uncle Frank came over to plan. They sat, by candlelight if we had a power cut which was often, talking softly.

I loved those times. They were insecure yet I felt secure, more than I've ever felt since then. I was cocooned and doted on by Uncle Frank and Aunt Rita. Uncle Frank was a pilot for Air Jamaica and on one of his trips he bought me a Barbie doll. She was different from the plastic yellow-haired pouty-mouth Barbies of the time. Her eyes were large and wide and she had real-looking blonde hair. I was the only child on the block to have this coveted piece of First World. I've never forgotten it and even after all that happened, I still think of him fondly.

Frank and Rita started to siphon US dollars out of the island slowly on Frank's trips. My mother warned my father to do the same but he complained that the dollars were hard to come by. My mother had wanted to travel to Miami and open a bank account. Frank could make monthly deposits so by the time we arrived, we'd have a large amount and could set ourselves up in a nice neighbourhood. My father said it wasn't necessary. He had a plan.

It was my mother who saved her salary, bought the US dollars from an Air Jamaica clerk and hid it away, locked it in an old suitcase on the top of the closet in an unused guest room. She trusted the Air Jamaica clerk because he'd been an old boyfriend of her sister's. Hopefully, she said to herself back then, hopefully that counted for something, because people were reporting one another and you couldn't 'talk your business' openly any more. These actions were to save us and later my mother would say, "In life, you have to follow your intuition. You can't wait on no man to guide you. They think they know everything but they don't know anything. They have two heads but they think with one."

Frank and Rita left first. They sold their house in Stony Hill and bought a house in South Florida. Uncle Frank still flew from Jamaica and commuted to Miami. Aunt Rita found work in a department store and she kept moving up, to manager and then moving on and opening her own retail store selling formal dresses. I know this because once, walking the malls with my mother in 1985, I saw her boutique, 'Rita's Fashion World,' and in the window was an emerald green, sweetheart neckline dress. I wanted that dress but my mother ushered me past the store, her body shrinking with distaste and the edges of her mouth pulled down as if she'd just had cough syrup.

"I would never buy anything from that witch."

"Who's a witch, Mommy?'

Her face acquired an anxious, worried expression.

"You remember Rita Scott, Frank and Rita Scott?"

I did and I missed them. My parents had no close friends in Miami, preferring to stick to themselves. I remember thinking how much life had changed, how much they had changed. My mother and I sat down in the food court and ordered hamburgers and French fries.

She leaned toward me on the small grey plastic table and whispered angrily, "Frank and Rita migrated first. I had been ready for years but your father, slow as always to make up his mind, hated change and did not make the decision to go."

She said the decision was made for him after a series of horrible incidents.

First, our house was broken into while we were in Negril for a long weekend. Our TV, stereo and my mother's jewelry were gone. My mother had gasped when we walked in.

"Don't touch anything," commanded my father. "They could still be here."

She didn't listen. She ran hurtling over the piles of clothes strewn on the floor around the room. She took the stairs two or three at a time and darted into the guest room. She collapsed to the floor sobbing with relief when she saw the suitcase still there with all the money. By then she'd saved two thousand US dollars.

Then, only two weeks later, coming home from Harbour View Drive-In, as we stepped out of our car, two men stepped from the bushes and held knives to my parents' throats. My mother, thinking she'd be raped, stood still while they cut off her thick gold chain. She thought about her grade school teacher and when she was a child and happy. She closed her eyes while they unclasped her gold bracelet and pulled off her rings and prayed they wouldn't hurt me, standing frozen by the car door. My father stood defenseless, weaponless, his face ashen grey. The incident had humiliated him. He had wet his pants. As quickly as the men came, they left, leaving us unharmed.

The final straw came six months later when a close colleague of my father's was murdered in his home one night. The papers said it was cold-blooded murder. It was then my parents decided it was time to migrate.

My mother stopped talking as we sat at the table in the food court of the mall. She didn't tell me why Rita Scott was a witch. Through the years I gleaned bits and pieces from her angry words along with my memories and came to know the story.

One evening back then in the spring of 1977 when the poui trees had shed their flowers like a Japanese garden and it had rained many afternoons keeping me indoors with paper dolls and colouring books, my parents came home early and giggled like school children over dinner. We'd eaten that night like a Sunday, with roast beef, rice and peas, cream-styled corn, salad and wine for the adults. An Englishman who lived in New York had bought our house with cash, in US. Thirty thousand dollars. We had the money to set ourselves up in Kendall near Frank and Rita. My father would open the business with Frank. Frank would still fly for the airlines and my father would be the operations manager.

My mother ran her fingers lovingly over the walls of our sold house and said she was a little sad but our country had hit rock bottom. In America, our new house would be bigger and better and there would be no need for grills, padlocks or gates. We would be starting a new life. The politicians were crooks, she said, and even people in business had begun to be dishonest. She was upset that a pharmacy she supplied declared bankruptcy so they wouldn't have to pay their suppliers the full amount they owed. These were the terms of the Bankruptcy Act, but my mother had a cousin in Cayman who worked at the bank where the owners of the pharmacy had stashed all their money. My mother always spoke about this because she'd been depending on that money to help fill her suitcase. "The world is small, Ingrid," she said. "There are no secrets. Not for long."

The problem then, was how to get all the money out of the island. The solution was determined over a stew peas and rice dinner with Uncle Frank one Friday evening. The bougainvillea rustled in the night breeze and a full moon hung low in the sky. I was sent to bed but couldn't sleep. There was tension and excitement in the air.

I sat at the foot of the stairs and watched the heads of the adults talking. My father's head, shiny and bald, nodded vigorously. Uncle Frank's head, a shock of shiny black curls and the dandruff I knew which powdered the strands, held his head erect. His face was serious and his thick black moustache twitched. My mother, running her fingers through short brown roller-set hair, seemed anxious. The money on the table, counted and put in piles and bound with a caramel-coloured elastic band, was put into Frank's suitcase. Chances are he would not be searched when leaving the country. He would keep the money until we arrived the following month.

The day we left Jamaica, I thought: I won't see my country for a long time. I won't see my friends, my teachers and the sea sparkling like diamonds on both sides of the Palisadoes Road. I remember it clearly because it was the first time I'd seen my parents fight, first time I'd seen my father speak harshly to my mother. He called her a stupid ass because she hadn't included the money from the suitcase, her two thousand, with the house money in Frank's briefcase.

My father spoke with clenched teeth, his voice low and ominous.

"It's trouble for us now. Pure trouble, and all because of one person's stupidity."

He kissed his teeth and continued his rant. "Fifty-five dollars is what we can take out and the foolish woman taking a chance. Stupid, stupid woman."

My mother sat silent and uncomfortable, two thousand dollars taped to her stomach. She wore a navy blue pantsuit and I smelled her sweat mingled with Chanel No. 5 perfume and the upholstery in the rented car we drove to the airport. I smelled the heat, the road, the sea and when we got to the airport, the perspiration of the crowd waiting in line to check in.

When we got through customs without being searched, my father's steps quickened in a run to board the plane. He squeezed my mother's hand.

"Let's not get too excited yet. We're not out of the danger zone yet."

My mother did not respond. Her face was stern and set, her jaw clenched and her eyes lowered. I had to run to keep up with them. The bright sunlight bounced off the plane and I shaded my eyes.

"Miami will be hot and sunny too," my father said, glancing back at me.

Frank and Rita picked us up from the airport. I knew at once something had changed. They were unusually quiet. My father, in the front seat beside Frank, asked if everything had gone well and Frank nodded gravely. We were to stay with them until we bought our own house, which would happen quickly Aunt Rita had assured my mother when they'd sat on our verandah on those cool dusky evenings.

When we arrived, I ran about Rita's house mesmerized. Everything was new and clean and large. They sent me outside to play on a perfectly manicured lawn with trimmed hedges bordering both neighbours. A taxi drove up and my mother and father came out with our suitcases. That was the last time my parents spoke to Aunt Rita and Uncle Frank.

My parents refused to tell me what had happened. In the hotel that night, my mother's voice came through the thin-as-paper walls.

"Look who's the stupid ass now, eh? Look."

My father's voice, low and weary: "Shut up."

My mother again: "If it wasn't for my money taped around my backside, we couldn't afford this hotel. Couldn't afford food for Ingrid. Who's the stupid ass now?"

I heard her crying that night but she seemed to have recovered the next morning. She said Uncle Frank had stolen our money and given some silly excuse but it was obvious he'd been lying because Aunt Rita had looked ashamed and guilty. There had been an argument and angry words were exchanged, words so bitter forgiveness wasn't possible.

A month later, my father told my mother that although he would never trust Frank again, it hadn't been Frank's fault entirely. He'd got heart palpitations that day and was sweating excessively so he couldn't fly. He thought he might have been having a heart attack but it had only been his nerves. He'd handed the briefcase to a stewardess he'd trusted with his life. At my mother's raised brows, he said Frank trusted this woman because he'd been having an affair with her for two years. She claimed she had put the briefcase on top of the rental car after she had arrived and forgot about it. Only while speeding down the highway two minutes later did she remember and realized it wasn't there. By the time she exited and circled around, the briefcase was gone.

This near-white uptown Jamaican stewardess wasn't a nobody. She'd had no reason to steal the money, reasoned Frank to my father. To cover the affair, Frank told Rita the briefcase had been stolen from the airport. Rita never found out about the affair.

"And who really knows," said my mother, "Frank could be lying about that too. You can't trust a soul."

My parents never recovered, neither financially nor emotionally. In 1980 when the JLP won the election and people, hopeful and optimistic returned home to rebuild the island, my parents stayed in Miami in a small apartment still trying to make ends meet. My mother cleaned for other people, a job I know humiliated her because she never told another Jamaican what she did for a living. My father pumped gas in an out of the way gas station. Their bitterness remained a stain on their souls, a deep wound unhealed by time. They still spoke of the Seventies as if it happened yesterday, as if they still had no choice in their lives today. They spoke as if some imminent threat remained on the island, some dark curse had ousted them from their rightful place and they behaved as though they were exiled.

I saw the same pattern in others: the construction worker I passed on a bench in my lunch hour passionately discussing the Seventies to his uncomprehending work crew. My middle-aged uncle in Toronto resigned to his role as a mere office clerk and a number, no longer the big man down at the head office in Kingston. The ones who healed moved on. They either adjusted to their new country or they returned home and dealt with Jamaica as it is now, new problems, some worse than the time in the Seventies.

My parents continued the pattern of bickering and insulting each other and still do to this day, except in rare moments, like when I was to graduate from high school. My father came home one evening and sat wearily on the sofa. He told my mother he'd seen Frank Scott that day. He'd filled his car for him. It was a new BMW. My mother said nothing, only held my father's gaze and her stern expression softened. I understood. Their jobs were among the lowest back home and even in the 'promised land' they had never moved up. They'd tried, but in my mother's words, "it had never worked out."

Another time, I sat, hot and uncomfortable in my graduating cap and gown while waiting for my name to be called. This time, I was graduating from medical school. My father had worked two jobs for ten years to put me through.

The girl beside me nudged my arm. "Are those your parents? That old man crying over there?"

I nodded.

My father was sobbing uncontrollably, openly and unashamedly. My mother, sitting regally in a red suit, had that same soft look of understanding on her face. Among the tears was the unmistakable glow of pride. I saw my mother squeeze my father's hand before she met my gaze and nodded with a soft proud smile.

LITTLE JAM BUSINESS

Miss Bertie's husband Robert believed in a religion that preached that only one hundred people could get into heaven. So when she heard the front door slam at two o'clock in the afternoon, she knew he had been fired from his job again. No boss wanted to hear that someone was preaching on the job when there was work to be done. No boss wanted to hear that drinking was wrong, that having too much money was wrong and that he should go to some obscure fundamentalist church on a Sunday morning and sit there all day.

"Alberta, I'm home. Is dinner ready?" Robert had a deep, gruff voice and once again, Alberta marveled that such a small man could speak with the roar of a lion. She was tall for a woman, 6 feet, and Robert reached her neck. She had to look down when speaking to him yet her voice was meek. She would do anything to avoid his bad temper.

"Alberta, woman! Where is my dinner?" he roared again.

"Hello, Robert. Dinner isn't quite ready yet."

Alberta put her baby on the floor and chopped some onion and put it in a pan. The smell of frying onions would fool him into thinking that something was cooking. He was home three hours too early. Her boys hadn't even come home from school yet.

Luckily Robert never came into the kitchen. He stood in the doorway and said, "When a man comes home, he wants his dinner." His voice filled the kitchen with tension.

"How was your day at work?" she asked without looking at him.

"Never mind about my day. It is easier for a camel to go through the eye of a needle than it is for a rich man to get into heaven."

Miss Bertie sighed. She knew that after a firing, she would have to listen to an afternoon of Robert's preaching which was more like ranting and raving about the injustices of life.

The front door opened again and slammed shut. Her boys were home. Albert was ten and Winston, seven. They walked to school five miles every day rain or shine. Winston ran to her and hugged her, burying his tear-streaked face in her skirt and soiling her white apron.

"What's wrong? What's the matter?" she asked.

He pulled away from her defiantly as if she were the cause of his tears.

"The boys at school teased me and said I was poor because the heels of my shoes are coming off and you cut a hole in the toe. No one else has to cut a hole in the toe. Everyone else gets new shoes."

Albert said, "That's why I don't wear shoes at all. I tell everyone I don't like them."

"You think people don't know you don't have shoes to wear? Everyone knows we are poor, Albert. Don't be stupid," Winston cried.

"I'm not stupid. You're stupid. You're a cry baby."

"I'm not a cry baby and you're not fooling anyone with that story."

Robert came to the kitchen.

"What's all the noise about?"

Suddenly the boys tensed.

"Good afternoon, papa."

The boys' downcast faces told Miss Bertie that they knew that the only reason their father was home was because he had lost his job again.

Miss Bertie lay in bed that night, her eyes wide open, staring up at the ceiling. She had been taught that the man was the head of the household, the person who provided for his family, the one who was always right and always strong. Although Miss Bertie was beautiful with long thick, dark brown hair that glistened in the sun and she had pleasant features, she had not had many suitors because of her height. Robert had been so confident and sure of himself. He always talked about business opportunities and living the right Christian life. He had always seen the world in black and white. Someone had to be right and someone wrong. Miss Bertie found out soon after marriage that he was always the person who was right.

She didn't want to entertain the thought that her sons might have to endure their entire school life with shoes that were too small or no shoes at all. Albert was bound to get worms from the soil. She spent the night in silent prayer and finally fell into a troubled sleep.

When the hot tropical sun rose that morning and pierced through the sheer white curtains in Miss Bertie's bedroom, she woke and had a vision of her own grandmother bent over a stove making peanut brittle and fudge or the delicious paradise plums that were sweet on one side and tart on the other.

Miss Bertie got out of bed, washed her face, brushed her teeth and got ready for the day. She took a quick look in the mirror to make sure she was presentable and saw that her hair was starting to grey at the roots. She knew what she had to do and if Robert said anything about it, she was going to say what her grandmother always used to say. "God helps those who help themselves."

She would no longer be the new bride, surprised that she had more wisdom than her husband, shocked that she had more strength, and helpless and terrified that she might lose her home and her land—land that had been a wedding gift from her father—if she didn't take matters into her own hands. It seemed these days that everything cost money. It was not like the old days when goods could be bartered. Good leather school shoes came from England and she would have to go into the town to buy them. The travel would also cost money.

Miss Bertie couldn't sew. She knew women who made good money sewing for the wealthy. She didn't want to clean someone's house. That would not buy shoes for her boys. But she had spent her childhood in her mother's and grandmother's kitchens. She could make jams and jellies, candies and cake.

That morning when Robert left early to look for work, she began. She worked feverishly until her fingers were sore. It was mango season and she went outside and collected the different mangoes, peeled them and boiled them down with sugar. Then she started making guava jam from the tree that grew outside her bedroom window. After leaving the jams on the stove to cool, she put on her shawl and set out to spread the word of her new business. Miss Bertie had to walk a long way but all morning and afternoon she visited friends and neighbours. She walked to the small town center and informed the grocer that she had candies and jams to sell.

Soon orders started to come in. Miss Bertie hid some of her money in a jar in the kitchen pantry. The rest of it, she put in a bank. Soon she had enough money to buy new shoes for the boys but no time to go into Kingston to get them. She sent Robert to town with the money. He returned home at nightfall. The boys were waiting for him on the verandah. The night was warm and Miss Bertie could smell the sea on the occasional wind that blew in from the coast. Robert strutted up the steps smug and self-satisfied. His hands were empty. The boys looked up at Miss Bertie expectantly.

"Where are the shoes?" Miss Bertie's voice was low and ominous.

"Alberta, I gave our money to the Lord."

"That's fine, Robert, but all of the money?"

"I am the head of this house, Alberta, and I will say what is to be done with the money. I've invested in our souls."

"Okay, Robert. Come inside boys. It's time for bed."

The next day, Miss Bertie, grumbling under her breath, set out to fill orders for three birthday cakes, two batches of fudge, an order of peanut brittle, a jar of paradise plums and her new specialty, two bottles of mint jelly that the wealthy woman on the hill could eat with her lamb.

Robert did not go out looking for work. He walked through the house running his finger on the dusty window ledge and pointing out the dust to her.

"Alberta, are you in the kitchen? Please come into the sitting room."

Then he held up his finger and showed her the dust. Later on, "Alberta, do you sweep under the rug daily? Come and look at this dirt."

Miss Bertie stirred the fudge holding the baby in one arm. She put the baby to sleep and remembered that she had dirty baby diapers sitting in a pail outside. It was a long process to clean diapers and she had woken early to wash them. First, she had placed the soiled diapers in boiling water. She was to then have rinsed them in bleach and hang them to dry in the sun during the heat of the day. The day passed quickly and her breathing became shallow as she saw the sun setting in the distance. The boiling water had long cooled and the baby would not have enough diapers for the night.

"Alberta, where is my dinner?" Miss Bertie didn't answer. Robert was calling out from the sitting room. If he wasn't quiet, he would wake the baby. "Alberta, bring me a glass of water."

Miss Bertie heard the baby cry and something inside her snapped. She picked up the pail of dirty diaper water and walked inside.

"You want water, Robert. Here is your water."

And with that she threw the dirty water in his lap and walked into the kitchen. She waited for him to come in and the harsh words and repercussions that would follow but there was silence, only the occasional sounds of the children playing upstairs.

After she prepared dinner, brought it to the table, and called everyone, she said, "I am a businesswoman now, Robert. Next year I'm going to open a shop. Tomorrow I am going to Kingston to buy shoes for the boys and you will take care of the baby. Mrs. Smith next door will pop in to give you a hand. Our boys will never go to school without shoes again. I am going to make sure of that."

Robert did not answer nor did he look at her.

Years later when Miss Bertie remembered that day, she wondered how it would have turned out if she hadn't taken matters into her own hands. Robert had never once mentioned the incident and he had stopped shouting for her and demanding his dinner. He still didn't help in the kitchen. Men of that era didn't do what they called 'woman's work,' but he played with the children while she worked and helped the boys recite their multiplication tables. Eventually she hired a woman to look after the housework and children while she worked in her shop.

But every night when she came home and said goodnight, she whispered in their ears, “You can do anything. You must believe in yourself.”

When Winston came home to visit after his second year in England at Oxford University, he brought with him his new wife.

“I’ve heard so much about you Miss Bertie,” the attractive woman beamed. “Winston tells me you own a shop and you export your sauces to England. How did you do it and raise a family?”

Miss Bertie tried not to appear smug but her ‘little jam business’ as Robert called it, had sent Albert to college in New York and he was now helping her to manage the business; Winston to law school in Oxford and her third child Elizabeth to a finishing school in London, Ontario. Her business had grown so fast that they had to move to Kingston where she had opened a factory so that her supply could meet the demand.

Before Miss Bertie could answer her daughter-in-law’s question, Robert looked at her with pride and said in his deep gruff voice, “This woman here is the most exceptional woman I know. Her little jam business has done good for all of us. We are so proud of her.”

SAVING GRACE

1969

The child named Grace pushed dark brown curls out of her eyes and leaned down and kissed her father tenderly on his forehead. That afternoon he had read to her then closed the book and called her his saving grace.

Grace gingerly removed the upright glass out of his hand wondering how the milky brown contents had not spilled onto the floor. He was sleeping soundly, snoring with his head lolled to one side yet he clutched the glass tightly in his hand as if it were the most precious liquid in the world. She supposed it was. He had a glass cradled in his hand every day when she came home from school. He told her it was chocolate milk for his ulcer but she saw when he poured it that it wasn't the same chocolate milk she got and his chocolate milk made him sleepy and sometimes sad.

The child was only 8 but bright. She had heard a friend of her father's say that she was bright beyond her years and responsible. Well, she had to be, she thought. She woke up her brother in the morning, got herself ready for school, sometimes she even ironed her own uniform on the bed since she was too small to reach the ironing board. And every night, she removed the glass from her father's hand or picked it up off the floor if it had slipped through his tired fingers. Then she'd put a blanket over him and let him sleep off the intoxication until he woke sometime during the night and went upstairs to bed.

Sometimes when she took the glass from his hand, he'd wake up and with glazed eyes, ask, "Enid, is that you?" Grace would say, "No, daddy, it's me, Grace." Then he'd say resignedly, "She's not coming back, is she?" Once he got angry and said, "She's no good, is she? What type of woman would be so cruel? She's no good." When Grace had mentioned it in the morning, he'd gotten angry and said he'd said no such thing.

Sometimes she felt a pressure building up inside her chest, something that threatened to smother and suffocate her, a heavy presence within her that made her want to fall to the floor and cry uncontrollably, and kick and stamp her feet in despair. But she swallowed it and instead memorized lists in her mind: her homework, lunch, helping the maid sweep, or sort the laundry, or tell her what to prepare for dinner. The lists and the mental checking off what needed to be done would keep the bad feeling at bay. If she felt at all tired, she simply made up a new list and memorized it, and that renewed the strength in her skinny limbs.

1968 Neville McPherson

When the alarm went off at 5:30 am, I jumped out of bed. Without thinking that I was tired, I dressed, made breakfast for myself and my two older children Grace and Andrew and sat down with them and ate at 7. I knew the live-in help Dorothy would gladly have made breakfast, but it was something I enjoyed.

Before leaving for work, I kissed my wife Enid on her forehead. Her forehead was slightly damp as it was July and the time was hot. Even with the fan on, the morning sun pierced through the window and the thin white drapes, heating up the bedroom and making us sweat beneath the sheets.

Enid's eyes were closed but I knew she wasn't sleeping since she was on her side breastfeeding the baby. She didn't respond but I didn't expect her to. She is a nurse and works nights at the hospital so that I can work in the day. We made this arrangement so that one of us would always be with the children although I know that the children are mostly with Dorothy during the day as Enid must get her rest.

That day was no different than any other day. I arrived at the clinic and felt a sense of satisfaction when the nurses greeted me brightly, "Good morning, Dr. McPherson. Good morning, Sir." The receptionist handed me the first chart and it was a physical.

The entire day was more or less routine, a case of ringworm, a baby's first vaccine, and four people with the flu who thought that by coming to the doctor's they would be cured.

Sometimes I went home for lunch. Dorothy always cooks a soup. Yesterday she made a delicious pepperpot soup. Enid was still in bed so I didn't wake her. I ate that delicious soup, picked up the two older children from school and went back to work. I pick up the children every day. Grace is 7 and Andrew is 4. The baby is 6 months old.

Grace is quick and bright and a true firstborn, very responsible and willing to please. Andrew is smart as a whip too but likes to do his own thing. Today, I didn't bother to stop for lunch but I still picked up the children, dropped them home and backed out of the driveway.

As I said, the day was no different from any other day. I was busy, the sun was hot, vendors sold fruit on the side of the road. Looking back, I didn't even get a sense that something was happening at home that would change my life forever.

I arrived home at 6:30 pm. I'll never forget that it was a Thursday and that the Bombay mango tree in the front yard was laden with mangoes. The grass was dry and turning brown. I turned the key in the lock and opened the door. Enid was standing there impatiently, as if she'd been waiting all afternoon. She was dressed in a pale blue linen suit and matching pumps. There at her feet were two grips bulging at the seams. I saw at once that she was agitated and kept licking her lips.

"I'm sorry Neville. I'm leaving."

"What do you mean, 'you're leaving'?"

"I can't do this. I can't go on like this. You know how I've tried to tell you that I've been feeling off since the baby was born. I can't stand to be here, in this house, any longer."

A strange sensation came over me and I couldn't make sense of what she was saying. Feeling off? I had no idea what she meant by it. She had made comments from time to time that she didn't know motherhood was so hard, or she felt she was missing out on things. It was normal to feel that way. I had felt that way myself.

"What do you mean? Where are you going?"

"To New York to spend some time with my aunt."

Tears welled up in my throat. I would miss the children terribly. I wasn't even aware that she had a visa to travel. I didn't know how long she'd stay but I knew it wouldn't be for long. I had known Enid from high school. We had both gone to Wolmer's. I knew Enid and I knew she would come home in no time at all. I tried again.

"Enid, I'm very confused. Where are you going and why? Where are the children? How long will you be gone?"

She looked away and then turned back but her eyes were focused on the garden outside the front door. When she spoke it was quickly but firmly.

"Listen, Neville. You have always been a better father to the children than I am a mother." She attempted a smile. "As a matter of fact, sometimes I think you're a better mother. The children are better off with you. I don't want to speak of love, Neville. It's not about love."

I tried to hold her hand and tell her how I loved her. Her hands were cold in the summer heat.

"I don't want to sit here and speak of love. I can't explain it. Maybe I was never in love. Let me go, Neville."

She yanked her hand away like I did her something wrong.

"Sometimes I feel that I'm going to hurt the baby for no reason at all. I have to go."

As if she had timed it perfectly, a taxi pulled up just then and a man hopped out and she dragged a suitcase toward him. She struggled with the other, got in the cab, and just like that she was gone.

Every year I thought she'd return. Every year I waited expectantly, especially at Christmas when I was sure the doorbell would ring, and Enid would be standing there smiling. I would've taken her back in a New York minute as they say. She never came back. I never saw her again.

But that was not my immediate concern. I now had three children to care for and to provide for. Providing for and caring for are not the same thing. I went to work every day as usual and my practice grew. But I had no time for any extracurricular activity of any sort and that included dinner and drinks with colleagues and friends.

Every morning I woke at 5:30 am and made breakfast as usual. Dorothy was beside me already making preparations for lunch, making the lunch boxes and taking out the meat for dinner. After breakfast I plaited Grace's hair and made sure Andrew brushed his teeth. Dorothy was never any good at ironing so I would sometimes have to re-iron Grace and Andrew's uniform. The baby whose name is Michael and who we all still refer to as the baby, was a fat thriving boy until Enid left. He became thin and whiny.

That afternoon, in my pain, I had forgotten about him. Dorothy came to me where I sat alone in my study, holding him close to her bosom, trying to comfort him, trying to shush his cries.

"Dr. Mac, Sir, di baby need formula."

The sight of Michael clawing at Dorothy's chest propelled me out of my stupor. I jumped into the car and drove to the grocery shop. I bought the formula and rushed home. By this time Michael was screaming.

"Dr. Mac, Sir, you forget to buy di bokkle."

In a state of anxiety, I rushed out again, attempted to overtake a Volkswagon, couldn't make it as another car was speeding towards me, so I tried to go back and ended up slamming my car into the VW. The woman driving couldn't understand why I was reduced to hysterical tears.

By the time I got to the shop and bought several bottles, it was nighttime. The house was strangely quiet when I returned. The children had thought that I too was leaving like their mother so Grace had convinced Dorothy to ask the neighbour Mrs. Smith to take them to the pharmacy and buy bottles for Michael. Thankfully, Mrs. Smith had fed Michael and the other two had had dinner and were in my bed. Dorothy said they had been crying all evening. I woke them up and told them that I would never leave them. I promised them that for as long as we all live, I would be with them.

The months and years after that were hectic. I had little time for myself. I had to cut down my practice and come home early to help with homework.

Mrs. Smith, our widowed neighbour taught Grace how to plait her own hair. She also passed on some of her better recipes which I in turn passed on to Dorothy. I had no interest in Mrs. Smith, or Joyce as I called her, nor any other woman. Deep in my heart, I despised Enid yet I still loved her.

I avoided my friends and all the gossipmongers on the island. I was ashamed. A woman, my wife, my life, had left me and the life we had made together. I was embarrassed. What had I done? What terrible person was I that Enid could heartlessly walk out like she did? In time, I came to understand that Enid was the problem, not I. I watched as devoted mothers brought their children in for vaccines and saw that these women would never leave their children.

I wanted to tell Grace, Andrew and Michael that their mother was dead, but I couldn't be sure she wouldn't walk through the door one day. Enid wrote the children letters from time to time and sent gifts. There was the dancing flamenco doll from Spain, jade earrings from New Zealand, shiny red Oriental outfits, stuffed animals like kangaroos and koala bears, and flags from countries to which she'd traveled. I took all these gifts and letters and hid them in a box. I never showed them to the children. It seemed cruel to do that when what they needed was their mother.

I introduced the children to good literature, to the classics. I tutored them with their arithmetic and history. I taught them to ride a bicycle and to roller skate. I made sure to take as many pictures as I could. I comforted all the tears and learned to really listen.

Do I sound like the perfect father? I'm not. I've neglected to mention that I took to drinking brandy with milk. I told the children it was for my ulcer. Most evenings after work I was passed out on the couch. In a drunken stupor, I sensed that every night Grace kissed me good night and that it was she who removed my shoes and socks.

At 8, Grace could wash clothes and I lowered the line outside so she could hang them to dry too. By ten, she could roast a chicken. By then it was Grace who was ironing the uniforms. It was Grace who took to correcting Dorothy when she came back late on a Monday morning or telling her she had to do a better job as there was still dust on the coffee table.

I saw the children through high school and they all attended the University of the West Indies. Michael eventually dropped out and came to nothing, cavorting with musicians who smoked marijuana all day and shifting jobs as often as he changed his underwear. He went to jail for five years and has never told me the whole truth of that day they held him at the airport. He still claims someone planted drugs on him. The other two did well. Grace works at the bank and Andrew teaches English at a high school.

Grace now keeps in touch with her mother. She doesn't tell me and I don't care to ask. When Grace's marriage failed, she and her two daughters moved in with me. Once again, I was plaiting hair in the mornings and making lunch boxes and breakfast. Grace still removes my shoes and socks and kisses me good night when I've passed out on the couch. I can't do without the milk and brandy. It's for my ulcer.

2006 Enid McPherson

When the phone rings I glance at the call display and see it's my daughter Grace. I don't answer it. I'll call her back later. She probably wants me to come to Jamaica to visit her and the children. I'll call her later and tell her to come to New York. I don't have anything against Jamaica. I simply have no desire to visit. It's become an uncivilized place.

I glance at the clock and see that it's 4pm and that I have to be at the clinic where I volunteer in two hours. I turn on the T.V. out of boredom and start watching a show about a woman who abandoned her son at a park. The son needs closure and called Dr. Phil. Although the situation is nothing like mine, the words of Neville from a letter he wrote shortly after I left comes back to me and is still painful. 'I still love you, Enid. Please come back. No normal woman abandons her family and her children like that. No normal woman leaves a child she is breastfeeding just like that. What did I do wrong?'

Of course I tore up the letter and didn't reply. I didn't feel I had to justify my actions to Neville. He wouldn't have understood. He still thinks there was another man, fool that he is. He wouldn't have understood that I could've been a doctor too. That I'm just as smart, if not smarter than he. My father pushed me into nursing when I should've stuck to my gut and pursued medicine. Neville wouldn't have understood how claustrophobic I felt in Jamaica and around him. I close my eyes wearily and I'm taken back to that time. It's so real that I smell Dorothy's cooking and I feel the island breeze on my skin.

Michael was born in January. I felt no connection to him at all. I waited for it. I waited for the love to come as it eventually did with Grace and Andrew but it never came at all. I breastfed him out of duty but I'd been playing the role of Neville's wife out of duty since we came home from our honeymoon. I felt as if society had forced me into the role of dutiful wife and mother. I couldn't explain why I hated it. I tried to explain to Neville that I wasn't feeling right but he always patted my hand and said he hoped I'd feel better soon.

I don't think I was depressed. There was a whole world out there that I was missing. But what convinced me to leave was the day I almost smothered Michael. He'd been crying continuously for four hours straight. Dorothy had held him for a while but when she handed him back to me and walked out of the room, a surge of anger came over me and I held the pillow over his little face. He was only two months old. In a second I realized what I had done and what I was capable of doing. I clutched Michael to me and told him I was sorry and that I loved him. But I don't think I meant a word of it.

I knew then that I'd leave. I hated seeing Neville with the children, how they ran to him when he came home from work and how they spent so much time outdoors playing together. The baby would smile instantly when he heard his voice. None of them were like that with me.

I planned to leave for weeks. I got my visa, packed my suitcases and hid them under the bed in the guest room. I tried to warn Neville several times but people only hear what they want to hear.

Once I quarrelled with Grace. She had come to visit with her two daughters. They are spoiled and indulged. I tried to tell Grace that she should not cater to their every whim. We were shopping and the younger one wanted some toy. She had a temper tantrum in the store. People turned to stare.

"Okay, I'll get it for a quiet life," said Grace to me.

"Don't spoil her. You are spoiling those children. In my day children were to be seen and not heard," I said.

"Mommy, do not tell me how to raise my children. How would you ever know what a child needs? You left us and never came back. You abandoned three children and worse, you were breastfeeding Michael."

I could not believe the audacity of Grace. She was shouting at the top of her lungs in a toy store. And she wouldn't stop.

She said, "Do you know what happened when I got my period? I didn't have a mother to show me what to do."

"Oh for God's sakes," I cut in. "In this day and age you didn't know that you were going to get a period? What the hell did your father teach you and him a doctor."

She started sobbing in the store. I was aware of the curious stares of onlookers.

"Of course I knew I was having a period. And don't you dare say anything about daddy. It's just that I didn't know you couldn't go swimming with a pad. I was the laughing stock of an entire pool party of fourteen-year-olds when the pad disintegrated and the bottom of my bathing suit was all lumpy with cotton hanging out of my ass."

I wanted to shake her. I was sick of her self-pity. Ever since she contacted me she has always let me know that I somehow did something wrong.

"Listen to me." I shouted. "I have been to the Taj Mahal, I've seen the Great Wall of China. I've lived in Germany and learned German. I worked in Norway, climbed the Eiffel Tower and swam in the Red Sea. My God, girl, I've been to Italy and France. I was Head Nurse at the hospital. Head Nurse! That's no easy feat. Which woman you know has had a life like mine? I have no regrets. You hear me. None."

And I turned around and walked out of the store, leaving her and her spoilt child sobbing in the baby doll aisle.

I TOO HEAR THE DRUMS

1975, Kingston, Jamaica

My grandmother is brushing and plaiting my hair. She brushes it so hard that the brush hurts my scalp but I know she is simply trying to brush out the knots and the curls. My hair cascades down my back but I don't think it's beautiful.

Beauty is the hair of those American TV women in the programs we get at night, straight, long, wispy hair, the type that falls into your face and you toss your head to get it out of your eyes. I ask my grandmother how come her sister has blue eyes and is so fair-skinned. She tells me that when they were growing up, they would visit their cousins in the country. Their cousins were practically white. The girl, Daisy Rose, would give my grandmother's fair sister the best dolls and my darker grandmother would get the dolls with the missing legs and arms. My grandmother laughs gleefully about this; she's simply telling me a story, a fact, and it doesn't bother her.

"Daisy Rose was one mean girl," she laughs.

Even at my young age, I sense the injustice. I get mad. I tell my grandmother that I'm angry and that it was terrible of Daisy Rose but she shrugs and laughs it off.

"Daisy Rose was just a stupid girl. There are lots of people like that. Where would I be if I let that bother me?"

I look at my grandmother and I see why this doesn't affect her. Of all her siblings she seems to be the favoured one, the smart one, strong, ambitious, wise, and beautiful with a strong dose of common sense. I am in awe of this woman.

1978, Kingston, Jamaica

My friend Anastasia has cut her long, dark, thick, unruly hair. She is sporting a pixie cut and it is miraculous to me that her once wavy hair is now straight. She looks cute. I want the same cut, the exact same cut. My mother takes me to her hairdresser Ann. Ann has been straightening my mother's hair for years, setting it on rollers and giving her American magazines to read while she sits under the dryer and tames her tight curls. My hair is long, wavy and wispy, light brown with blonde highlights from weekends at the beach. I don't mind seeing it loped off and fall to the floor.

I don't want to sit under the dryer, my hair pulled tight in rollers anymore. That is not freedom.

When Ann is finished, hot tears of shock and anger burn my eyes.

"You don't like it," she purrs.

I shake my head. My mother tries to console me.

"It looks cute," she says. "Tell Ann thank you."

"Thank you," I murmur.

But when I get into the car, I explode.

"I hate it. I'm never going back there. I'm growing it again. It's an Afro," I scream and release the tears of anger.

Gone are the blonde highlights. This new hair on my head came out of nowhere. It is dark and coarser and curly, very curly. It feels alien on my head. This is the beginning of a love-hate relationship with my hair that goes on for decades, from extremes of relaxing it to tame, cutting it crew cut short during pregnancies, bathrooms filled with products to defrizz, detangle, decurl and now, in my forties, products to volumize and frizz and curl.

"Anastasia has different hair from you. It's straighter," my mother says.

I can't answer because I'm crying so hard.

1982 or thereabouts: The Greatest Invention Ever - Hair Mousse

1984, America to Jamaica

My family return to live in Jamaica. I am distraught. I have an American-Puerto Rican boyfriend who I think I'm in love with and although we promise to write letters and to be in love forever, I know this isn't true. It can't be. We will be miles apart in culture and distance. I promise to stay a virgin and return to America as soon as I can.

But when I get off the plane with my sixteen-year-old body dressed in American clothes with a slightly punk edge, my hair cut in a bob, a big blonde streak in the front, I am elevated to a status that I've never known. This is a new Jamaica where I am a goddess. My golden brown skin is sought after. I am bathed in glances of longing and admiration. This sudden glamour is abnormal. I've gone from being a spic, a nigger, a number, an 'other,' to a princess. I am no longer laughed at and ridiculed for my hair, my skin, my accent. I have now become what I thought I could never be. Popular. Rich white girls, Jamaican old money, glare at me. Black girls treat me with contempt.

It's fine. I'm surrounded by hundreds of other goddesses, that fusion of DNA that churns out the most exquisite beauties. Someone, a man, said to me once, "You brown people all look alike." I was surprised. Never have

I seen such diversity. You're wrong, man. We can have brown eyes, dark like ackee seeds or yellow like the eyes of a wolf. Our eyes can be midnight blue to pale grey, forest green to mint. Can be slanted, almond, round. Our noses, Nubian, Greek, Roman, snub, hawk, retroussé. Our hair, never mind colour now, can be kinky as the blackest woman or straight and thin as the whitest one. Our skin shades are like an artist's palette, from milky white to chocolate.

We goddesses play a game, parading around each other, sometimes forming lasting friendships, other times spreading wild gossip about each other, stealing each other's boyfriends, fooling our parents about where we're going while we live our young lives in hedonistic nirvana, at beaches, parties, movies, plazas.

1986, Toronto, Canada

I am excited to be in Canada, 'foreign,' as we call any white country. Excited about new beginnings. If you stay too long on an island, it gets stale.

My parents drop me off at York University. I chose York only because a guy I liked was going there. A friend of mine chose York because it has the highest population of blacks, the Canadian version of D.C.'s Howard.

This is where I taste my first bit of anger. Someone calls me a black cunt because we have a disagreement at the fast food restaurant where I am working to earn a little extra money. I decide I have to be black. I seem to have little in common with white Canadian girls who go beer drinking as a hobby and head to the ski slopes for March break. I have to try too hard with them. I head to the Caribbean Student Association where I am told that I cannot join. It's a club for West Indians, I am told.

"But I am Jamaican. I was born in Jamaica. I am West Indian."

The guy I'm speaking to is Dwayne. I know this because someone in a red, green and black t-shirt walks by and greets him with the fist to fist, 'respect.' Dwayne, tall, muscular and black, also donning a t-shirt with a Bob Marley face spread, has that typical Torontonian-Jamaican accent. I can tell it's been cultivated. Has this jackass ever even been to Jamaica? He tells me I don't sound Jamaican. I've heard this many times before but usually it's said with interest, surprise. People assume I've been living in England. No, people, I want to shout, I went to London once for two weeks, hardly enough time to acquire a British accent. But this coming from Dwayne, is accusatory, angry.

"I'm from Jamaica," I insist again.

"Prove it," he says. "Can you hear the drums?"

I am taken aback. I feel slapped in the face.

"Were you born in Jamaica?" I ask.

"No, but I can hear the drums."

"I can hear the drums," I say, "but I don't need to wear my culture on my t-shirt. It's in my blood. Screw your association."

When I walk away, I think, what fucking drums? He wasn't in Jamaica for the brain drain, the political riots, the empty supermarket shelves, the senseless murders where we all knew people who died. He was in rich North America learning how to be Jamaican second-hand.

I spend four years at university never once attending the Caribbean Students Association. I feel strangely disconnected from any race. White guys treat me like an exotic fruit, some are brave enough to taste, but mostly they wrinkle their noses. Black guys like me eventually, when they discover I really am Jamaican. Their line is always, "You don't look Jamaican." When I hear this, I too put them in a special category. Ignorant. They say this same line to my Jamaican friends who look Chinese or Indian or white.

These are the people who don't know Jamaica at all, don't know its rich history, know nothing about the many immigrants who set foot on its sandy shores, don't know our motto is 'out of many, one people.' Yeah, ignoramus, screw your association.

1995 Toronto, Canada

I get a job. I finally get a decent job that doesn't include serving drunken pre-adults or lecherous old men. I am teaching English as a second language at a small private college outside of Toronto. I spend my days teaching not only language but Canadian culture. It all goes smoothly until I take the students on a field trip to Toronto and they see a white girl lip-locked in a passionate embrace with a black boy. They are around seventeen, maybe more. Who knows these days. Then the students see an Asian girl holding hands with a black guy. They gasp at these couples and tell me it's not right. Black should be with black. All races should stick to their own. I take a deep breath and try to explain apartheid. I try to convey that their views are wrong, out-dated, and totally alien in this new land to which they have come.

My students are all from India and no matter what I say, I cannot change their views. I think, 'Oh no, my children will go to school with their children.' Why come here then? Why use Canada as a hotel for its freedoms while keeping yourself in a prison?'

At first, I tell myself it's just their upbringing but I get mad when they tell me they don't like black skin colour, they don't like black hair and they bring their fingers up to their head and make a disgusted face. They don't see me as black because I look like them. When our arms touch, my skin is no different from theirs. It's my hair that is different and even then, they don't see it as 'black' hair. I notice this. I don't look black so people feel they can say anything. I am mad, mad when they see a blonde-haired girl and they tell me she is beautiful when I see that she is just a plain Jane. I get mad that they don't see that the blood of Africa runs through their veins, that their DNA contains the genes of those first people who set foot out of that continent. I get mad that they've brought their 'us' and 'them' mentality, that they don't see that one big bang explosion created us all.

This anger makes me weary and I wonder how those great men of history kept fighting for justice through all the dissension.

2002, Toronto, Canada

I get married to a mixed-race man and we produce two more mixed-race people for the world. A boy who is darker than the girl, his hair is thick and curly. His skin colour is like honey, golden reddish-brown. The girl could be white, creamy, except for the giveaway hair, wildly curly from roots to ends, a fuzzy pale halo around her head. To me, they are mesmerizingly beautiful. People will ask them, what is your background, where are you from, what are your parents, is one white and one black, what are you really? They will have to explain the whole thing.

Or, maybe not.

Maybe they'll grow up in a Canada where cultural differences are no big deal, and where nobody really gives a damn if they hear the drums of a place they've never called 'home.'

Our new country

I met a Bangladeshi woman today. She looks like 30, but she's really 45 and a virgin. How do I know this? My Trinidadian babysitter tells me so. She tells me the gossip on everyone in the neighbourhood, so that I come to feel as if I actually know the people she's talking about.

The Bangladeshi woman and I talk: how it's so hard, how we had it better at home.

"I miss mangoes," she says, and I marvel that we have this in common. "But you wouldn't believe the persecution against women 'back home,'" she continues. "I just wanted to wear jeans and not have my head covered all the time. If you're a woman or a child," and here she shakes her head sadly, "and the religious persecution...I just wanted to be myself."

For a moment she seems lost in her memories, the way I get lost in mine. The Bangladeshi woman is really pretty: nice skin, chocolate, with dark doe-eyes. I think she feels something went wrong in her life and that she could have had so much more. She says the future is unclear, like trying to see down the road during the monsoon season. I say it's like walking in the desert during a sandstorm. We blame our old country. We blame our new country.

My Trinidadian babysitter comes over to babysit as she does most Saturday nights. She surveys the apartment like the most keen-eyed hawk, her black eyes narrowed to slits, and notices signs of a male presence.

"Ooh, she get she boyfriend to move in. How you manage dat, girl?"

She is overly dramatic in her gestures, slapping her thighs lightly, jutting one hip forward, raising her arched brows and pursing her lips. I deeply regret a rare mood of openness one evening when I admitted I wanted my boyfriend Kevin to move in. Now I feel weak and exposed. I grin awkwardly, biting my lip. I hope Kevin doesn't hear. The sound of the bathroom pipe hisses and I pray he doesn't hear because maybe he'll think I'm one of those conniving females trying to lure him into a trap. My Trinidadian babysitter is making me out to be like this when I'm not at all that way. Humiliation rages throughout my body.

She speaks loudly and is still speaking at the top of her voice when Kevin comes into the living room and we walk out the door.

She calls out, "Put on a hat, *chile*. It cold outside, you know."

I don't want to wear a hat. I'm not about to mess up my hair. What is wrong with her? Doesn't she think I'm old enough to know whether I need to wear a hat or not? I'm 37. And the neighbours will hear everything. They'll know my business. I mumble "hmm hmm" and rush out the door feeling like my night is already ruined.

We go to the movies but I'm worried the whole time because I don't really trust anyone with my children.

Kevin tells me, "For Christ's sake, Amber, let go."

I pretend to let go and smile, but I'm still thinking of my children all alone with the Trinidadian babysitter, quaking under her black-eyed razor-gaze and thundering vocal chords. I think, what if she leaves them? What if she hacks them? What if she steals them? Kevin doesn't care enough. After all, they're not his. Who can understand a mother's fears? Who can you trust in a land as large as this?

We get home and they're alive. The Trinidadian babysitter tells me they've vomited.

"It's the fruit you gave them." It sounds accusatory, a screech in my ears. "It's the acidity, you know. The fruit is acidic. Too much fruit not good, *chile*."

I want her to leave immediately after I've paid her but she stays a while chatting about inconsequential things and I wonder if it's to cover herself because she's sprinkled poison on their food. I wonder if she's capable of that degree of wickedness because she pretends to be a friend of all children but I don't think they like her much.

I tell Kevin about the poison and he says, "It's funny you said that, because the same thing ran through my mind."

I promise myself not to use her again, but I've made this promise before. Who else is there? At least she's from the Caribbean too and there's some kinship. I don't understand the Iranians, the Indians or the Canadians. When the Trinidadian babysitter leaves, I wonder what gossip she'll carry about me to the outside world.

The Trinidadian babysitter told me she only left Trinidad because she came here for school and in those times, it was easy to stay. They wanted people then, she said, but now, there are too many coming. Not enough jobs. Not enough apartments. But she could go home any time, I once suggested, Trinidad is not like Jamaica. But she made a disgusted face like she smelled something bad.

The Trinidadian babysitter said she held a good job for years and retired with a good compensation package. Her rent is low because she's lived in the same apartment for so long. I knew she wanted to ask me what rents are going for these days but I changed the subject.

After I pay rent, I have one-hundred-and-fifty-two dollars left for bills and food. That means I don't subscribe to cable, even though the cable company calls me during the evenings and tries to make me try one month for free. I now recognize that sick, money-pilfering, marketing ploy and won't be taken for a ride. It means that when I go to the supermarket, I'm careful. I'm so careful I tiptoe in the aisles and when the cart fills up, I put things back, afraid I won't have enough to pay for it.

I never add things in my head. I tried once and got sick. The numbers kept jumping from memory and I grabbed at them but they ran away, out of my head, out of the supermarket, laughing and shrieking in glee, like the ones on the children's television show where the numbers and letters have stick arms and legs.

The Trinidadian babysitter, not just her, everyone I meet, wants to know why I left Jamaica. Was it the crime? Was it the economy? I tell them yes. I want a better life for my children. It's the truth and yet not. I left so I could lock my memories in a box and leave the box in one country while I floated away to another. That's what an old friend of my mother's told me, that I should put my negative thoughts in a box and bury it in the backyard. I did. I used one of those small wooden boxes with the picture on top, of a market woman walking on a country road. I visualized my negative thoughts going into that box and I closed the lid on it. It's still there near the root of a tree, the soil above it dry and dusty in the hot months and sodden in the rainy months when the rain beats down and doesn't seem to let up for days.

But it is amazing how a single memory can erupt like an underground fountain that bursts through the soil and spews in the air. I wonder if the wood of the box is permeable and my thoughts have simply seeped up out of it, up through the soil and followed me here. I will be looking in the mirror and combing my hair and the light will shadow my face a certain way and all of a sudden, I see my mother. She used to stare at herself in the mirror, tilting her chin this way and that, plucking a fine hair from her chin, arching her eyebrows, smoothing an imaginary wrinkle.

She would say, "Amber, it's not enough to be beautiful. Being beautiful can be a curse. By the time you realize there are other choices than just getting married and being someone's wife, it's too late and your beauty is gone."

Sometimes she'd say, "Amber, being a woman is a curse. You don't realize it's a curse because it's not 1920, and we're not equal. We thought we could make out alright but we can't. We are burdened with too much."

The weekend passes by uneventfully. I lock myself in the bathroom and chant, "Damned if I do, damned if I don't." This means I wish I'd done something. Anything. I wanted to go out and I wanted to stay in too. When I look back, almost all my weekends pass this way. I want to do something but bone weariness overcomes me and I am unable to leave my bed.

Kevin goes for a morning jog and comes home and wants sex. I do it of course, but my heart is not in it. My heart is not in my body at all. It is hanging from a hook on the wall, pumping blood, exposed and vulnerable and I watch it while having sex.

It's been two-and-a-half years since Kevin and I have been dating. It is one of those relationships that take a while to establish, where the man seems unreachable. His cell is off, the phone rings interminably. You wait and hate yourself for waiting. Your friends tell you to keep busy but you are constantly reminded that each distraction (and a failed one at that) is a thing you'd rather not be doing because you want to connect with that elusive man.

But finally he's moved in. It happens one day in the spring when the first breath of warmth tantalizes my skin, promising long walks and green trees and a kiss under the stars. It happens because Kevin can't pay his rent. He needs a place to crash while he finds himself, and he loves me too, he adds offhandedly.

It doesn't matter that his dirty pants and shirts are our bedspread and that the laundry basket is filled to overflowing that we don't see it anymore. All that matters is he is with me. He is someone to come home to. He is permanent and of course, I love him. Or, at least, I think I do.

It's Monday morning. I drop my kids at daycare. They don't run in gleefully like the other children. They don't cry. They look up at me with such longing, their large eyes opened wide, promising not to shed tears. They look at me with such hope that I curse inside. I curse that I can't gather them to my bosom and hold them the entire day. I curse my own painful, awkward existence.

A childhood memory erupts and showers me with heat and smell. I am 3. My mother drops me off at daycare, what we'd called nursery school, and her face is set in grim determination to get to this place called work even though I get the feeling she doesn't want to be there. She puts my tiny hand in the thick-skinned, pudgy palm of a woman with a fat, square face and she hands me over in an obligatory, grateful way, her head slightly bowed, her eyes not looking at me but at the woman and thanking her, as if to say she wasn't paying for the nursery school and the woman is doing her a big favour.

We eat from pale, pink, plastic bowls that retain smells. The oats porridge I eat in the morning smells of chicken soup from the day before and when I eat the raw-smelling chicken soup for lunch, it will smell of oats porridge. I am not happy, nor am I childlike and free. When people say they wish they could be a child again, problem-free, I nod in agreement but I do not agree. I cannot recall these feelings. Chicken soup makes me feel abandoned.

I leave the comforting dry heat of the daycare and dash out into a rush of cold air. The white apartment buildings along the street all look alike, lined up row by row and they are deceiving in their ugliness. Inside they are not so bad. I heard they were at one time roach-ridden, this was before I had moved to Canada. Since then management had so many complaints and tenants leaving that they had to fumigate and renovate the place. One company owns all the buildings.

I notice a young, slim, well-dressed black woman sitting on a cracked cement block outside one of the buildings. She has the fine features of a Somalian or Ethiopian. She is dangling a set of keys in her hand and I recognize the white plastic card similar to the one I use in my office. But then I notice something odd about her. Instead of going to work, she looks as if she's idling, talking to herself, head bent, mumbling under her breath. White frothy spots mark the corners of her mouth. I want to run to her and ask what's wrong. A whole street of people walk by. No one does more than glance nervously in her direction, so neither do I. I walk on. Have to get to work.

The Filipino man who guides our children across the street every morning is directly in front of her, but he ignores her, intent on the task at hand, holding one pudgy arm up to stop traffic, holding the red stop sign in his other hand. I feel empathetic towards the Somalian woman, but not enough to help. Why did she bother to curl her hair so prettily, to dress so nicely with that multi-coloured scarf around her neck and a blazer to boot, to fall apart on the curb? Wouldn't it have been easier to fall apart in bed? To not even get up? To call in sick? To sink her frothy mouth in the privacy of her pillow?

I am not so judgmental or self-righteous as you might think. I know there is something for all of us, the one thing that will send us over the edge muttering madly to ourselves and frothing at the mouth. I want to find out about the Somalian woman but maybe she is cuckoo and will attack me at the throat. Maybe today is that day, the day she will end her pain. Since there is nothing I can do to stop it, I cross the street and hurry to the subway.

It's an outdoor subway station so I'm cold. I stand behind a thin pole to avoid the wind but it comes at me, ripping me open and exposing me. I move and stand to the side of the pole, leaning up against it, but there's no hiding from the wind. It still rushes at me full force like an evil spirit and I feel like my face is covered with tiny scratches and my pants feel like they're wet. When I get on the subway, the blood oozes from the scratches on my face and runs down and warms my cheeks.

I eat lunch at a café on the corner near my work. A hint of some spice sends me reeling back to my childhood home and suddenly, I am overcome with a surge of emotion. Suddenly I am grateful for all the times my mother cooked for me, set the table just right and sat down watching me closely while I ate, saying, "Life won't be easy, Amber. It's important to know this from early. I realized this too late. It's a long, hard road to walk alone."

A tear rolls down my cheek. Not now, not now, I urge myself. This is a cold world and there is no time for tears. People will think I am crazy like the Somalian woman. I eat quickly; the food tastes like dust in my mouth, and read a magazine for half an hour but the memory of my mother blinds me to the words. Unbidden I see her sit across from me smiling. I smell her warm fruity breath from across the table. She sighs, "The day you were born, your skin, your eyes, your hair were all the same honey colour. They won't let me call you Honey, so we call you Amber, a precious jewel."

"Mom..." It's a question, a whisper, a sigh and a longing. But before I can reach out and touch her, she's gone and all the emotions pull at me, ripping my body to shreds so that I'm scattered. I want to hold tight to her but I get angry and it's just like the night before her death. A week before, she had fought with my father every night. She attacked him with her fists, accused him of having an affair with a woman at work. She said she works tirelessly cleaning our house. She said we were leaving for good this time. She is resolute. But we don't go anywhere. My father leaves us for days, quietly packing a small bag and saying before he goes, "She loves us, you know. She just can't..."

"What?" What does he mean to say? I never find out but I rehearse the words at least a dozen times a day. I sit with her, watch her try to leave her bed but it's as though her limbs are underwater. She does not eat. She does not sleep. When I see her again early the next morning, she is dead, hanging from a tree in the backyard. She looks unreal, like a scarecrow, her hair unkempt, her nightclothes in disarray, her face a bulging purple-blue. It is an image that remains deeply embedded in me, resinous and unchanging, decade after decade.

I'm in no rush to get back to work. When I leave the café, twenty-two pigeons sit on the ground with their chests puffed out. They look like fat round birds, all puffed out like that. I think it must be from the cold and wonder if our ancestors who resembled the apes puffed out their hair to keep warm. I read the people who survived the first migrations north were the hardiest. The others froze to death. Idly, I wonder if my jeans weren't so tight, would my pubic hair be puffed out. I wonder if I'll get used to the weather as some say I will. I wonder what's the use of a life, but I brush that thought away. I can't be pulled under today.

Sharon from work sits in the cubicle next to mine. She is from Jamaica and is Chinese. We don't really have much in common but her mother has recently died so we feel now that we have that in common. She shows me her lottery ticket and kisses it. Now that both her parents are dead, she says, they are bound to help her win this time. We go through this every week. Optimism when she buys the ticket. An appeal and prayer to the spirit of her dead mother and father. Concentration when she checks the Lotto Website. Anger that her parents are forsaking her in life and now in death. A bitter whisper that the stinking rich get richer and the dutty poor get poorer. Anger that God is letting her suffer. A fall to despair that lasts all day and encompasses her life, her work, home, weight, children. Sharon wants to leave her emotionally-abusive husband but she is scared.

Just do it, I say.

"I can't," she snaps, "how will I survive?"

It's funny how I see other people's fear tangibly like a hat on their heads. I wonder, do they see mine?

On my way home from work, I see the Bangladeshi woman again standing at the bus stop. We jump back when the bus comes and drives through the huge puddle in the road, splashing everyone already shivering on the sidewalk. I take a chance and ask her if she has a boyfriend. She tells me she's never had a boyfriend. I ask if she thinks she'll meet somebody. I hope so, she says and smiles coyly.

"I see you walking with yours. He's so handsome."

Thank you, I say and feel proud, as if my boyfriend being handsome is one of my great accomplishments.

Kevin and I are at a restaurant having dinner. He tells me over lukewarm pasta that this country is as racist as the best of them.

"People here speak in a patronizing way when they hear you have an accent." Kevin stabs the pasta and says people here must think he lived in a mud hut or a tree. He said the doctor asked him if he'd heard of Advil. He said he's sick of their pasty skin and condescending attitudes.

I pipe in, "It's like when I went for that job interview and the short bald man in the crumpled suit asked in a most offensive way, 'You have a degree?' 'Yes, I do,' I told him. 'I studied History at the University of the West Indies.' He smirked and asked if that was a real school and said he didn't know they had a university down there. I didn't get the job because I didn't have Canadian experience even though I was over-qualified. It was a slap in the face."

I wait for Kevin's response but he's looking at the pasta with a bored expression. It's a look that says it's neither here nor there, I'm neither here nor there. It's a look that says he's pretending to care about me chatting away to him but I can see he's already somewhere else.

Kevin has been trying to get a job for five months. Before that he held four jobs in six months. He left one because they didn't pay him on time. He left another because his boss spoke to him badly in front of a customer. He left another one because he didn't feel like going in one Monday morning and didn't call in and Tuesday he didn't call in and by Wednesday he got so worried that he hadn't called in that he decided not to show up at all. He left his latest job because he said it was beneath him and he wasn't going to have miserable people look down on him all the time when he was better than them.

He said this is the year he'll be making changes. Big changes. I'll see, he says, the cream sauce dribbling from his chin. He's said this before, but today his voice is tinged with indifference and for the first time I wonder if I'll be included in these big changes. I brush the thought away because the anxiety it provokes gives me indigestion.

My children are different from each other. One girl is introverted and doesn't seem to question her life. She goes along, eats what is put in front of her and I am grateful for her calm, easy spirit. She even looks like me, tall with slightly hunched shoulders to hide her height, brown hair, brown eyes, mousy, nondescript, the type of person you never notice in the streets, or if you do, you notice her only because of her plainness. The other girl is like fire. She bounces through life, full of optimism and determination and then crashes into the abyss. She reminds me of my mother. Uneasy, I monitor her every move, handling her like hot potatoes when she falls from her high to the abyss.

I have a photo of my children on my dresser. Sometimes I don't picture my children as they are. I picture them as they were in that photo, taken one Saturday morning at the beach, before we left Jamaica, before their father left forever. Before their lives changed irrevocably. Before grief, pain, uncertainty, disappointment and fear introduced themselves into their lives.

When I look at the picture, their innocence is pronounced, clear as day. They are tanned from the tropical summer sun, playing in the sand, looking happily into the camera, their hair lightened from a season outdoors, their bodies round and soft with baby fat. They are 4 and 2. They are angels and the sun touches them and lights up the photo in a way that makes me feel they are specially blessed or should be. They should never have to feel pain at all. Their father took the picture a month before he decided a family was not for him. Looking at the picture fills me with grief and I can't escape the feeling that I should be able to go back and change things or even recapture what I had, what we were, but I can't. The past is lost forever and innocence along with it.

The 2-year-old, now 4, finds a picture of my mother. "Who's that?"

"My mother."

"Where is she?"

"In heaven."

I truly believe this. Once I went to a party, a formal sit-down affair where people discuss politics and literature and the hostess uses the good plates, and some loudmouth mouthed off about how people who commit suicide don't go to heaven. I said yes they can. We argued the unknowable, the unprovable, with him saying that I hadn't read the Bible or studied theology like he had. But all I could think of was my good, gentle mother barred from heaven through no fault of her own. I threw down my plate and tossed my drink at him. From the anguished looks on everyone's face in the room, you would've thought I was crazy.

I ran out of there, and Kevin came after me. He told me he was completely and utterly humiliated and that I needed help.

I remembered one summer night when my parents had a party. I woke up and the music was off but everyone was still there. Everyone was watching my parents.

"Calm down, Eleanor, just take it easy," my father's voice was saying.

It was obvious she had had too much to drink. It was obvious something had upset her and my eyes were drawn to a tall, slim woman in a one-piece red jumpsuit. Her hair was pulled back tight in a ponytail and she seemed to me to be smirking, glad that my mother was getting this negative attention.

My mother, Eleanor, was yelling, but I didn't hear what she said. It sounded unintelligible.

"You're washing your dirty laundry in public. Calm down now," said my father.

She threw a glass at him and it crashed into the wall behind him. I remember people leaving. I remember my father pulling her out of the room and shouting, "You need help." I remember her face filled with shame. I remember the woman in the red jumpsuit smiling and whispering to her friend.

"Is she with God?" My daughter asks.

I don't answer. Instead, I say, "You remind me of her."

One day my daughter will ask me how my mother died. That's the great thing about a new country. I can be a different person. So can my mother. I will say she died from an illness, and even this is partly true. I'll say she was a happy person, the way I knew she wanted to be. Instead of trapped inside her despair. Trapped by my father who didn't understand how to deal with her illness. In our new country, we can all be completely different people.

The weeks pass by, each one as blurred and indistinct from the rest. Kevin calls the community colleges checking out business courses. Nothing changes. I get tired of picking up after him and maybe it shows in my face. He gets tired of my sighing and it shows in his face, the way he tunes me out and watches TV. Our lives and relationship are a bit like housework, everything has gotten so messy that it's hard to know where to start to clean up and fix it. Should we start in one small area? Or should we just do a general tidying up so that things look better even though we've shoved all the junk in the closet. But it's so messy that we get overwhelmed and instead of doing anything at all, we do nothing. Because doing something small doesn't seem to make a difference and when it doesn't make a difference, it's easy to get disheartened.

Tonight is different. Kevin takes me to dinner at a cozy Italian restaurant on Yonge Street. It feels good to get out of the apartment. It feels like we're a normal couple like the other couples I see at dinner, leaning towards each other and holding hands, the light of the candles giving each face the soft warm glow of contentment. It's been a long time since we've been out.

Over dinner he tells me he's gotten a job. I say congratulations and sing that song from the childhood musical Annie, the one that goes, "Easy street bom bom bom bom/Easy street." I sway in my chair and move my hips to the "bom bom bom" like the wicked Ms. Hannigan in Annie, but then I notice his face looks funny and he's not smiling. I mean, he is smiling but it's a pitying sort of smile that tells me something is wrong.

"What's the matter?" I ask concerned. "Aren't you going to take it?"

He tells me he is going to take it, for sure, he is. But it's not in Toronto.

Heck, it's not even in Canada. He looks sheepish for a moment but it doesn't faze him because he says quickly, lest I get the impression I'm coming along, "It's my dream. I'm going to be traveling a lot, based in England with my Uncle Edward. He got me the position. I did the interview over the phone. Connections, you know."

I nod.

I'm happy he's going to be living his dream, I tell him. But really, and not so deep down, I'm angry. I know the break-up conversation is coming next, the one where he'll say it doesn't make sense, the long distance thing, London England, Toronto Ontario. Why couldn't it have been London Ontario? But it's not.

He's starting the break-up conversation but I'm not listening. I'm thinking if I'd known it was going to end, I wouldn't have started it. I mean, I ended so many other ones before they started because I couldn't see a future. I saw a future with Kevin. Now he is telling me there will be no future. Maybe there would've been a future with another one that I ended it with. Maybe I'd be securely married by now. It's all so confusing and unfair. Unfair that we're not given the chance to see an outcome. Then at least we could choose better. There's no figuring out destiny. I've stood at forked paths many times and made conscious decisions which road to take. I just got on the wrong road this time.

We are well into the break-up conversation now and I see his jaw forming the words but my ears won't accept them. He's saying something about a fair, an amusement park and a ride you get on but it's going too fast and you need to get off but can't. Now he's getting off.

We exit the restaurant and I squeeze past Kevin into the street. I feel as small as a child of 3. I want to hold his hand. It will stop me from running in the street, it will protect me from getting lost. But I keep my hands clenched so I can be sure of my body. I need to be sure this isn't a dream. I clutch my purse tightly into my side.

All those conversations where we talked about "us" and "we" and having a child of our own, they were all lies. They had to be. You don't have those conversations and take a job in London England. Maybe London Ontario which is already bad enough.

"Amber, say something."

Oh, he's talking to me, asking if I'm going to say something. I thought I said all of it. I'm amazed he hasn't heard me. I thought I was screaming at him. I thought I was telling him that I wouldn't have let him into my life, into my children's life if he wasn't going to be permanent. He wants me to speak. It's all so sudden, he knows, but the job starts immediately. I think it's incomprehensible how things can remain the same for years when all you want is a little bit of change, when you think you're dying if something doesn't change and then wham bam kazam, there's so much change you're sure you're dying in that suffocating whirl-wind. And yet, the things that should remain permanent never do.

"That's great. You should live your dream. That's so great. I'm happy for you."

Is that really my voice? It sounds so foreign to my ears. That's really me pretending to be happy, giving advice on migrating to a new country since I've recently done it. I'm walking but my feet are made from air and the next minute, of lead. My mouth aches with my smiles and I finally see the future. Yes, it's clear. I see it ahead of me like a long clear road. Are you thinking I may end it? I won't. I will be permanent for my children. But I see clearly fifty years of long winters. I see my scratched and bleeding face every time I leave the house. My children leave home with barely a look back. Barely a call and I think, those girls would be family-oriented if they were raised in Jamaica instead of our new country. I see a sigh escaping my cracked lips, a useless regret forming on the tip of my tongue.

My girls will marry strange, incomprehensible 'foreigners': a redneck from Sudbury, a loudmouth of Serbian descent. No place for me in their sterilized world. My girls tell each other: 'we'll never get divorced. Look how hard mom had it.' Their guilt will guide them to the phone.

See that old woman who fell on the ice? That's me with a broken hip. I only stepped out to get some bread. Alone in my apartment, stooping at the front door to pick up the pension cheque which slid through the rusty brass mail slot. I stand for hours looking through dirty windows at the trees without leaves, the landscape bereft of green, the snow turn to mud and slush.

We are almost home. It is a cold and clear winter's night. It is not snowing but the wind is strong and it blows the settled snow from the tops of a low-rise building. The wind blows the snowflakes to a frenzy and they swirl crazily above my head, in my eyes. I stop and watch it, caught in a magical moment under a streetlight watching these swirling diamonds of light. It's beautiful. It's like tiny pieces of broken glass. Broken glass in my eyes. That's why my face is wet. I'm bleeding from my eyes.

Kevin holds me and tells me I'll manage.

WATER UNDER THE BRIDGE

Francis Ross was getting dressed for his daughter's wedding. He called out to the woman with whom he was living.

"Iris, bring my shirt nuh man. What tekking you so long to iron it?"

Iris came in and put the shirt gently on the bed. Francis grabbed it.

"Don't put it on the bed. It's going to get crushed again. You got the creases out of my jacket?"

Iris nodded and walked out of the room to get the jacket.

"Hurry nuh man," Francis called to her.

Iris came back in and tossed the jacket at him. "You mek youself late, watching TV till all hours of the night and cyah wake up in the morning time."

Francis winced because she pronounced 'hours' with the h.

"How many times I have to tell you the word is 'our.' Jesus!"

Iris kissed her teeth but said nothing more. She sat quietly on the bed and looked up at him while he straightened his tie. Her voice was meek when she spoke.

"Francis, how come Amanda didn't invite me? Don't she know we are like man and wife?"

Francis looked in the mirror, straightened his part and combed his hair, smoothing down his soft curls with oil while he spoke. He was proud that his hair was still jet black unlike so many of his contemporaries.

"Iris, don't bother me with this now. I told you it was a small wedding and she only invited close family."

"But two hundred people invited. I heard you say so on the phone to your friend the other night."

"I can't tell my daughter who to invite. Her mother will be there and maybe she doesn't want her to feel uncomfortable."

"It's you who don't want to feel uncomfortable, Francis. You don't want anybody to see you with me, especially your high and mighty ex-wife and your high colour friends."

"Woman, stop your foolishness. Can't you see I'm late?"

Iris started crying.

"It's not foolishness. I heard you on the phone and I heard you call the name Trisha and you said your wife. You didn't say ex-wife and it's how many years you're divorced now? Fifteen."

Francis handed Iris a handkerchief, kissed her forehead, and told her he would bring back a piece of wedding cake for her but he had to go. He knew it would have made her happy if he had said he loved her but he had never said those words to anybody and he certainly wouldn't be saying them to Iris. He wasn't even sure he did love her so he said the next best thing.

"See you soon. We'll watch a good show on TV together. I'll borrow a good movie."

And he rushed out to walk his firstborn down the aisle.

He drove like a madman weaving in and out of traffic. It was a miracle Amanda had asked him to walk her down the aisle. He had always thought there would be no doubt that he would walk his daughters down the aisle on their wedding day until his other daughter Laura, proud and rebellious, informed him some years ago that he certainly wouldn't be walking her down the aisle.

"First of all dad," she had said, "You are not giving me away. If I get married and I doubt I will, I will be entering an equal union of my own accord. Second of all, you were not around when I was growing up. If I get married, Bill would walk me down the aisle."

Francis had been hurt. After all, Bill could not love his daughters like he. Trisha had probably turned them against him. He had smarted from that comment for a long time and he secretly hoped Laura would never get married so he wouldn't have to endure Bill walking her down the aisle.

Francis screeched into the church parking lot almost hitting down a small barefooted boy in ragged clothes who was begging at the church gate. He saw a small huddle around Amanda–Trisha, Bill, Laura and her grandmothers, their heads craning towards the gate, no doubt looking out for him. He saw Trisha stamp her foot impatiently. He slammed the car door and rushed toward them, straightening his tie and smoothing down his hair.

"Did you have to be late?" Francis' own mother berated him.

Amanda looked relieved. Trisha didn't say as much as hello to him. She glared at him and turned to Amanda.

"Well, we can start now. The rest of us should take our seats."

Bill took Trisha's hand and led her to the front of the church. Francis wanted to tell Amanda he was sorry he was late but he couldn't speak. He was not used to showing emotion but she was so beautiful and she looked exactly like how Trisha had looked when he had married her in 1967. Francis wanted to cry. It was just yesterday Amanda had been born, a perfectly-shaped baby with dark, curly hair, skin the colour of the palest yellow flower, and hazel eyes like his own. Sometimes he had wanted to stay at home and hold her but she cried for her mother and his friends expected him to come out with them. Now Amanda stood looking at him with those huge hazel eyes, her thick black hair cut short, emphasizing her perfect features. Her skin had the rosy glow of youth and happiness. She had perfectly sculpted cheekbones and a pointed chin with a nose that was slightly long like her mother's.

"Do you like my dress?" she whispered. He hadn't noticed her dress but when he stood back and surveyed her, he recognized it as her mother's wedding dress. It had been restored and fit her perfectly. It had always been Trisha's wish that one day her daughter would wear her wedding gown. The dress was simple and elegant, white and long, with beads and lace lining the bodice. It clung to Amanda's waist and hips and then flared slightly to the floor. Instead of a veil, she wore a tiara.

"You look beautiful, like a princess." Francis fought the tears that threatened to spill over. He used to pick her up and call her his princess until one day at age ten, she told him not to call her that anymore. He took her arm and walked up the aisle.

The church was filled with people, a lot of whom he hadn't seen since he and Trisha divorced. He was glad he had come without Iris. It wasn't that she hadn't been invited. Amanda had asked him if he would bring her and he had said no. He wanted to share this moment with Trisha only, to reminisce and feel nostalgic together. He had forgotten that she was still cold towards him and of course, that Bill would be there.

Francis proudly led Amanda down the aisle, kissed her and stepped aside. He almost walked over and took his rightful place beside Trisha. He started in the direction toward her but he saw Bill. Everyone said how happy Trisha was with Bill. Francis felt alone. It wasn't that Iris didn't count but she would not have fit in with this crowd.

Francis walked to his seat. He barely heard the ceremony because it was as if he walked through a doorway to the past.

He found himself back in 1967. The priest was talking but he hadn't heard a thing except the cadence of the priest's voice rising up and down. All Francis could think about was that Trisha was now his and all the waiting they had done would now be over. Although they hadn't really waited because the weekend before the wedding, she had finally given in.

"Just this one time before the wedding," she had said, "since it's only one week away."

He couldn't wait to experience that blissful experience again. Then just like that, the wedding and honeymoon were over. They settled into a rented house. They got up every morning and went to work. They came home and had dinner. His friends called and he went out.

"Where are you going now?" Trisha would ask.

"Out with Wray and Nephew," he'd replied. It had taken a moment for her to realize he meant he'd been drinking rum again.

It became habitual, going out all night, or leaving home from Friday after work and staying out all weekend. Sometimes other women were involved but sometimes he was just too drunk to come home. As the group of men woke in the morning, they started drinking again. Francis didn't see why Trisha got upset. All his friends were married and they were all doing the same thing. He had never had access to so many women. It seemed that the day he got married, women became available. They didn't care that he was married. If anything, it made him more desirable. He had a long four-year affair with one of these women before Trisha got wind of it.

During the time of the affair, he had his two daughters Amanda and Laura. They bought a house and a second car. He spent more weekends at his mistress' house than he did at his new house with his own family. He didn't think of it as a double life. All his friends had other women.

One Sunday when he walked in slovenly and smelling of the other woman, Trisha asked, "Where have you been?"

"Out with Mr. Walker."

"Who is Mr. Walker?"

"Johnny."

She threw her plate of food at him and the children screamed in fright.

"Stop telling me crap. You think I don't know about her? You think I'm stupid."

Before he knew what was happening, Trisha left. She left everything in the house, even most of her clothes and moved in with her older sister in a tiny house in Havendale. He would go there and bang on the door, screaming her name to let him in. He called her every day to tell her to come home and that she better bring his children home, but she hung up the phone. He realized he loved her more than ever so he drank more and carried on with more women. Sometimes Trisha called him to pick up the girls at school and when he did, he realized he didn't know them. As far as he knew, Trisha would one day come back to him.

One Saturday morning, she called to tell him she was getting married. He didn't believe her at first but the wedding came and went, and he eventually met Bill at Amanda's ballet recital. Bill was there at every school event and his name always came up when he saw his children. He finally accepted that Bill was there to stay but sometimes Francis left the present and returned to the past where he concocted his own memories and his own version of events. When he returned to the past, Trisha was always there. She would never think of leaving him, no matter what he did. In time he settled down and they sat on the verandah together and laughed about their early days and his roaming ways. Trisha always said she loved him too much to leave him and thank God for that because look how they had each other now.

After the ceremony, the posing of the pictures, the reception and sit down dinner, Francis roamed around the garden feeling left out. He seemed to have nothing to say to anyone and making small talk was painful. He saw some old friends and all they had in common was the past.

"Wh'appen Ross? Remember when we used to kick some ball back when we were younger and fitter?" or, "What a way time fly! Remember when..."

He left a group of men talking and went over to Trisha. He caught her alone.

"Will the mother of the bride dance with the father of the bride?" She hesitated and he said hurriedly, "It's just a dance."

"Okay."

As always, all he wanted to say was stuck in his throat but something told him if he didn't say it now, it would be the last chance. He started with, "We have a beautiful daughter. You've done a great job. Don't think I haven't noticed all you've done."

"Thank you." She smiled but didn't look him in the eye. He got the feeling she wished the dance were over.

"Trish, only time makes you realize how...I did a lot wrong...I didn't realize things...you were a good wife, a great wife. I messed it up...I was young and stupid..."

"It's okay, Francis. It's all water under the bridge. I'm happy with Bill. Maybe it was meant to be like this."

Francis didn't say it but he felt it should never be like this. He muttered "maybe."

After he danced with Trisha, he walked casually over to his daughter. "My baby is a married woman now."

"I haven't been a baby for a long time, Dad."

Once again, he felt misunderstood. He tried again.

"That man of yours seems like a good man. Men these days are different, more into family. I haven't always been a good father."

The tears that threatened to erupt escaped. He hugged his daughter so she wouldn't see. Finally he said the words that had never left his lips.

"I love you, princess. I'm sorry how it's been with me and your mother. It wasn't meant to be like that."

She murmured, her voice sounding reminiscent of Trisha's, "Oh Dad.

I love you too. Stop thinking so much about the past. It's all water under the bridge."

AFTER THE INCIDENT – PART I

In his dream, a raven, black as night was perched atop a dark evergreen tree. The landscape was stark and desolate, the trees stripped of their leaves, scarecrows against a dull grey sky. The asphalt road was a melancholy washed out grey, the houses a forlorn echo of each other, a sorry sight to eyes that had feasted on the bright blues, sunny yellows, and lush greens of the Caribbean—where sounds, sights, smells assaulted the senses all at once.

In this tunnel of grey there was silence, except for the caw caw caw of a raven, an eerily lonesome sound that pierced the air. There it was again, an omen, but what did it mean? It was as if there was a message he was meant to decipher but the meaning was lost in the wind.

In his dream, the landscape shifted and Eddie Harrison was back in Jamaica, a teenager again, and playing football on the beach with his friends. They were all there, Ronnie, Warren and Paul.

"Pass the ball, Eddie," they shouted. He ran on the sand stumbling slightly on its uneven surface. Some girls in bikinis sashayed by, hips undulating, holding a tray of fish and festival. It was Hellshire beach, back in the old days when it was the hot spot on a weekend, filled with Hawaiian Tropics oil-slicked bodies scorching in the Caribbean sun.

One of the girls was his wife Sue-Ann, the way she used to be when he had first met her, long, thick, dark hair, tanned tawny skin and always smiling. She was tall, almost the same height as he, and she came up to him in the dream and stuck her hand down his pants. He shuddered and they went into the water. Then a wave came and carried him out to sea. He found himself alone, standing waist high in shallow water. The short, squat, red-skinned people on the beach in grass skirts appeared to be Arawak Indians. They waved to him and he waved back.

He was about to go onshore to ask how to get back when a kick from Sue-Ann woke him.

She said brusquely, "The alarm went off and you didn't even hear it. Aren't you going to get up?"

He swallowed his irritation, swung his legs over the side of the bed and rubbed his eyes, determined not to let the dream edge past his consciousness into forgetfulness. He needed the memory, the smell of the salty sea, the heat of the sun on his body and the erotic touch of his wife on his groin. He realized that it had been six months since they'd made love.

Eddie pulled on his robe and mentally prepared himself for the day. He changed and fed their ten-month old baby Abigail, and made lunch for his older daughter Sydney. Caring for his children had become second nature to him. Although he constantly complained that he had no time for himself, he was secretly proud that Abigail cried for him, had eyes only for him, and would fuss when Sue-Ann tried to take over. Eddie was the one who fed her, changed her diapers, played with her and spoke and sang softly to her. When the role was first thrust on him, he had felt useless. Sue-Ann would come home and shout that he had forgotten to change Abigail's diaper and bathe her, that Sydney's hair needed combing and that he hadn't organized dinner or done the laundry. Now he had a routine: cook dinner as soon as he came home, throw in a load of laundry, help Sydney with her homework, load and start the dishwasher, get everyone ready for bed.

After Eddie showered and dried the beads of water that ran down his legs, he straightened up and looked at himself in the full-length mirror. My God, how he'd changed. He had always been tall and lean but now his frame felt lost in the pudgy skin on his thighs and buttocks, and he had a paunch. He viewed himself sideways. He looked like his father. Old. His skin looked blotchy and mottled and his curly brown hair, kinky in some areas, was streaked with grey. Stooped. He'd had the tendency to round his shoulders as if he wanted to mask his height and blend in with the world. Now he felt weak abdominal muscles pulling down his frame to his middle. Defeated. His blue-grey eyes were watery and red with fatigue.

When he first came to Canada, he had taken a job as a security guard, a job to him that was as menial as a bag boy in a supermarket. It was all he could get, and he prayed that no one from Jamaica would spot him. He told his friends he wasn't working rather than tell them what he was doing. He could see the gossip. Hawk eyes and eager mouths stretched wide in anticipation of the newest juicy tidbit. Eddie Harrison from upper St. Andrew, former executive, yes, the same one who migrated for a better life to the great north, now not only a lowly security guard, but freezing his ass off for essentially nine months out of twelve. The very same one who was up to his elbows in Red Stripe and rum, and Sundays in the hot sun at the beach, and late night domino sessions with the boys on Fridays, now up to his elbows in dirty diapers and laundry, lunch boxes and vacuuming, and walks to the park, one eye watching his children on the swings, his other eye turned inward in regretful reflection.

He kept in touch with all his friends and still knew every 'important' event that was happening in Jamaica, the weekend jaunts to Negril or Ochi, the Frenchmen's parties and the latest gossip. Sue-Ann on the other hand couldn't care less what was happening in Jamaica which she referred to as 'down there' with a contemptuous sneer on her face. She had started jogging and going to the gym every day, in all types of weather. Eddie reflected that that was what made one a true Canadian, not the blue passport with the symbolic coat of arms on the cover with the apt Latin motto *a mari usque ad mare*—from sea unto sea—but the ability to go outside in all types of weather as if the weather itself didn't matter at all.

Sue-Ann jogged when it was raining or snowing. She jogged when it was morning or night. She jogged when there were five loads of laundry to be done and four hands would've been better than two. She jogged when bedtime stories needed to be read. She was at the gym when dinner needed to be cooked and he'd be damned before taking the kids to fast food restaurants every night.

Unlike him, she got more beautiful every day. She looked strong and athletic, lean and finely sculpted like a model from the cover of one of those fitness magazines. If he ever felt angry or resentful, or if the thought even surfaced in his mind that she was selfish, he suppressed it guiltily because she had been through so much. She had every right to keep busy. She'd told him she had to. It made her forget the incident.

The incident changed everything. If only the incident hadn't happened. Or, if only it had happened the way he replayed it in his mind, where he was a hero, saving Sue-Ann and killing the men. In Canada, they called it sexual assault, ambiguously tidy words to mask the violence of what happened five years ago in their bedroom. Rape was a better word. It conjured up all the hate and violence and horror and dread and insanity of the act.

The dogs had been barking that night but he'd taken no notice of it. Once one dog in the neighbourhood started up, then they all did, a cacophony of barks from every household, some barks high-pitched, others low and deep in the throat. He'd woken up that night and walked downstairs for a glass of water. He'd grabbed a kitchen knife, rushed back upstairs, and fought those two men before they had a chance to do the unthinkable and killed them both with his bare hands.

But of course, that was what he imagined. What really happened was that he hadn't heard a thing. Didn't grab a kitchen knife, but walked back into their bedroom where two men stepped from behind the door and held a gun to his head. Then they bound and gagged him with a filthy, foul-smelling scarf and kicked him into a corner. He watched with an odd sort of detachment while they took turns raping Sue-Ann. After they had gone, Sue-Ann limped from the bed, untied him and looked at him in disgust when she saw that he had shit his pants.

When they went to check on Sydney who was three at the time, they found her under her bed crying soundlessly, staring wide-eyed at them. She didn't speak for a month and they had never found out how much she had seen. Sue-Ann hadn't wanted to talk about it nor get help of any kind. She simply said that if he wanted to be married to her, he would have to come to Canada for good. She would be leaving the hell-hole as soon as she could.

Within a month, she'd wrapped up her life in Jamaica, cutting all ties that bound her, quit her job, cancelled all Jamaican credit cards, closed all bank accounts, sold all the furniture, paid the helper three months' salary, gave away their cat, and told the landlord from whom they rented their house, that he could kiss her ass, she was breaking the lease and too fucking bad. He could keep the deposit and stick it. In that same month, she'd taken blood tests, taken medication to prevent HIV should that unthinkable possibility occur, and had hidden the entire ordeal from everyone including her parents. She was adamant that no one would ever know.

The incident would not change her; the incident would make her stronger. No one needed to know her business to then go and carry news all over the island and have people looking at her, pitying her, and saying, "she's the one they raped." He'd gone along with it even though his heart was breaking and he woke in a cold sweat every night. She had been fine the first night, and even the night after. It was the third night that she woke and started screaming. The scream came from low in her throat and rose and rose to a high-pitched fervour that wouldn't stop. Even after he had held her rocking in his arms.

When Eddie came home from work that day, he tidied the house and threw in a load of laundry, fed the girls scrambled eggs and put them to bed. He cooked a quick stir-fry with chicken and broccoli because Sue-Ann liked it. Usually she would come home, wolf down dinner, berate him for some chore he hadn't done and head to her class but today she was going to school straight from work and coming home late. She was taking a Masters at the University of Toronto. Since they'd migrated to Canada five years ago, she had been taking a constant stream of courses in addition to working full time, and keeping herself fit. She reminded him of a racehorse that never ran out of steam, a powerhouse of energy. People didn't believe him when he, half-complainingly, half-proudly, told them how she swam twice a week, ran most mornings before work and on weekends, and worked out at the gym. Eddie wondered what his carefree, rum-drinking friends in Jamaica would say if they saw him now, up to his neck in domesticity, stirring the food around in the wok in faded blue slippers with a protruding belly like some old bachelor man.

Sue-Ann came through the door sighing.

"You're home early," he said. She looked exhausted. "I wasn't expecting you until later."

"I decided to leave early. I missed you guys."

"The kids are already sleeping."

"The house looks good."

It was a first. She'd never noticed his efforts before. She just expected the housework to be done. He came behind her and massaged her neck, then gently slid his hands down her back and around her breasts. She reacted as though she'd gotten an electric shock.

"Eddie, I just came home." She turned to face him and kissed him lightly on the cheek. "And I'm so tired. Not tonight, hon."

"Which night then?" She looked at him accusingly but he continued in a soft voice. "Every time I try, you're tired. I'm tired too. When are we not going to be tired?"

"I don't know. It will be better soon. After I get my Masters, I'll earn more money and we can get out of this stupid townhouse and buy a real house with a proper garden for the kids to run around in."

They sat down in front of the TV and he handed her a plate of the stir-fry dinner he had cooked.

He sighed. "I don't want you to overdo it. I know you are doing a lot. Maybe I'll get a second job." He changed the subject. "Warren is having a party this weekend at his new house in Jacks Hill. He says he can see all of Kingston from his balcony." She didn't say anything. "He said there will be two dance floors, one with oldies music and one for the younger crowd."

"Since when are you a big dancer?"

"It's going to be a great party. Wish I were there with the guys."

"What do you care? You don't dance."

"Just making conversation. It's not about me dancing, Sue-Ann. I miss home."

"Nobody is stopping you from going back."

Why did the conversation always have to take a turn for the worse?

"You know I'll never go back."

He treaded carefully with his next words.

"But why do you get so angry if I even mention home. I'm not the enemy, you know, and bad things happen here too."

"Go back, then."

"I'm not going back." He was exasperated.

"Well I'm sick of you always talking about what's happening there. Even when you talk to Jamaicans here. I heard you ask Belinda Carmichael the other night if she was missing the Air Jamaica office party. Do you think she cares? She's been here seven years. She has a life here. You talk about Jamaica as if we just left. God. You don't realize it, but you always do it. One foot in the past. And you asked Belinda's husband, whom you hardly know, by the way, if he wanted to go drink a rum. No one has time for that. People are busy."

"I was just being social. Christ, we live five minutes walk from them."

"Well, that's how it is here. And for God's sake, stop telling people you'd love them to drop in. No one drops in here. You want people to drop in when the laundry is being sorted on the floor or the bathroom hasn't been cleaned? I don't want anybody to drop in."

"I think we should go for counselling. To deal with... everything."

"You mean me. You mean the incident. You mean, I should go for counselling. Forget it. I don't need to talk about it. I don't need to be reminded of it. I'm fine."

"Okay."

He didn't tell her she had changed and that there was an ache in his heart that wouldn't go away and an unbearable guilt that made him constantly replay the events in his head. What if he hadn't been thirsty? What if he had carried a glass of water up to his room from earlier as he usually did? Why didn't he that night? What if he'd had a gun like so many of his friends who carried guns strapped to their ankles in holsters or bulging from their waists like some absurd Twenty-First century Western, where half the men who carried guns didn't even know how to use them? What if he were stronger, had been more careful? What if they had rented another house where the grills on the windows were screwed in to the inside-fucking-wall instead of the outside?

His daughter seemed okay. When they had first arrived, they'd go walking down the street and if she saw a dark-skinned man walking toward them, she'd cling to him and hide her face. When he pointed it out to her and asked why, she'd shrugged. He asked her what she had seen that night. She said warily that she didn't remember. He pointed out to her that they were all different shades of black and he didn't want her to be afraid of anyone. She'd shrugged again and ran off to play. He couldn't get any more out of her.

So many times he left things unsaid. They were all lodged on the tip of his tongue and sometimes he felt he would choke on the words. He wanted to talk about the incident, to shout to the world, "this is what happened to my family, to my wife, to me, and it's changed us, hurt us. I want to go and find the sons of bitches and kill them." So many times he wanted to do something, anything to get out of the house: walk the malls, run, see a movie alone, but he couldn't. He worked all day and came home to look after the children while Sue-Ann pursued all the things she wanted to do. And she was fooling herself if she thought that her rat race behavior would make her forget. He knew that if he got twenty Masters, five PhD's and ran around Canada twice, he would never forget the incident.

After Sue-Ann finally got her Master's degree, she earned five hundred dollars more per year. She told Eddie she could potentially earn much more but she liked her job. "If I go somewhere else, I might not have ten sick days nor such understanding bosses when it comes to time off. You need to look for another job. Belinda's husband Darryl only came to Canada four years ago and he's already earning over a hundred thousand a year."

Eddie looked for another job.

"I swear it's my accent," he told Warren over the phone. "I swear that when people hear me, they are not interested in even seeing my résumé."

"Bwoy, Eddie, better you than me. I couldn't deal with that. Yard is best. I'll visit foreign but I wouldn't leave for good."

Every time Eddie emailed a résumé, he thought of Darryl and his one hundred thousand a year. He wondered what made him different. If Darryl Carmichael could do it, surely he, Eddie Harrison, could do it too.

Eddie Harrison heard a baby's cry from far away. He had been in a deep sleep and thought he was still dreaming. He had been dreaming that he was in some alternate world where Muslims ruled and he had broken a law by not bowing down in front of a mosque. He tried to reason with the police but they held back his arms. He was screaming but no one would listen. He was trying to explain that he didn't know that he had to bow before approaching a mosque. He didn't know that particular law but he would try harder to remember in future. He didn't deserve to be beheaded for not knowing. He didn't deserve to die just because he was Catholic.

A child and her mother were being executed inside the mosque and he heard the child's crying screams over the caw of a raven. As the axe came down, he jumped out of his sleep and realized the crying child was Abigail. Eddie rushed into her room. Her face was blotchy and she was out of breath. She must have been crying for a while and even though he knew this, a part of him was glad he had been able to get some sleep. It was Monday morning and the same old routine was about to consume him. Sue-Ann had already gone, doing what he thought was insane: going to the gym before work.

"Daddy have you seen my library book?"

"It's on the table underneath the newspaper."

"Daddy can you sign my math test?"

"Pass it here."

The phone rang.

"Sydney, can you get it? Is it mommy?"

"No, it's a woman."

He took the phone and patted her head. "Hello?"

"Hi Eddie. It's Belinda Carmichael."

"Hey Belinda." He was cheerful, happy that it was almost the end of winter, the end of people hibernating like bears in a cave. He thought she was calling to invite them over. "How are you guys?"

"I'm quite fine, Eddie, but can you please tell your wife to stop fucking my husband? Darryl has no intention of leaving me for her, contrary to what she might think, and frankly, I've had enough of it. Eddie? Are you there? Surely you know. It's been going on for years. So do me a favour and tell her."

"Okay."

He couldn't believe that "okay" was all he said. Okay, then he'd hung up the phone. What does one say to a statement like that? He kept telling himself, okay. He could calm his anger. Okay. He could think it through. Okay.

He called Sue-Ann on her cell. "Come home now."

"What's wrong? Is it the children?"

"The children are fine. Come home now."

"No. I just started my workout. Then I'm off to work. Whatever it is, deal with it, Eddie."

"How long have you been sleeping with Darryl Carmichael? His wife just informed me." He heard her sharp intake of breath. "I'll see you shortly."

"So do you love him?"

"I don't know."

"Why, after everything, why?"

"Don't know. It just happened."

"Nothing just happens."

They called in sick. Eddie didn't feel guilty. He was sick. The churning in his stomach would not stop. He felt like his intestines were being wrung like a wet rag. When he dropped Sydney to school and Abigail to daycare, he couldn't bear to see them off. He felt like he would never see them again. He clenched his jaw to keep from crying.

That day Sue-Ann and Eddie talked honestly for the first time in years. They agreed everything had changed after the incident. It might've gone differently had the incident not happened but it had. Sue-Ann said she would always love him but she couldn't stay with him. She didn't want a sour break up. She knew he was an exceptional father and she wanted to share custody. She didn't know why she couldn't stay and she couldn't imagine why he would still want her to. Yes, she still loved him too, but she didn't want to go for counselling and she felt she had gotten over the incident. She also knew in her heart that it wasn't going to work. Her biggest mistake was the affair and not telling him sooner.

Eddie wanted to tell her that he would never forget the affair, but he would forgive her. Eddie wanted to tell her that they could start over and if she wanted to pretend the incident never happened, he would be glad to go along with it. Eddie wanted to say that living in a foreign country without her by his side seemed useless but that he couldn't go home, knowing he would hardly ever see his children. Eddie wanted to say so many things but he had become used to holding the words on the tip of his tongue. Eddie wanted to blame Sue-Ann but he found himself blaming the incident and the two men.

After Sue-Ann had gone and had emptied the house, emptied it of toys and chaos, mess, candy wrappers, Barbie dolls, doll houses, emptied it of laughter and demands, joy and the gentle, innocent smiles of his children, the silence closed around him like hands around his neck. There was nothing to do, no laundry nor homework, no questions to be answered, no dishes to load in the dishwasher and no dinner to cook for anyone. He made himself a sandwich with stale cold cuts and cheddar cheese that had turned orange and hard. It didn't matter. His senses were dulled so that he couldn't taste nor smell nor see nor feel. If his shell cracked, he knew he would collapse on the floor.

He thought of calling Warren but he didn't want to talk about anything. The energy it took to talk, he needed so as to put one step in front of the other. The house was becoming more and more oppressive. He tried to take a deep breath and came up short, gasping for air like a strangled fish. He clutched at the black turtleneck he wore, and tried to pry it off his neck. The panicked feeling was getting worse. He tore off the turtleneck over his head, flung it down and rushed to the back sliding door that opened onto his garden. He ran outside in a t-shirt, and felt the cold air prick at his skin like tiny little needles, darting in random jabs on his face and arms. One of Abigail's sand pails peeked out from behind an empty flowerpot, the only spot of colour in the garden.

Holding his heart, Eddie sat down slowly on the garden bench until the racing stopped, until he could breathe deeply again. He sat shivering in the cold for five minutes and as he stood, ready to go inside, he heard an eerily lonesome sound. Caw caw caw. It was a raven, perched atop an evergreen tree hidden almost by the branches. Eddie looked up at the grey sky and squinted. The raven looked down at him and as if in answer, the sobs rose from Eddie's throat and erupted in an anguished cry. Eddie shook his fist at the bird who seemed to stare through him with one eye. Then Eddie sank to his knees in the snow and held his head in his hands. The raven cawed again, the sole witness to Eddie's breakdown.

After the Incident – Part II

Eddie Harrison, unable to sleep, watched the spider slowly descend its web from the light fixture to six inches above his chest. The spider was larger than usual, about the size of a walnut, but such was Eddie's depression that he didn't care whether it landed on him and gave him the bite of death. Eddie couldn't see the web so it seemed as though the spider was suspended in mid-air. Then without warning, it scampered up again. Eddie watched the spider for a week, wondering why it decided to descend. It was as if it were playing a game of catch-me-if-you-can, but Eddie, drowning in self-pity, thought, "Even a spider doesn't want to come near me."

At the end of the week, exactly seven days later, Eddie slowly eased himself off his bed, picked up his tattered bed slippers and slowly and carefully clapped the spider between the slippers. That act of destruction brought him out of his stupor and he got out of bed, cleaned the gunk from the bottom of his slippers and went into the kitchen to make himself a cup of coffee. It was only then that he realized that it was winter again, one year later.

Eddie had been vaguely aware of the seasons changing. Winter had turned into a wet spring but he hadn't seen the first green buds peeping out of the ground nor heard the birds as they built their nests and laid their eggs. He woke up, went to work or sometimes didn't, so that sometime around early spring, he lost his job.

He stayed in bed all spring and watched television. He washed his clothes, flung them in the dryer and piled them on his bed unfolded so that clean clothes got mixed up with dirty clothes. His bed sheets stayed on for months. At one point his older sister Juliet had come up from Jamaica and tried to coax him out of his depression.

"Lots of people get separated, Eddie. You have two children to think about and if you don't get your life in order, Sue-Ann is going to get sole custody of Sydney and Abigail."

It was obvious that she thought that the threat of losing his daughters would have jolted him out of his state but he remained seemingly oblivious. He couldn't explain to Juliet that he was worried about all those things, that his heart sometimes beat so fast he thought it would explode, that he'd wanted to get up and take action but a sloth-like weariness overtook him and made him remain inert on the bed. At least he could will himself to sleep. It was easy. The panic made him tired so he would empty his mind, stare at a blank wall and when he came to, several hours would've passed. That was effortless, the easy passing of time through sleep.

He thought he would've gotten himself together by the summer. While lying in bed, he'd thought of all the places he would take Sydney and Abigail, Niagara Falls, Centre Island, Exhibition Place. If he hadn't been fired, he would've even taken them to Florida to see Disney World. But summer came and went and he'd hardly noticed. His daughters came over and visited as was specified in the separation agreement and he took them to McDonald's and watched movies with them at home. He loved those moments but it took a lot out of him. The pain he suffered when they left was too much to bear and he thought he understood why some fathers never played a role. It was perhaps easier not to see them at all.

Eddie only realized summer had turned to fall when there was an aggressive pounding on the door one morning and he opened it and looked out blearily into a bright sunlit morning and saw the canopied trees alight with umbrellas of red, gold, and orange.

Sue-Ann stood there looking belligerent and shoved a piece of paper into his chest.

"If you're not going to play any role at all, I'm filing for sole custody."

"I give you all the money you ask for," he said beseechingly.

"It's not enough. Sydney gave you a permission slip for a fieldtrip and you took it, didn't sign it, kept it and she missed out. She had to sit at school while all her friends went. You idiot!"

"I'm ss...sor...sorry," he sputtered. He knew from years of living with Sue-Ann that this amounted to a travesty of parenthood. God forbid her children should miss out on anything. She had Sydney up and down and across town doing every single activity a kid could do. Sydney was only seven and involved in gymnastics, swimming, tennis, soccer and voice coaching. It was too much. Abigail, almost two, was doing what Eddie thought a money-wasting activity, swimming for tots. Sue-Ann insisted he take Abigail every Sunday morning and he complied. He took her into tepid, heavily-chlorinated pool water for 45 minutes and sang songs in a circle with other parents who sometimes tried to make conversation with him, excruciating small talk. He had no energy for them and their happy lives.

He was glad to be with Abigail but why did everything have to run on a strict schedule? Sometimes he wanted to simply be with his children without outside interference, in the warmth of his home and if he took them out, why couldn't it be a place of his choosing? Sue-Ann acted like she couldn't trust him. She forgot that when they were together, he was the one who raised the girls. Had she so quickly forgotten that it was he who looked after Sydney and Abigail while she got her Masters, went to the gym, and screwed around with shiny-bald-headed Darryl Carmichael so that his wife Belinda had found out and called him one morning?

Eddie had found out later that Belinda had become suspicious when she came home from work and found Sue-Ann in her house slightly disheveled, claiming to be looking for her. She had found it odd. In this new country, miles apart in distance and culture from Jamaica, no one really dropped in unless it was some sort of emergency. Belinda had asked Sue-Ann if everything was okay and everything was, so she became suspicious. It was unlike Sue-Ann who never dropped in on anybody and who loathed it when people dropped in on her. Belinda had subsequently hired a private detective. As she told her friends, she wasn't going to lower herself by searching through emails and cell phones or waiting outside the house in the cold, waiting for some hint of suspicious activity. The pictures the detective took told her the whole story.

As far as Eddie knew, Darryl and Sue-Ann were over, and Belinda had stayed with him. It was shocking for Eddie and Belinda that this affair had gone on for three years. An even bigger shock for Eddie was that he still would've taken Sue-Ann back and forgiven her but she wanted out of their marriage. She wouldn't even stay for the children.

And now it was winter again. He had spent a year in hibernation on unemployment insurance and now it was time to emerge from the darkness. Eddie had a year to catch up on. He cleaned his house and sat down to write a résumé. At the end of the day, he had sent out twenty résumés, called old contacts, cleaned his house and shaved. He worked feverishly to restore order to his life. He also called his doctor and got a prescription for an antidepressant that, he was told, would take three weeks for noticeable change. But Eddie felt a change already. He couldn't let another year slip by unnoticed, wasted and causing irreparable damage to his career and his relationship with his daughters.

He called Sue-Ann and asked to pick them up. Yes, he knew it wasn't his weekend but he thought he would take them into Toronto to Nathan Phillips Square to go ice-skating. He thought she'd be glad so he was surprised when she rounded on him.

"Why should I? I plan to take them out this afternoon. Why should I drop my plans because you suddenly feel like taking them ice-skating? Get your act together. We came up with a schedule and you need to stick to it. I plan things six months in advance. I need notice."

"Oh come on. What's the big deal? You make such a big deal out of everything."

This was the wrong thing to say to her. She slammed the phone down and refused to pick it up when he called again. The following day she called him and asked if he wanted the children that day. He told her yes and hated how grateful his voice sounded. On the way to Toronto in the stuffy overheated car, Sydney told him that she had begged her mother to see him that weekend. He smirked inwardly. His children still loved him no matter what. They loved him even when he couldn't get himself together. They loved him even when he hated himself.

The drive into Toronto was easy and peaceful. Eddie played Abigail's music and they sang the nursery rhymes together. A large expanse of cirrus clouds like white truck tire tracks filled the sky. Eddie felt sorry he hadn't planned outings like this while he and Sue-Ann were together. It was difficult not to slip into regret.

The rink was crowded and it was late afternoon so it would be getting dark soon. Eddie was glad Sue-Ann had dressed them well, in hats that covered their ears and tied in a bow below their chins. He led them to a bench and put on their skates. He had to take off his thick gloves to tie them and his fingers, stiff with cold, burned as he strung the laces in through the holes.

"Wait, Sydney. Don't go running off. I have to put on my skates and Abigail's skates."

He couldn't believe Abigail, not yet two, had pink plastic baby skates. She was unsteady and he had to bend down and hold her tiny arms. He found that he couldn't do that and watch Sydney at the same time plus he was a little unsteady on his feet.

"Hold on, Sydney, wait for daddy," he shouted.

He spotted her as she weaved among the adults. She did a half turn and skated back to him.

"Please stay with daddy," he implored. "This place is full of strangers. You know not to talk to strangers, right?"

"Yes, daddy," she said dutifully and held his hand.

They skated unsteadily, holding hands, Eddie's eyes downward to watch Abigail when suddenly he felt the ice move out from under him and he found himself sitting on the cold hard surface, legs sprawled out, looking up straight into the narrow black eyes of Darryl Carmichael. Eddie didn't know which came first, seeing Darryl and falling, or falling and then seeing Darryl.

"Hello, Eddie. Are you alright, man?" He extended his arm to help Eddie up.

The man had some nerve to even say hello. Eddie wanted to get up and hit him.

"Yeah man. Yeah. I'm alright." Eddie got up clumsily and then he saw the petite frame of Belinda Carmichael behind Eddie.

She smiled wryly at him. "Hello, Eddie. How are you?"

The way he said, "I'm fine," a little too insistently, suggested he was not fine at all. Eddie didn't want to prolong the awkwardness but Darryl seemed insistent on talking to him. He sounded contrite.

"What a cold winter we seem to be having this year." Darryl looked at Sydney and Abigail. He had a silly grin on his face. "The girls have gotten big. Any news of back home?"

Eddie glared at him. Belinda wasn't saying much. Eddie saw her glance at the girls and look away. Then she bent down and retied her laces. It was absurd how Darryl didn't simply walk away. Was he a glutton for punishment or was he trying to punish him? Eddie hated confrontation but it was unavoidable.

"I don't think we have much to say to each other, Darryl. I th...think..." Eddie started to stammer and his eyes felt hot. "It's im...impossible to ignore what has happened. My marriage has broken up and my children..."

He couldn't go on. His children no longer had a stable home. He looked down and saw that his hand, numb from the cold, was still attached to Abigail. He looked around for Sydney's pink and purple hat. Panic's iron grip wrenched at his heart when he realized she was not near him. Mentally, he reassured himself. She couldn't be far and he stretched his gaze over the entire rink. It was impossible to see because of the crowd. She was three heads shorter than the adults and people weaved and bobbed at an alarming speed.

Eddie gasped, "Sydney, where's Sydney?"

He saw Belinda shrug nonchalantly but Darryl broke away.

"She was just here a minute ago. She can't be too far. What colour is her hat? What colour is her jacket?"

Belinda mumbled, "I'll look after Abigail. You guys search for Sydney."

Darryl took charge. "I'll cover this end of the rink. You go the other way."

Eddie hated that he felt grateful to Darryl. If anything happened to Sydney, Sue-Ann would never forgive him and worse, he would never forgive himself. On the rink, the skaters kept going blurry before his eyes and he found it hard to focus. Colours swirled together, a dissonant mix of hats, gloves, jackets, scarves. Oh God, where was the blue jacket and the pink and purple hat? An unpleasant tinny taste in his mouth when he swallowed made him want to vomit.

Without warning, a panicked cry erupted from him. "Sydney? SSyyydddnneeeey?"

He impulsively grabbed a man who was skating with his children.

"My daughter," he gasped. "My daughter is missing. She's wearing..." He promptly forgot what she was wearing. "Help me find my daughter."

He took a deep breath and the cold air filled his nostrils and the words tumbled out as fast as he could speak coherently.

"Seven, light blue ski jacket, pink and purple hat, dark brown hair, dark brown eyes, slender, brown skin."

By then a small crowd had gathered. Eddie was surprised that the normally reticent local people, usually aloof, swarmed around him getting details and passing it on from person to person as if on an assembly line. Men, women and teenagers called out Sydney's name and rushed from one end of the rink to the other searching for the little girl. A buxom blonde woman called out to a cop. Instead of saying, 'Excuse me, sir,' she said, "Hey! Officer! A child is missing."

Eddie wondered why he even noted such trivialities at a time like this. He even noted that her skin looked coarse, hardened as if she were a heavy smoker and had a hard life. It occurred to him that this woman who he had pre-judged was the one taking charge to help him. She roared Sydney's name, took his hand and led him beyond the rink.

"We're going to find her. Don't you worry," she assured him. "Don't you worry."

It seemed these events played out for hours but he realized after that only seven minutes had passed. They were the longest seven minutes of his life. The thought of calling Sue-Ann sent beads of sweat down his back and he thought he would rather have jumped off a bridge.

Then, like the superhero in a fantasy movie, Darryl came striding toward him holding Sydney in his arms. It was surreal how time slowed to a crawl after that and he thought he saw Darryl walking in slow motion grinning triumphantly, his winter jacket making his arms look more muscular and larger than they really were. Darryl was the unlikely hero—portly, bald-headed—what did Sue-Ann see in him? He, Eddie, was better-looking and taller. It had to be one of two things, money or sex.

But how could he be thinking these things at this time? Darryl was holding his precious Sydney in his arms. Eddie was so grateful he wanted to thank him profusely but he hated him at the same time. Then everything seemed to happen quickly. The officer was striding towards him and talking to Darryl. Sydney had skated to the other side of the rink and had come off the ice because her feet were hurting. Then she had hobbled over to the hot chocolate stand balancing on the narrow blades and away from all the commotion.

Eddie felt light-headed. He took Sydney from Darryl.

"Thank you, Darryl." He turned to Sydney and his anger erupted. "Why did you leave? A wha wrong wid you, pickney? You know better. You should never have left daddy."

"Easy now. It's okay. Everything's okay." That came from Darryl.

"No," he shouted. "Everything is not okay. You hear me? It's not okay."

Abigail, who was in Belinda's arms, started to cry.

Belinda stepped in. "Hi Sydney. Are you okay, honey?"

Sydney nodded. Eddie's heart was breaking. He wanted to hit Sydney and hug her at the same time. He lifted her chin and stared into her eyes. Her lips trembled and his eyes watered in response.

The news that Sydney was found, spread through the crowd and he felt people patting him on the back, shaking his hand, with the women telling him to 'thank God.' They reached down and patted Sydney's head. They told him their own stories of when they lost their children in grocery stores, department stores, and how they had felt and how it all turned out all right. He was glad for the distraction. None of these kind strangers knew that he was filled with equal amounts of love and hate. Why were Darryl and Belinda still standing by him when he just wanted to be alone?

"Well, I think we're going to be off," Eddie said.

"But Daddy, we just got here."

Eddie was grim. "We'll come back another time." He turned to Darryl. "Thanks again, man. Bye, Belinda."

He turned abruptly and walked away.

Eddie debated on the drive home whether or not he should tell Sue-Ann what had happened. Nothing happened really. He had simply run into the man she had been sleeping with, he had been so shocked that he hadn't noticed his daughter running off and then he had spent a heart-wrenching seven minutes thinking she might've been kidnapped by some pervert and gone for good.

Sue-Ann opened the door as if she were annoyed to be interrupted, as if she couldn't wait for him to be gone.

Eddie screamed at her, "Why did you do it? How could you?"

She looked surprised. All through the mediation he had been oddly calm. He had agreed to all her terms, never questioning, never getting angry, just letting Sue-Ann dictate what weekends she wanted, what holidays, how much money she wanted.

"You were my girl, you know." Eddie started to cry. "You were always my girl."

"Not in front of the children." She ushered Sydney inside and took Abigail from his arms.

"But why Darryl Carmichael with his big, bald head? Three years? I should've known." She started to protest but he held up a hand to stop her. "Tell me nuh? Was it his dick? Was it big enough for you? Did it fill you up? Mmm? The fancy car?"

"Eddie, stop it! Shame on you! In front of the children! Get out. Leave."

"Go on. Treat me like a dog." His angry tears turned to resignation. "It doesn't matter anyway. You never gave us a chance. You never wanted to work it out."

"It was over, Eddie. Everything changed after we came to Canada."

Eddie shook his head and turned his back on her. He got into his car and drove off. It was dark as he steered toward the exit and merged with the highway traffic.

It started to snow, a light sideways falling snow that swirled around on the road like duppies rising from their graves and making the road slippery. It was eerie like some horror movie. The wind lifted and gathered the snow from the road, making it rise, swirl and fall, to rise again. Eddie's windshield was momentarily battered, perhaps from the snow falling from the truck in front of him or an onslaught of hail. It mimicked the strange heavy beating of his heart and gave him a feeling of powerlessness.

The end of his marriage had nothing to do with money or sex, Darryl Carmichael or moving to Canada. It was over back in Jamaica, after the incident, from that fateful night those men broke into his house and raped Sue-Ann. He recoiled in his seat when he remembered her eyes after she'd untied him. She didn't avert her eyes when she saw he'd shit himself. She'd looked at him with aversion. She had decided then to hate him. Maybe even to blame him. And she hated herself. That night he had tried to hold her. He wanted her to see into his soul, to see how he loved her and how horrified he had felt at the incident. But it had been too late, even then.

Eddie took a deep breath and looked up. The sky was black and clear. It had stopped snowing. The only sign of snow was on the roads where cars had not yet driven and on rooftops and treetops. All was calm. And the landscape was utterly changed.

After the Incident – Part III

According to Eddie Harrison's friend, Migo, there was only one way to get over a woman and that was to find another woman. It would be easy in Jamaica where there was *punaani* in abundance, willing to give it up to a man with money, *punaani* of all colours, shapes and sizes, available at supermarkets, nightclubs, parties, the beach...

"I really can't make that trip right now, Migo. I looking job," Eddie told him annoyed.

Sue-Ann had always said Migo was a man who had never and would never grow up.

"Don't take up with those Canadian women! You'll end up losing half of everything you own. Plus you'll end up doing all the housework while they go off gallivanting to gym and club and class. You need a sweet young thing," continued Migo, oblivious to the fact that Eddie had stopped talking. "If it's the airfare, I can get it for you. No problem, man."

Eddie had felt a sudden and unexpected rage.

"It's not the *bumbaclat* airfare. I can buy my own ticket. It's the timing. It's a bad time."

"Easy man. Just trying to help."

"I don't need your help," Eddie told him brusquely. "I can find a woman on my own. I'm not even sure I want to, seeing that they are usually hypocrites and liars." Especially Sue-Ann, he thought. If someone had told him Sue-Ann would've been unfaithful, sleeping with bald-head Darryl Carmichael, he would've laughed and said, no way. Not my wife. But she had and it had cut him to the core. He was just now recovering from a year-long depression.

But after Eddie hung up the phone, he found himself on his computer researching on-line dating services. He felt there was no easy way to meet a decent woman in Toronto. Decent women didn't go to bars till all hours of the morning picking up guys. He chose a service and plugged in his information, already despairing at the lack of details requested that couldn't possibly describe who he was, nor anyone else for that matter. Nevertheless, he forced himself to go through with it.

Name: Eddie Harrison

Gender: Male

Age: 43 (feels much older, some mornings feels like 80)

Location: Toronto (not exactly but close enough)

Body type: Slim (supposed to be slim but now carrying a paunch, still slim, though, but not toned)

Ethnicity: Prefer not to say (if you say Jamaican, people stereotype you; if you say mixed, it sounds like you have no idea what the hell you are)

Hair: Salt and pepper (was a nice shade of dark brown before The Incident)

Eyes: Brown

Profile: I am seeking a woman

For: Dating (what else would he be seeking a woman for?)

Drink: Socially (but there is no one to drink with so has taken to drinking alone now and then)

Marital status: Divorced (in paper only. Still madly in love with ex-wife and strongly feels that she threw away what could've been the best marriage ever, even after The Incident, because with counselling, people have gotten through worse, through war, death, anything)

Profession: Manager (a big boldfaced lie. The correct response is, nothing. What you were in one country means nothing in another country where you have to prove yourself all over again to different people with different backgrounds. The real answer should've been 'full of potential if only given a chance.' But which woman under-stands that?)

Smarts: College (a business degree, utterly useless in today's world)

Do you want children: No (but I still don't want to date an old woman past her childbearing years. I'd like a young and beautiful woman who is willing to love my children. Does she exist? Probably not)

Do you have children: Yes (the two most beautiful girls in the world who I hardly get to see and when they're with me, they act like I'm some stranger they've just met and every time they visit, I have to start all over again like we're a family with short term memory loss)

Do you do drugs: No

Do you have a car: Yes (I have wheels that move)

Interests: Movies, relaxing with a bottle of wine, great conversation, the beach, traveling, sailing, soccer (women want a sporty guy), cooking, reading, enjoying life. (I haven't actually done any of these things in a long time. I've been watching TV. The only thing I've been interested in is watching TV)

This information couldn't possibly tell someone that he, Eddie, had plummeted straight to hell, that he had seen his lovely wife raped by two hideous men and the incident had tormented them, taken them away from their island home, cast them adrift on unknown shores, torn them apart so that their marriage became one of convenience and even that had crashed like a roof collapsing on a house and destroying everything in it. The information could never say that Sue-Ann sought solace from another man, Darryl Carmichael—the name still left a bitter taste in Eddie's mouth, like bile that rose up unbidden and soured everything around him.

A week after posting his profile, Eddie got a date. Her name was Flavia and she was somewhat attractive with hips that swayed seductively as she walked. Eddie tried to imagine how her hips would conform to his and move under him but he couldn't get past the kiss. Her lipstick was a bright orange-pink colour. Sue-Ann never wore lipstick.

"I love your accent," she said too many times and he wanted to roll his eyes. "You don't look at all like the Jamaicans I know. I work with a Jamaican guy. When he gets mad, no one understands what he's saying."

Eddie sighed and shrugged. "Jamaicans are mixed up. I mean, we're not mixed up, we're mixed, many races." She'd laughed. "Everyone is mixed up."

There was a long pause. Eddie remembered his first date with Sue-Ann. They had been so young, teenagers, but there had been no pauses. They'd laughed a lot at everything. And they went out and danced and when he had kissed her, he'd known she'd be the only woman he'd ever love. A man could screw a lot of women but for him, she'd always been that special one. Flavia bored him and he suspected he bored her. He didn't want to explain how Jamaicans were mixed or why he'd moved to Canada or where he was or wasn't working. It was too much work. He didn't want to make the effort to get to know someone new.

"So you have two girls. Tell me about them," Flavia had asked, rambling. Eddie watched her orange-pink lips moving but barely heard her words. "I once dated a man with a child but she hated me. I guess she still hadn't gotten over her parents' divorce."

Eddie wanted the date to end and when it did, he took Flavia home and didn't say he'd call her. He told her he'd had a nice time and that she seemed like a nice person. She asked him if he wanted to come upstairs and he told her maybe another time because he had to go to work early the next morning.

"Tomorrow is Sunday," she said disbelievingly.

"I know, and I have to work," he said firmly and that had been it.

A week later, Eddie joined a gym. He felt he was being conned the moment he sat in the office opposite the muscled salesman who told him that he needed a personal trainer in addition to the monthly membership.

"I think I'll be fine just coming and working out," he told the salesman. The salesman looked in his eye. "You won't see the results you want. You need to first strengthen your core. Your core is your center. It's where you first need to be strong. The rest of your muscles can't function without a strong core."

Those words had a greater effect on Eddie than the salesman had intended. Eddie not only booked a personal trainer for six weeks, but that Sunday he went to church for the first time since he'd taken his first communion as a boy in Jamaica. Eddie realized it wasn't only his muscular core that needed strengthening, it was the core of his soul. A strong man wouldn't have shit his pants and even if he had, he would've found a way to keep his wife and his children together. And even if all those things were beyond his control, a strong man wouldn't have lain in bed for a year under a debilitating depression, unable to get up and work. Eddie knelt down in the church pews among strangers and hid the tears that ran down his face.

"God, I'm begging you as I've never begged before, make me whole, make me strong, show me what to do. Help Sue-Ann. Help us."

Desperately, he watched for signs that his prayers were being heard. So when that week, he turned on CBC radio and heard a program on forgiveness, he saw it as a sign of hope. A man being interviewed talked about forgiving the terrorist who had killed his child. Eddie figured if a man could forgive such a huge loss, he could somehow learn to forgive Sue-Ann for leaving him, for sleeping with Darryl Carmichael. He could forgive the men for raping her, although he didn't know how, and he could forgive himself for not doing anything, for not being able to do anything, because, he reasoned to himself, if he had tried to do anything, they might not be alive right now. He wanted to say that to Sue-Ann. He wanted to say to her, 'we're alive dammit. We're alive. We could be dead but we're alive.'

One morning a few weeks later, Sue-Ann showed up on his doorstep out of the blue. He was so surprised he stood gaping at her.

"I know I didn't call before, but I wanted to talk to you. And I thought you might like to see the girls," she said. Then she stared at him, her glance going up and down. "You look great, by the way. Are you working out?"

"Yes, I am working out." Eddie hugged his daughters as they came in.

"Can I come in too?" she asked.

"Of course. It's just so unexpected." She walked in and surveyed his place. He saw it through her eyes, still sparse since she had left and taken mostly everything. His gym bag was on the floor, the contents spilling out.

"I haven't had a chance to tidy up," he said apologetically.

"It's not bad," she said, and sat down.

"Would you like a drink?" he asked.

"A beer, please if you have it." Eddie raised his eyebrows slightly. This was unlike Sue-Ann.

"I know this visit is unexpected. I had to come in person. I had this strange dream last night. It was so weird. In the dream, I came to your house to talk about Sydney because you know she's having trouble at school," she said as she sat down on the sofa.

"No, I didn't know. Why didn't you tell me?"

"Well, I didn't know if it would make a difference but the guidance counselor says she is suffering from post-traumatic stress disorder. She cries at school and tells her teacher she wants her parents back together." Sue-Ann glanced quickly at Eddie. He remained silent. "Anyway, in the dream, we came to visit you. You were in this large house and I was sitting on a bed in the basement with Sydney and Abigail. You looked down at the floor and there was this huge snake, this huge, thick, red-and-black snake. Maybe a boa. You grabbed the snake. Of course, in the way dreams happen, the snake turned into a red and black Barney."

"Barney?"

"You know, Barney, the purple dinosaur. But it was still a snake and you wrapped your arms around it and told me to get the girls and run. You told me to run to safety. Then the Barney boa turned its head and bit you on the arm. It took out a chunk of your arm but you didn't let go. You were bleeding and everything and it left a gaping wound in your arm but you continued to wrap your arms around it as it attacked the crap out of you until we got out of the room. I woke up and realized immediately what the dream meant. It meant you would do anything to protect us. You came here for me, to Canada I mean. I've been thinking a lot, you know, and I don't know if 'we' will work and I don't blame you if you don't want me to come back and I'm not even sure if I want to come back. I wanted to come over and tell you I'm sorry for everything that's happened."

The words tumbled out fast like she needed to get them out.

"Why did you sleep wid Darryl?"

"Why do we have to bring that up?"

"Come on, Sue-Ann. How can we not bring that up? Dat was the last straw. I mean, it started from the incident. Do you want to not bring that up too?"

Eddie found himself feeling stronger. He found that he was shocked at the words coming out of his mouth from deep within him. It almost seemed like the crunches and planks, all those exercises that strengthened his muscles had also strengthened his resolve.

"We're alive, Sue-Ann. I wish I could've stopped those men but I was tied up. I wish I'd had a gun but I've never believed in violence. I never thought anything could happen to us. Do you see now that I did everything I could? I was terrified. I've never felt terror like dat before, not for myself, but for you and Sydney. The entire time I kept praying dey wouldn't find Sydney. I was begging God to let us all live."

"I know that. I know you love us." Sue-Ann shifted herself closer to him until their thighs were pressed together.

"I'm sorry that happened to you. I'm really sorry." Eddie turned and took her hands in his.

"I'm sorry, too," she whispered. "Do you think we can be a family again? Sydney is doing so badly in school." Sue-Ann started crying. "I don't know what to do. I just know I can't do it alone."

"We'll always be a family. I will always take care of all of you. But I can't go back to how things were. Maybe before I could've, but not now."

Eddie had always thought he would've taken Sue-Ann back in a heartbeat so he was shocked as the words came out of his mouth.

"I want to be friends, and I'm not just saying that. I mean it. We raise the girls together. We get together for special occasions and if someone else comes into the picture, we deal with the situation then. But I can't forget Darryl Carmichael just like that. Our marriage wouldn't be the same. I don't know if I could trust you again. I want to, but I can't erase the past like dat."

Sue-Ann started to sob.

"Sweetheart, listen, what is it you want?" asked Eddie.

"I want you to forgive me."

"I have forgiven you. I forgive you now. But I still haven't forgiven myself. I'm working on it. But I don't see this as the end for us. It's another beginning. But I need to get myself together before I make any decisions on what I'm going to do. That doesn't change how I feel about you or that we are still a family."

"How did you get so strong?" Sue-Ann's tear-stained face looked up at him. "You're seeing someone else, aren't you?"

"No, I'm not. I'm not saying I won't ever, but I'm not seeing anyone at all right now."

"Everything hurts so much. I started seeing Darryl because I wanted to forget all the hurt. Every time I looked at you, I remembered that night."

Eddie wanted to take her in his arms and tell her all was forgiven. But would that change anything? Would she still look at him and remember that night? Would she go off and sleep with someone else, hurting him even more?

He had to ask the question: "So when you look at me now, do you still remember that night?"

"It will take time to forget."

"Do you remember me as I was that night?"

"Yes. But I want to give us another try. I want to try and make love with you again."

Eddie wanted her but he heard himself saying, "And what if it doesn't work? What if you go off again and sleep with someone else?"

"I won't but isn't life a risk? Aren't all relationships risky?" she asked.

Eddie shook his head.

"No. I won't take that risk. A long time ago, I suggested counselling. Maybe if we'd done that... but I can't give us another try, not right now."

Sue-Ann nodded. She got up and walked to the door.

"You haven't really forgiven me, then."

"Yes. I have. And I'm finally learning what it means to forgive myself."

After Sue-Ann left, Eddie sat down, poured himself a drink and put his feet up in front of the TV. Tomorrow he would start sending out those résumés. He would go to the gym. Then he'd check out one of those sailing courses. He would teach his girls to sail with him. He would start enjoying life until the sharp pain that surrounded him eased and became a dull thud, until eventually it would disappear.

That was what he hoped—that one day he could think of Sue-Ann without that pain. One day she would look at him and she would see him as he was, not as the impotent husband who couldn't protect her.

As his eyes closed sleepily, he clasped his hands on his shrinking belly and felt content and calm for the first time in a long time.

THAT I VANT

I met him in Toronto, at the corner of King and Jarvis, on my way to a job interview. It was noon in late August and the weather was warm; blue skies with cirrus clouds moved slowly directly overhead. People in T-shirts and shorts sauntered in and out of cafés. I didn't pay him any mind because he was dressed like a hoodlum in baggy jeans with a black sweatshirt with a hood. He was large and black and he eyed me down, so I stared straight ahead and watched him from the corner of my eye.

I wore a blue pinstriped suit, with my hair slicked back in a bun and high-heeled shoes. He made an appreciative smacking sound with his lips. I was annoyed but, at the same time, felt a warm, familiar feeling.

He said: "You can't even return my hello." He had a Canadian accent.

"Hello," I said. "I'm in a rush. Cyah stop."

"Wait. Did I hear right? Are you a *yardie*?"

"Yes."

"Really? You couldn't be. You don't look like a Jamaican."

"I am."

He licked his lips and smiled. "Can I call you?"

"No. I have a boyfriend. Sorry. I have to go."

I saw him a week later on King Street again. I was waiting for the streetcar.

"Hello, Miss Jamaica. *Yardie* girl."

"Hello."

"Did you get the job?"

"Yup. Hate it though."

He told me he worked at the Toronto Star. He wasn't a journalist but he'd try to get me in. I gave him my résumé and my number.

He called me early in September and we met in the park. People sat in groups eating sandwiches and chatting animatedly. Grey-and-white pigeons, their chests puffed out, hovered nearby and pecked at crumbs. We sat on a bench and stared straight ahead.

"Don't worry, *Yardie* girl. You'll get another job fast. You speak good English. When I came here, man, it was tough. I was 10."

"Didn't you speak English?"

"No, man."

His mother had left him in Jamaica when she came to Toronto. She'd left him with an uncle who had beat him, shouted at him, and treated him differently from his own children. By the time his mother sent for him two years later, he was already full of fight and hate. His memories were painful; he looked down often and fidgeted on the bench. The Canadian children teased him and laughed at the way he spoke. His teachers pretended not to understand. They laughed along with the students and ridiculed him in front of the class. He didn't know his father and he loved his mother, but he didn't like her.

"I don't know what was wrong with her, man, but she was always angry, always shouting and beating me. For nothing."

He told me about the time he got into a fight with an older white boy who'd been teasing him. He said he taught that boy a lesson, not to tease him no more. But his mother took the teacher's side, he said in disbelief.

"She always took everyone else's side over mine. Always. Why am I telling you this? I haven't thought about this in years."

He was a grown man and he looked like he was about to cry. I was embarrassed.

"Even after they suspended me, I came home and she beat me."

He looked away. We were silent. Then he turned back to me abruptly and smiled.

"I always wanted a girl like you, Jamaican with that brown colour, or like you but mixed with Chinese, or just Chinese, Chinese-Jamaican. Yeah. Only a Jamaican girl would understand me. I'm getting outta this place... soon. I'm going back to Jamaica to build my big house in Red Hills. But first, I'm going to New York to pursue my acting."

"You have the look for it," I lied.

"Yeah, I'm getting out of this shithole. This is no place for a black man. The system works against us. I was in jail once. My ex-girlfriend wanted to cause trouble for me. She wanted me out of the picture so she called the cops. Told them I beat her. They threw me in jail, man, no questions asked."

"That's terrible."

"Yeah. A girl like you beside me, then I'd be fine. I guess your boyfriend has a lot of money. I had a lot of money once. A lot of money."

"Really?"

"Yeah. I don't know where it's all gone. I blew it. I did the drug thing... dealing. I had enough money to buy a house, a nice car, but I wasn't thinking. I blew it on friends, restaurants, going out all the time, that kind of stuff. One time I had over two hundred thousand Canadian, cash."

"That's a lot of money. You should've bought a house."

"Yeah, I should've. I'm out of that business now. It's too dangerous. I don't want to get killed or go to jail."

"Too bad you couldn't do the drug thing one more time...to set yourself up?"

"Naw, I'm out of it now. Gotta look after my kid. I've got a little girl. She's four. My goal is to be a good father and an actor. I see her every week."

He called me a few weeks later. He was going to New York to check out some acting prospects. He said he'd call when he got back. When I called two months later, he was gone.

The aesthetician who did my manicure was 23-years-old and came from Romania. Her hair was glossy black and short and her skin was vampire-pale and acne-scarred. Her face was long and her black eyes were framed with short, thick lashes. She never smiled. She spoke with a short, gruff manner and her accent was thick: Eastern European with a Spanishy ring. When I told her my boyfriend gave me a day at the spa as a birthday gift, she sighed and said I was lucky.

"Yes. He is wonderful," I said. "Are you married?"

She sighed. "Yes."

"Is he Canadian?"

"No. He is Romanian too."

"How wonderful. Then you understand each other. My boyfriend is Jamaican and we really understand each other."

"My husband, we no understand each other."

Her husband, at 57, was only two years younger than her father. They did not think alike. She didn't love him but she couldn't have stayed in Canada without him. She couldn't leave him now because she had no money and he was sponsoring her mother.

"I would stay if he was rich but he not even that. Yes, I could be happy with some money, but he old and poor." She changed the subject. "People like you, I love. I love this skin you have, this mix of black and white. I see men like you, but...I am already married. I see young men. I vant. That I vant."

I told her I'd been married too, that it was hard to leave, but she could do it.

White lab-coated aestheticians walked back and forth. The place reminded me of a research centre. I wondered how often wealthy women came for all the treatments: the massages, facials, salt glow scrubs, the manicures and pedicures. The Romanian broke my thoughts by saying her job was very poorly paid.

"I don't normally say this," I said, "and I don't believe in it myself, but maybe you should have an affair with a young man."

"My husband, he will kill me. He say that already."

But the prospect must have been enticing to her because she blushed and smiled. I told her to open her own bank account and prepare for the day she would finally leave him. While she clumped pale pink nail polish on my fingers, we plotted and planned together. She'd send the money to Romania where the interest was higher. She wouldn't have any children for him even though he kept pushing her to do it. He thought she was trying but she hid her birth control pills taped to the bottom of an old cooking pot in the drawer in the bottom of the oven. He never went in the kitchen anyway. He was one of those who couldn't find his own socks. He couldn't cook a meal or make himself a cup of coffee. He disgusted her. She'd wait till her mother was sponsored and, meanwhile, she'd look for another job. She started to smile.

"I know how you feel," I said. "Every morning I woke up and asked myself, 'Is life like this?' I was so unhappy. Now, I'm always happy. You will be, too."

"Yes," she replied, her dark eyes shining. "I will leave him. I will wait. What language you speak in Jamaica?"

"English."

"No! I tink broken English, no?"

"Well, ah, we speak English. Some people speak broken English."

"Ah. I will leave him. I will wait."

I left her a generous tip even though the nail polish was thick and gooey and smeared within the hour.

The first taxi left and I waited half-an-hour for the next one. It was a cool, busy Friday night in October. Couples came out of the building hand in hand, laughing, dressed up for a night out on the town. A light persistent rain fell. I held one sick child in my arms and gently pushed the other sick child ahead of me into the taxi.

"Are you the jerk who left me after I specifically told you to wait and that I'd be right out?" I said as I got in.

"No, no. Dat not me. I heard dispatcher call now and I come now."

"Oh."

"Do not be angry. It is such a nice night."

I didn't answer. The dispatcher's voice, staticky and cracked, came through the radio on the dashboard.

"Pick up at Queen Street. There's a large dog."

A European accent: "I'm not picking up a large dog. It will make bad smell in taxi."

The Canadian dispatcher: "OK."

An Indian accent: "This is driver 101. What was the address again?"

The Canadian dispatcher: "Write it down. Write everything down. That's why I keep telling you people to write everything down. Now you've just wasted a good six minutes circling around. It's 4220 Yonge. See why I tell you people to write everything down."

The Indian: "You said 2042."

The Canadian dispatcher: "Oh, I did, did I? So now you're calling me a liar, driver 101? Play it back for me, driver 101. Play it back. I want to hear exactly what I said."

The Indian: "I erased it."

The Canadian: "Oh God, 101. If you're gonna lie, at least don't get caught in it. Write everything down."

I giggled. "Sounds like my boss."

The taxi driver replied, "Work, work, work, here. All work."

The taxi driver was from Pakistan and we talked about the fact that mangoes in North America were tasteless and we had so many delicious varieties in our countries. His brothers were doing well in Pakistan, better than he. The life was better there. He had young children but he had decided not to raise them in Canada. He worked seven days a week to save money so he could take them back. The houses in Pakistan had eight or nine bedrooms and everyone helped. It was too hard here. His wife had no help. Back home if you needed help, he said, you shout and soon, someone will come.

"I know what you mean," I said. "Here, we are all slaves."

"Yes," he shouted in his enthusiasm. "We are slaves. Work, work, work, work, work. And they won't give you a job without Canadian experience."

"And how will we get Canadian experience if someone doesn't give us a chance?"

"Exactly," he shouted, "back home I'm an engineer. Here no work so I am a taxi driver."

"All I do," I said, "is get on the subway, like a cow herded on a truck, packed up close with strangers coughing and sneezing up the place."

We sighed and were silent.

"You know, I didn't feel free in Jamaica. I couldn't walk on the road at night or ride a bicycle in the day. I can here yet I'm still not free."

He couldn't believe that I'd left my husband and come with my children alone.

"He beat you, no?"

"No, no. It just didn't work."

He didn't understand.

The rain pelted the windows and I felt warm and safe in the cab with the black interior and the driver's picture pasted on the seat in front of me. Underneath his picture was a statement that said I had a right to a safe and comfortable journey and the driver had to respect my right to silence. I leaned forward suddenly and asked, "What are your dreams?" The question shocked him. It was too intimate.

"My dreams?"

A second passed.

"I want a big house in Pakistan. I want my children to be successful, maybe a doctor. I want my family to be happy. I want to taste the fruit in Pakistan in the summertime. I want to know my nieces and nephews. I want my children to grow up as I did. Yours?"

"I want to be a writer. A good one. And of course I want my children to be successful too," I added as an afterthought.

The taxi stopped at the curb.

"We're here. This is it."

He jumped out to help me. I woke the older child and shuffled out with the younger one, her head flopped to one side. It was still raining and the tail lights of the cars in the distance were hazy and blurred.

"Good luck," I said.

"Good luck," he echoed.

I walked into the After Hours Doctors Clinic and sat down. Four women in saris and two African women, their heads covered and their long dresses trailing to the floor, waited with their children. They looked careworn, weary to the bone. Their tired, sad eyes watched their kids distractedly.

Looking at them, I wondered if they too had dreams that had gone astray. Dreams of a better life in the Promised Land that had not quite panned out as planned. I wondered if they yearned to escape this tired life, to chase some secret dream.

The aesthetician's voice played-back in my head: "Yes, that I vant."

Within your class

When people gossiped about Heinz Goldberg, they said his life was a mess, a self-inflicted tangle of problems he brought on himself and therefore deserved. How could a man, they said to each other, so professional in his work, so accomplished and debonair, be so downright stupid when conducting his private affairs? And now he had a child to look after, a little brown-skinned girl, the union of Heinz and a local prostitute.

That relationship was over now, but here was Heinz, carrying on with his helper and taking her to all the functions in town. He had told his business partner that he was going to make her a lady, to push her status up to middle-class. Heinz's middle-class friends were outraged. They pointed out that it could not be done. Things were simply not done that way.

Heinz Goldberg was Austrian by birth but he had grown up in Germany and Denmark. He came to Jamaica first on vacation in the late Seventies, and when his parents died, he took his inheritance money and his wife Marit and came again in 1982. He stepped off the plane and the island's smell rose to greet him: heat, tarmac, earth and a faint whiff of fragrant flowers. He saw the ocean, turquoise, blues and greens, shimmering in the distance and white caps in scattered dots on the surface. He imagined himself in a large white villa overlooking the sea, sitting with his feet up, tanned and relaxed, sipping a long fruity alcoholic beverage, while visiting friends from Austria sat across from him, sighing, openly envious.

He had come at a good time, some of the locals had told him. The government had changed hands and the island was improving economically. Heinz opened up a business with his inheritance money and settled down to life in his tropical paradise.

The first few years were turbulent, but Heinz thrived, improving his English, learning the local dialect, and making money.

Heinz's wife Marit had never left Denmark. She enjoyed Jamaica for one week, until it came to her suddenly that Heinz intended to stay. It had been the end of that first week and Heinz and Marit had been walking on the beach. A Rastafarian approached them with a tray of black coral and small wooden carvings. He said something that they didn't understand, so he put down his tray and motioned them over. He changed his accent so it resembled an American twang.

"'Ave a look, 'ave a look, nice lady, black coral found only in Jamaica."

Marit fingered the small black pendants and rings, then told the Rastaman in a haughty manner, "No, I'm not interested."

They walked away, but he trailed after them. Heinz turned around and waved his arms forward and backward as if he was shooing away a stray dog.

"Get away, go, go!" he bellowed.

The kind, gentle expression on the Rastaman's face quickly hardened and he became aggressive. He cursed them, called them horrible names in a language they didn't understand, and would not leave them alone. Marit was frightened. She held onto Heinz's arm and whimpered, "Please don't hurt us."

Eventually the Rastaman walked off, still shouting curses after them.

The incident meant nothing, Heinz had told her. He understood these people. You had to be harsh with them: treat them badly and they respected you. A brown-skinned middle-class Jamaican businessman had told him this. Never show your weakness and they will respect you. Heinz said the Jamaican businessman, whom he had met in a bar, had actually said the worse you treated them, the more they respected you.

Marit didn't believe it. Nothing in this island seemed right. It was too hot, and she felt like sleeping all the time. The mosquitoes were horrid and she had never seen large brown flying cockroaches before. She found the people tiresome for she could not go anywhere without someone calling to her, "Psst, ay, whitey." The supermarkets were dirty, and the service everywhere was terrible. She felt they had traded civilized Europe for a backward, barbaric island.

After her first month in Jamaica, she felt like someone close to her had died. She had not known that homesickness could feel so traumatic, spiraling her into depression, so that she saw life unclearly. Everything was bad about Jamaica. Every black man was waiting to pull her into a bush, rape her or slash her throat.

Marit spent most of her time at home. Heinz had bought a house and hired a housekeeper. Marit spent her days in bed reading and writing long letters to her family in Denmark. The elderly housekeeper Nora brought her breakfast in bed and kept her house tidy. Slowly, Marit began to open up and talk to her. She asked Nora about her family and learnt she had seven children and five grandchildren. Sometimes, Nora said, there wasn't enough food to feed them all.

Marit soon found a reason for living. These people were being exploited by the Jamaican middle and upper classes. They were ignorant of this and it would become her job to help them. She never said any of this to her own helper, but at every available opportunity, when visiting the houses of friends and acquaintances, she asked the helpers and gardeners how much they were earning and told them, after calculating and comparing the minimum wage to Denmark's, how much they should be earning. She told them she was on their side, and to stand up for their rights. It was a terrible, terrible injustice that they could not sit with the family they worked for and eat their lunch. It was an entrenched wrong that maids' quarters were so small and hot and uncomfortable while the masters of the household lived in such extravagance.

"Why should you be treated like a nobody?" she asked countless helpers, gardeners, bartenders, and waitresses. Unbeknownst to Marit, hundreds of service employees became noticeably insubordinate, leaving their jobs at the smallest, imagined or not, slight, arriving late and leaving early, and taking a little extra here and there.

Two years after moving to Jamaica, Heinz came home from work at noon to collect a wallet he had forgotten. He found Marit and the gardener from next door in his bed. He stood at the entrance to his bedroom and observed his wife's pale, blue-veined legs wrapped tightly around the sinewy muscles of the gardener's back. She was pulling him to her fiercely and moaning with pleasure.

Heinz was amazed at his calm. He strode over and pulled the gardener off, beating him severely, and backhanded Marit across the face several times.

"Thought you didn't like the black boys," he barked at her. "Looked like you were raping him."

The marriage was over. They had both known it. Since they moved to Jamaica they had been living separate lives, had become separate people, and now she told him why she had done it. It was their smell, she said. She couldn't resist their shiny black skin and that earthy natural smell.

When Heinz told his friends what had happened, why Marit had suddenly returned to Denmark, they were horrified.

"What? The gardener!" The women exclaimed aghast. They looked with horror as if he had said Marit slept with their Rottweiler. But he did not feel that way. He slapped her only because she had been unfaithful to him. It was over only because she exhausted him. She was like a large heavy sack he had to carry around day after day for the rest of his life. A complaining, nagging, dissatisfied person. He was glad for the excuse to put her on a plane and out of his life.

Truth was, black skin intrigued him too. He remembered the bartender in the bar, her smooth black arms well-muscled and strong, her legs taut and long, her cheekbones high and her teeth white; and he wanted her.

He remembered the prostitute he had seen. She had approached his car, hips swaying, arms akimbo, eyes defiant. She was beautiful with long, finely braided hair down to her waist, the darkest skin he had ever seen, full lips, breasts high, waist small, stomach muscular. He wanted her.

The day after Marit left, Heinz woke before the dawn and lay in bed a minute, listening to the whirring of the ceiling fan and the high-pitched whine of mosquitoes above his head. He felt renewed and excited, as if he had gotten an extra source of energy. He jumped out of bed and put on his jogging clothes, as he did every other morning. Heinz was a short, muscular, stocky man, with thinning light brown hair. His skin was scarred from acne as a teenager and the only remarkable feature on his face was his eyes, which were a piercing vivid blue. His smile stretched wide, but his lips were thin and cruel. He had large, hairy hands and a gruff manner, and he was extremely ambitious.

His parents had come from the mountains, uneducated, coarse country folk who had shown no love or affection to their children. They were harsh disciplinarians who ran a Spartan household and beat their sons regularly. Heinz's mother was a grey-haired, grey-faced, thin-lipped woman who regretted every moment of her life since wedlock, but she had seen that Heinz was different. She convinced her husband to send him off to the city during the week to live with her sister and her husband, who were doing very well financially, so that Heinz could go to school and be raised a gentleman. When his uncle's job took him overseas to Germany, Heinz went with them. Now he spoke five languages, English, German, Danish, French and Italian.

He was completely different from his brother Helmut who had remained in the Austrian mountains. Heinz thought Helmut an undisciplined moron with no ambition. Helmut had already been in jail for disorderly conduct. Helmut had gone to town one night, drunk too much beer and, on his way home, kicked a policeman in his face. Helmut had always been a troublemaker and he had to be the center of attention. The latest Heinz had heard was that Helmut had been showing off to his friends, lighting petrol to see how high the flames would go, and had burned his face so badly that he was unrecognizable. The flames had spread quickly, burning down Helmut's cottage and the house next door and killing an old lady's Siamese cat. Heinz had not returned when he had heard.

That was almost a year ago. In moments of reflection, Heinz recognized that, had he not been sent to the city, he might have ended up like Helmut, a peasant and always in trouble.

After Marit left, he made many changes. He fired Nora because he thought she had the most undesirable combination in a human, ignorance and stubbornness. She did not like to be corrected or told what to do, and since laundry day was Wednesday, nothing was to upset that routine, even if there were no dirty clothes. She burnt lasagna and turned up her nose at pasta sauces, and she couldn't read or write. Heinz had to admit her memory was excellent and he didn't discover her illiteracy for two months. He stumbled upon that fact when he sent her to the supermarket to do his shopping one Monday morning. He sat in the car looking over some accounts, waiting for her, but finally got fed up when he realized an hour and a half had passed. He walked into the supermarket and saw her and the bagboy, their heads bent low over the list, and the boy reading and pointing out the items.

He had kept her on, though, but the one thing he could not forgive was that, after his daughter was born, she did not look after her properly. She seemed annoyed that she had to care for an infant, or was it that the child's mother was a prostitute? Heinz didn't know and didn't care. He had come home one day and heard Nora shouting at his precious Carolina. He had fired her at once, his face distorted by rage, throwing her and her clothes out on the lawn.

Heinz' daughter Carolina was the only person he loved and he was going to protect her from everything. Her mother, Ena Beckfort, was never mentioned. When Heinz thought of her, he still got a bad taste in his mouth. Ena Beckfort was young, short and slightly plump with light brown eyes and mahogany skin. He met her at Pulses, a local bar run by a German fellow, frequented mostly by prostitutes and European men living on the island. He never loved her. She was convenient and happy, that is to say, he never saw her in a bad mood. She said she did what she did because of her circumstances. She never spoke much about what those circumstances were, but she said she was ready to leave the business behind. She had been going to his house every Friday night routinely. Then she started making breakfast in the mornings and tidying his house. Suddenly, it seemed to Heinz, she had moved in. After a while she became pregnant.

"Of course, I am not stupid," Heinz told his business partner Dean Kavanaugh, "I will get a paternity test."

He did and the child was his. She was a beautiful mix, with brown skin and green eyes. "She have good hair," laughed Ena. "She what dem call a browning."

Nora and Ena did not get along. Ena complained that Nora thought she was better than her.

"She must si feel say she is princess," she would complain daily, and she asked Heinz to fire her. Heinz never noticed any such snobbery, but Ena said Nora would not do what she asked when they were alone. However, it was Ena who would be the first to go.

Looking back after that incident, Heinz wondered how he never saw any changes in Ena's behavior. It had been a Wednesday, a hot summer day when the humidity was stifling and his shirt was soaked. He had told Ena he would be driving to Kingston on business, but he had gotten held up at the bank, waiting in line for 45 minutes; and then the air conditioning in his car had broken down, blowing hot air. He decided to go home, change his clothes and switch cars.

He heard Carolina crying when he opened the front door. Not her usual cry, it was a hysterical sob, a sharp intake and gasp for breath. He went straight to her airy powder-blue room with stars and the moon, Humpty Dumpty and Alice in Wonderland painted on the walls.

Carolina lay in her crib hyperventilating, her face red and wet, her eyes wide and abandoned, her diaper full, faeces leaking out from the elastic hugging her soft, plump thighs. It had been Nora's day off. He bellowed for Ena. There was no answer. He picked up Carolina, the faeces soiling his shirt, and strode from the room.

He smelt the smoke before he saw her. She was sitting with another prostitute he had seen at Pulses, with a drinking glass covered with foil in her hand. Cigarette ash covered his cream carpet and the room was filled with smoke. Heinz remembered he held Carolina in his arms. He was rational and unemotional in his abuse.

"What is that? Tell me, you bitch. What the fuck is that?"

Heinz knew it wasn't marijuana. He took a little drag now and then with Dean Kavanaugh but he had never rolled a joint himself. He pulled Ena's hair yanking back her head.

"You didn't hear the baby crying? What is that you're doing?" He grabbed her arm and twisted it so she cried out in pain and he brought his face close to hers. "Get out. Don't ever come back here," he hissed, and his spit flew in her face. Carolina doesn't want a crack-head for a mother. Don't come back. I'll kill you."

And she didn't.

He didn't see her after that. He stopped going to Pulses and he stopped picking up prostitutes. He had a child to look after. If she ever asked for her mother, he would say she had died, from cancer–so tragic, because she had been so young.

Ironically, he met Lorna through Dean's wife, Morganne Kavanaugh. Morganne's helper had a younger cousin who needed work. This younger cousin had graduated from high school and had taken a secretarial course, but she could not find a job. When she came for the interview, Heinz hired her immediately. It was not only that she was attractive—a damn good-looking girl, Dean Kavanaugh later said. It was a gleam in her dark eyes, an energy and ambition that Heinz recognized in himself. She said she loved children and she was good at anything she put her mind to. She said, surprisingly, that she would only stay if she was treated well. Heinz told her she could try the job and that he would kill her if she stole from him. Her eyes flashed, angry and indignant.

"I wouldn't do that, sir."

After that, the malicious gossip flew around town. 'Heinz Goldberg is screwing his maid.' 'Heinz Goldberg comes home and drops his pants so his maid can suck his cock.' 'Heinz Goldberg, for all his money, is just a country boy himself, with no pride or decency.'

Heinz lived in a sprawling white house overlooking the bay. Over a short time (and he was proud of telling this to his friends) he had added a fourth bedroom, a swimming pool, a bar and a small two-bedroom villa for houseguests. Lorna had never seen anything like it. The work was hard because the house was large but she felt like a princess in a castle. Lorna was smart and she saw opportunity in the job. She stopped searching for secretarial work on the side and treated the child Carolina like she was her own. She catered to Heinz and revered him in a way no other woman had. She was there waiting for him when he came home in the evening, with a rum and coke in her hand, ready to hand it to him. Eventually he offered her a drink too, and they sat on his verandah. Heinz reclined in a colourful Guatemalan hammock, Lorna on a white wicker chair, her feet up on a hassock, so absorbed in their conversation that they hardly noticed the rapid change from dusk to night, the scattering of stars in the midnight blue sky, and the bougainvillea and the rose bush around the verandah fading from sight into the darkness. Occasionally they were aware of the screech of an owl and Heinz, coming from a land silent at night, was always amazed at the cacophony of sounds in a Jamaican night, the cicadas, the whistling toads and the occasional croak of a lizard sounding close to his ear, right above his head. Lorna imagined she was his wife, that she belonged there in that house. When they put Carolina to bed together, it almost seemed true.

Lorna was the youngest of four girls. She was often left to herself so she became more introspective and observant than she naturally would have been. She saw that her mother worked long hours, sitting in the Craft Market all day and coming home late evening complaining that the tourists 'look but don't buy' and that all the stalls sold more or less the same items.

Lorna never knew who her father was, just as her mother never knew who her father was; she saw her three older sisters repeating the same pattern. They already had children, none were married, and all the baby fathers had taken off. She saw that even though a woman without a child was a mule, a failed woman, nonetheless children were a burden, and she insisted to her sisters that she would only have one or two.

They laughed at her and her ambitions. She told them one day she would go on the cruise ship that came into the harbour to let off the tourists and she would leave Jamaica and 'go a foreign' to seek her fortune. She saw that the brown-skinned people and the tourists were different, somehow, but it was hard for her to pinpoint exactly how. It was a confidence she saw in them, as if they were saying, 'The world is mine and I have no fear.' She saw their children jumping into the sea and swimming like fish while the children of the poor hung back in longing and awe. She wanted to be like one of those rich children, fearless and haughty, feeling like the world belonged to her.

She saw also that her sisters continued to do the same things that got them into trouble. They lived for Saturday nights, when they would gather in the streets, the loudspeakers towering over everyone and booming throughout the district. Inevitably, one of them would have a new baby father.

So when she saw that Heinz was lonely, she made sure she was the one who was there, and their relationship went smoothly from employer-employee to lovers where they were discreet, to boyfriend and girlfriend where Heinz no longer felt he had to be discreet because Lorna was just as smart and beautiful as everyone else, and she could learn.

Heinz began by sending Lorna to Kingston to the Alliance Française to learn French and to the German Society to learn German. He was incredulous when, after one month, she came home and held a conversation with him in German. Of course, her accent was not quite what it should be, but they understood each other.

Then he asked Morganne Kavanaugh to teach her how to be a lady, simple things like how to speak properly, how to eat properly, and the type of clothes she should wear when going out. Morganne agreed, smiling brightly that it was a wonderful idea, but she told her husband in confidence, "Between me and you, Heinz is crazy. The Pygmalion thing never works.

But I'll do it." She shrugged. "After all, he is paying me."

Morganne Kavanaugh was an attractive copper-brunette with fine features and curly hair. She went to the hairdresser's religiously every month to straighten her curls, what Jamaican women called 'cremed or relaxed hair' and Americans call a perm. She insisted to everyone that her ancestry was Latin, and most certainly not African, and she wore on both forearms, all the way to her elbows, gold bracelets and bangles which she said came from her grandmother in Spain.

She told her friends in a way that suggested she was a kind, helpful person about her arrangement with Heinz, mostly as it was something new to talk about and to throw in that hint of gossip at the same time. She invited her friend Fiona Chilvers to tea to talk and vent her frustrations.

She sat in her penthouse apartment on the balcony, sipping green tea, and said to Fiona, "I hope Heinz uses a condom."

"He would be a fool not to," answered Fiona.

"Because HIV is spreading like wildfire on this island and I'm sure his helper has done it with countless other people already. And you know the masses, they feel they have to have a million children with a million different men."

She scowled and looked out to the bright blue sea and some children playing in the sand.

Morganne had always been an exaggerator and was a little dramatic. She got very excited when talking and moved her arms wildly so the bangles jingled. Fiona did not want to talk about something so distasteful to her as HIV so she changed the subject.

"How is your mother-in-law?"

Morganne sighed. "I spent the entire day Friday taking her to the doctors, and then her shopping. You see how life is," she said with conviction. "She treated me like dirt in the beginning because I wasn't Arab and now I'm the only one who pays her any mind."

Fiona had heard it before, so she nodded in agreement. She knew what was coming next.

"To think that my great-grandfather owned most of the land in this town and his son gambled it away. It makes me sick to think about it. And Dean's ancestors came to Jamaica poor as church mice, higgling material from a donkey cart in the streets. Now they have money and they think they are better than us, classifying themselves as belonging to high society." Morganne shook her head. "My grandmother said when she was young, a person like Mrs. Kavanaugh couldn't get into Liganea Club in Kingston."

Fiona smiled in agreement. She knew it made Morganne feel better to say this. Morganne and Dean had struggled through the years and were just now, in their fifties, doing better financially.

"Anyway, my dear," Morganne continued. "And so it goes. Money talks, even when one doesn't have a shred of class."

Fiona nodded sympathetically, the required response. She was a tall, very dark woman whose grandparents had migrated to England, and so she had grown up there. Her mother had been a lawyer and her father a judge, so she did not have the same hang-ups as Morganne. She had grown up in an affluent household, had studied law herself, and had travelled widely throughout Europe. She was childless, and had returned to Jamaica when she was 32, after divorcing her husband, an Englishman. She had met Carl Chilvers at a society function. He was tall, handsome, light brown, not quite a member of the island's nobility, but polished and successful. He saw Fiona and was taken in with her sophistication and quick-witted response to his questions. He wondered what she saw in Morganne Kavanaugh, whom he thought was a silly woman and full of careless chatter.

Fiona sipped her tea and told Morganne her orchids were beautiful. Morganne glanced at the pink and deep purple flower hanging from her balcony and nodded her thanks, then turned the conversation back to Heinz.

"And you remember you're invited to dinner next weekend? So is Heinz, and he better not bring that girl."

"No, that would be distasteful," agreed Fiona.

Heinz walked into the Kavanaughs' living room with Lorna. Immediately, he saw that Lorna was inappropriately dressed. She wore tight black Capri pants and a small midriff baring halter-top. Morganne floated in a long flowing, black dress, and Fiona, always elegant, wore black slacks and a long-sleeved black blouse. Morganne greeted them with a smile of chilly friendliness. Lorna was quiet most of the time, and, before dinner, placed herself close to Fiona when the men walked off and segregated themselves by the bar.

At the table, Lorna grimaced at the food and said, "What is that? I'm not eating that."

"It's smoked marlin. Try it," cajoled Heinz. "Try everything. Eat." He emphasized.

When asked later if she saw how Lorna ate, Morganne could not answer because she refused to look at her. She excluded her from the conversation and kept her face looking straight ahead. Lorna sat with her elbows on the table, wearing the expression of a small child listening to incomprehensible adult conversation. Heinz tried to draw her out but she did not have anything to say. She focused on the tablecloth, white embroidered linen, and the cutlery, which was an unusual shape. She was glad when it was over and they left for home.

Two weeks later, the Kavanaughs sat in the Chilvers' living room before dinner.

"Can you believe he brought his maid?" asked Morganne emphasizing each word.

"Did you see her eat?" asked Fiona, raising perfectly plucked brows.

"All she could talk about was Beanie Man," scoffed Morganne.

"Shocking," offered Carl.

"Heinz really has to do better than that," Fiona said.

"Sick. It's just sick," hissed Morganne.

"Ladies, come now, don't be so wicked." This, from Dean.

"No!" Morganne held her arms up in the air, the bangles dropping to her elbows. "I want no part in this. He's not to come to my house again if he's going to bring her."

"Don't get hysterical, Morganne. He didn't bring a leper," said Dean irritated.

"For God's sake, Dean, people must know their class. I can't have her calling me Morganne."

Fiona and Carl looked at each other. They read each other's eyes, which said, Morganne and Dean are heading for a fight. Fiona silently implored Carl to steer the conversation away to something else, but Carl could not resist. He turned to Morganne.

"I hear you are going to show Lorna how to speak and eat, and all those things."

Morganne answered sourly. "A child's basic character is formed from ages 0 to 5. I seriously doubt whether anything I do will have an impact." She turned to Fiona, "I hear she sucks his..."

Dean interrupted quickly, "Don't, Morganne," and shot his wife a look of distaste. She could be so crass. Carl looked pointedly at Fiona. They remembered one of their intimate bedside conversations, when Carl insisted that Morganne was a prude. Carl turned to Dean and said, "Well, at least she is getting an opportunity. If only the government gave each person equal opportunity..."

Dean interrupted heatedly. "No, no. There will always be an underclass. There will always be people who won't amount to anything."

"Not saying no. Just saying give the masses education."

And so the conversation continued, about politics and the plight of the island, about crime and religion, gossip and economics. When the couples parted, late in the night, they each left with a feeling of discontent, like something was very wrong in the world in which they lived.

It was ten years since Lorna Goldberg sat at the same table as the Kavanaughs and the Chilvers. She had not seen them since then, and she wondered why she was remembering that night with such clarity. After that dinner, she knew she would never be one hundred percent comfortable with them, but she vowed that one day she would be better.

She sat now in Gatwick Airport waiting for her connecting flight. The lights were bright and she sat on a red vinyl seat looking around her at the Body Shop, the Tie Rack and, above her head, a McDonald's fast food counter. Some people were rushing around; some waited, sitting wearily, with closed, stony expressions on their faces.

Lorna observed a young black woman walking rapidly behind an older white man, her high-heeled shoes obviously new and uncomfortable. She remembered her first time in a foreign airport, walking quickly, trying to match Heinz' pace and staring wildly all around, at the newness, the cleanliness, the order. She heard an announcement for British Airways boarding now from Gate E to Kingston, Jamaica, and she closed her eyes and thought of the past.

Heinz had married her and fallen out with Dean Kavanaugh. Dean had been taking money on the side to finance Morganne's trips to Europe, because she complained bitterly, "If that maid can spend summers in Paris, why the hell can't I?"

Heinz and Lorna rented their house in Jamaica and moved to France. Lorna studied Physiotherapy and was now a trained physiotherapist. She spoke French and German impeccably, although she had to concentrate when speaking proper English. When she was relaxed 'hot' became 'ot' and the 'h' was pronounced in 'hour.' She had a slight stammer, but, strangely enough, only when speaking English. She eventually outgrew Heinz, seeing him as coarse and crude, and was now on her own.

It was ironic, she thought, that she was about to board a plane to go skiing in the Austrian Alps with some medical friends from the hospital where she worked. She owned a house in France, drove the latest model of a Pajero and took two holidays a year. It had been years since she saw Heinz.

One cold winter day in the middle of February, she passed a girl on crutches in the emergency ward of the hospital and recognized Heinz' daughter Carolina. She had broken her leg skiing. From then on, they kept in touch occasionally. Carolina had asked her once if she knew her mother. Lorna thought it best to say no. She told Carolina she had met Heinz after, and he had told her Carolina's mother had died of cancer.

Lorna rarely thought of Jamaica, and when she heard the flight announcement she wondered idly if she should visit. She still owned that villa on the hill. Then she grinned and shook her head, dismissing the notion as an idle, indulgent thought. Of course she would not. She would holiday in Martinique or Tahiti instead. It was hassle-free and so much safer.

And of course, and here she smiled wryly, there would be no reminders of the old class barriers and prejudices which still held sway in Jamaica. They meant nothing to her in her new life. Absolutely nothing.

TIMES A-CHANGING

Miss Imo trudged up the steep hill and down again to get to the bus stop on the main road as she did every morning from Monday to Friday. She'd wake at dawn, boil water and make herself a cup of tea to wash down a slice of bread and get ready to go to work in a freshly-starched dress and good walking shoes. Before she left, she'd wake her two children, her son Mark and her daughter Sharon and tell them to do their chores before going to school.

She also told Mark as she had every morning since he was seven years old, to look after his younger sister and to make sure he walked her all the way to school. Mark sighed, "Yes, Mommy." He was now fifteen and Sharon thirteen.

Since it was only 5 in the morning when Miss Imo left home, the air was cool and sweet, smelling like the night before and the day to come, full of promise and possibility, rich with the scent of the land and the fruit and the morning dew. Miss Imo walked with purpose. She could have done it with her eyes closed, avoiding the trees, rocks and bracken in her path. She had been doing this for six years, leaving the countryside in the early morning to get to Kingston where she worked for one Mrs. Escoffery.

It took her three hours to get to work and by the time she got there, three buses and an uphill walk to Jacks Hill later, the sun would be hot in the sky and Miss Imo would be sweating and smelling like the work men on the buses. She knew she smelled because when she arrived at work, Mrs. Escoffery made a face like she smelled rotting garbage, told her to hurry and change into her uniform because she was late and to wash her hands properly and not to forget to scrub her underarms because, as she would say in her uptown suburban snobbish tone, "Imogene, I don't want you to feel a way but you are handling the children and the food we eat. You must be clean at all times."

Miss Imo felt insulted when Mrs. Escoffery said this. After all, she too was a grown woman and was raising her own children. She knew she had to always wash her hands before cooking and eating or the children would succumb to the dysentery that might kill them before they could get to the town doctor. Miss Imo also felt that if she had to call Mrs. Escoffery 'Mrs. Escoffery,' then why shouldn't Mrs. Escoffery call her Mrs. Baker? The least that should happen was that Mrs. Escoffery's children Mas William and Miss Lorraine should show an older woman respect and call her Miss Imogene or Miss Imo, but that wasn't the way it was. When Miss Imo complained to her niece who also worked as a helper about this, her niece kissed her teeth and shook her head.

"But Miss Imo, is only you don't know dat times a-changing. You think when I go to work for Mrs. McGregor dat I wear uniform? No ma'am. I go to work in my jeans and I change my shirt. That's all. You think I would call Mrs. McGregor's rude pickney Mas' Andrew and Mas' Ian? No way. Those two rude boys are Andrew and Ian. Mr. Michael Manley say times a-changing and it's our time now."

When Miss Imo's niece spoke about the Prime Minister Michael Manley, her face changed and became reverent. She carried a cut out newspaper picture of him in her wallet and she would periodically take it out and study it carefully.

"Times a-changing, Miss Imo, times a-changing," her niece would chant.

"Imogene. Imogene. You just walking in? I don't see why you are late every morning."

"The Kingston bus was late, Mam."

"I suppose the Kingston bus is late every morning."

"Yes mam. It is."

"Make haste. After you change into your uniform and freshen up, start on lunch. I'm having some ladies over for one o'clock. I'm going to ask you to make the sandwiches. Take out a chicken for dinner and season it later. Oh and don't forget to dust and vacuum the formal living and dining room. We'll be using them for lunch."

"Yes mam."

This was in addition to cleaning the four bathrooms, cleaning the five bedrooms, cleaning the kitchen, washing the clothes, hanging them up to dry and then ironing them, fixing lunch for the children when they came home from school, making sure they had school uniforms for the next day and whatever else needed to be done. It was back-breaking work and Miss Imo did it uncomplainingly.

But every night when she went home to her own family, her feet sore and her back aching, she recited her mantra, "Mark, Sharon, you see how it is for me? I don't want it to be like this for you."

They answered dutifully. "Yes, Mommy."

"Listen to me. I don't want you to be a maid or gardener, working for little money, so little bit that it can't stretch. You must go to school every day. Education and hard work. Education and hard work."

Miss Imo had high hopes for her children. It was her niece who told her that Mr. Manley was building and opening up new colleges every day.

"Listen Miss Imo, Mr. Manley making it possible for all of we to succeed. It's our time now."

Plus Miss Imo had never forgotten the time she had heard Mrs. Escoffery refer to her as The Maid. She'd been on the phone and said, "We have a decent girl with us now but we still have to be careful. You know how these maids are." The dictionary said: maid, a female, domestic servant. But Mrs. Escoffery used it differently. There was a tone in her voice that meant the word meant someone lowly, not worthy, not trustworthy. In her beloved country, a maid was something bad, even though her mother had been one and her grandmother before that. Miss Imo resolved that she would rather die than have Sharon become a maid. She never worried as much about Mark. He was a boy and smart. She could see him working in an office in Kingston after he'd finished school and he was almost done already.

When Miss Imo went home that evening, she fell into a chair as she always did and rubbed her feet.

"How was school?"

Fine, they answered.

"You did your homework?"

Yes, Mommy.

"Mark, you walked Sharon into town?"

He didn't answer.

"Mark, I'm talking to you. You walked Sharon into town. Straight to school?"

"Yes mama. Why you have to ask me that every day?"

Miss Imo didn't answer. She kissed her teeth and continued rubbing her feet.

"Boy, I'm tired. I'm so tired," she muttered softly and fell asleep in the chair until the next morning when she woke at dawn.

That summer was a hot one. There was a drought and the grass went brown and crops wilted under the searing sun. It seemed to Miss Imo that the sun was hot from the moment it rose and her feet sweat and slid in her shoes on her way to work giving her painful blisters. When she came home in the evenings, Mark would be out and Sharon would be sleeping. Dinner would not be prepared.

"But what is this? What is this laziness? Why you always sleeping girl?"

"A tired Mommy."

"Tired from what? You don't know tired yet."

Then Miss Imo noticed that Sharon often didn't want to eat.

"But you love yam and dumpling," she coaxed. It was the tiny telltale swelling of Sharon's belly that set off alarms in Miss Imo's head. "Sharon, a pregnant you pregnant?"

"No mama."

Two days later. "Sharon, is pregnant you pregnant."

"No mama."

One day later on a Saturday morning when Miss Imo was home, she woke to the sound of Sharon retching. Her suspicions now confirmed, she rushed out of bed.

"Sharon, you is pregnant. Sharon, how you could do dis to me? With all you studies when you find time to be pregnant? What about all those colleges Mr. Manley building? How you going to go to school with you belly swell out so?"

Miss Imo rounded her arms in front of her and waddled forward. She had a million questions but the most important one was this: "which fool fool school boy do this to you?"

"I don't know."

"Girl, don't let me box you between your ears. Is so many of them that you don't know?"

"No Mommy."

"Well, I'm going to sit here with you until I find out so you might as well tell me and you better tell me the truth."

It had started four months ago. Mark had stopped going to school. He'd made Sharon promise not to tell their mother. He didn't need school, he had insisted. A group of young men like himself were moving to Kingston where they would share a place. Every morning, he went into town after Miss Imo caught her bus, to set up business as he called it, and then got a ride home before she came in. His business was secret stuff but he was going to make a lot of money.

Those mornings that he went, Sharon walked to school alone. None of the school boys had paid her much attention. She looked young for her age and hadn't sprouted breasts or hips yet. Every morning she passed several small shops on the way. One shop owned by a stout sleepy-eyed woman sold beauty products and cosmetics. Another man sold clothes. He had jeans and shirts hanging from every wall. Then there was Mr. Barnett who sold juicy fruit, grater cake, paradise plums, icy mints and other delicious sweets. Mr. Barnett was married and sometimes his wife was in the shop helping him. He also had a daughter the same age as Sharon who went to her school.

Mr. Barnett called out to her as she walked by, usually when his wife was not around. Sometimes he told her to come into the store where he complimented her and gave her free juicy fruit chewing gum. One day he said he had something to show her in the back of the store. Sharon didn't see when he locked the door of his shop and turned on her, clamping his hand over her mouth to stifle her screams.

When Mark came home Miss Imo pounced on him with the ferocity of a wildcat giving no thought to the fact that he was taller and stronger than her. As he came in the door she sprang forward and boxed him hard across his face. His face registered shock then anger. Before he had time to say anything, she hurled her angry words at him, gasping for breath, crying and tearing out her hair all at once. You left Sharon to walk alone. All these mornings, you didn't follow her to school and Mr. Barnett trouble her and now she pregnant. Your fault! Your fault! That nasty old man trouble my daughter. Her words tumbled out in a crazed rant.

"Don't worry. I will take care of it," he screamed. "I will take care of Mr. Barnett."

"You will do no such thing. I will take care of Mr. Barnett."

Miss Imo dressed herself that Saturday morning and marched up the hill and down again to Mr. Barnett's store. His wife was there.

"I have business with Mr. Barnett," she stated.

Mr. Barnett would be returning in five minutes, she told her.

When Mr. Barnett saw Miss Imo, the startled guilty look on his face confirmed it. When she told him Sharon was pregnant, he laughed.

"Miss Imo, who is going to believe that young girl? Any school boy could have done it. I have nothing to do with the matter. The police? Lady, the chief of police is my best friend. What him going to do? Tell my wife? She will never believe it. She's in the shop. Go on. Tell her."

Miss Imo returned home defeated. She trudged up the hill with a heavy heart but by the time she got home, she had resolved that Sharon would continue in school and when the baby was born, she would look after it. That was just what mothers did.

Miss Imo never had to do that. Sharon lost the baby three weeks later. It was probably all for the best, said Miss Imo when she told her niece. One minute Sharon was pregnant. Then she had cramping and suddenly, she wasn't pregnant anymore. Life could change suddenly, Miss Imo mused. One minute you were on a path. Next minute you were on a completely different road. Sometimes it was hard to prepare for life when you couldn't see what was coming around the corner.

More changes were to come. One day Miss Imo went to work and was told to help pack boxes. "I know you will find another job," encouraged Mrs. Escoffery, "and I will write you a good reference but we have to get out of this country. Michael Manley is carrying it down to the depths of hell. It's already gone to the dogs as far as we are concerned. All the good, decent hardworking people are leaving."

Mrs. Escoffery was not one to be left behind. So Miss Imo helped her pack up her home and waved goodbye when she left for the airport two months later. Miss Imo thought she saw a tear in Mrs. Escoffery's eye but the sun was hot and glinting off the car metal so she couldn't be sure. Then Miss Imo returned to the country not bothering to find another domestic position. She wanted to keep an eye on Sharon, make sure she finished school and to encourage her. She couldn't do that from Kingston so she stayed in the country and grew yams to sell at the local market on weekends.

Mark came and went, depositing money on the table.

"You can turn up your nose at it all you want but this money can pay for that fancy university in Kingston."

In the end, Miss Imo had to take Mark's drug money for no matter how many yams she sold, there was not enough money for tuition and room and board. She asked God for forgiveness but if that's what it took for Sharon to make something of herself, then so be it. For some strange reason, Sharon wanted to be an animal doctor.

"Why not a real doctor?" Miss Imo asked over and over again.

"Mama, I want to be a veterinarian. You always said I could be anything I want. This is what I want."

Miss Imo agreed that an animal doctor was certainly better than working for the rich people in Kingston and earning minimum wage.

One morning in the rainy season Mr. Barnett was found dead in his shop strangled with a telephone cord. Miss Imo made sure to bring Mrs. Barnett cooked food and words of comfort. When she mentioned the incident to Mark, he had a look in his eye that she didn't like. He never made it to that office in Kingston but he was a grown man now and made his own decisions. Miss Imo had done her best.

The years had deepened the lines on Miss Imo's face. Even though she didn't have to clean anymore, she polished and mopped and dusted and scrubbed Sharon's house till it gleamed.

"Mommy, will you stop cleaning for God's sake. Why do you think I hired Lisa?"

"These young girls from the country are not half as thorough as we were," Miss Imo replied. "I'm just lending a helping hand."

Sometimes Miss Imo took a taxi to Sharon's office. She liked to sit there amidst the yapping dogs and cats sitting on the laps of the well-dressed moneyed women and think, they are flocking to see my daughter. Then when Sharon was finished, they'd travel home together.

One day as Miss Imo sat in the waiting room, the older but unmistakeable form of Mrs. Escoffery sauntered in, clutching to her chest a tiny dog with sharp features. She had gained ten or so pounds and the lines around her eyes and mouth had, like Miss Imo's, deepened. Her pale skin reminded Miss Imo of delicate writing paper, the kind with the slight bumps and lines to make it look pretty. Mrs. Escoffery kept her eyes straight ahead and sat down beside Miss Imo.

"Ms. Escoffery, mam, is it really you?"

"Imogene Baker? What a surprise!"

It turned out that the Escofferys had moved first to Florida and didn't like it, then moved to Canada and didn't like it.

"You are 'a nobody' when you move to foreign. Everybody is just a number," she complained to Miss Imo. So they'd returned to Jamaica some years now since the government had changed and the future looked somewhat hopeful.

"Anyway, Imogene, what you doing at the vet's? You have a dog?"

"No mam." The 'mam' slipped out before Miss Imo could stop it. Some habits were hard to break. "I'm waiting on my daughter to finish work."

"Oh wonderful! Your daughter is helping to clean Dr. Baker's office. I'm sure she appreciates the help."

"No mam. Dr. Baker is my daughter."

Just then Sharon walked out and handed a file to the receptionist.

"Sharon, Sharon," Miss Imo called out. "Look who it is. Mrs. Escoffery."

Miss Imo felt as if her dark face was as bright as the sun with sheer joy and pride as she assessed the incredulous look on Mrs. Escoffery's face. Sharon came over and shook Mrs. Escoffery's hand like an equal and then she cooed softly to the dog on her lap.

"I'll be with you in a moment," she said and returned to her office.

Mrs. Escoffery tried to recover but couldn't. A range of emotions flashed across her face ranging from disbelief to envy and she muttered, "Your daughter is the vet. What a way times have changed."

"Yes," agreed Miss Imo, literally bursting with pride. "Times have really changed fi true."

DEAR JEAN

My dearest Jean,

You must be wondering how my letter has been so long in coming. I have been in this beautiful island for three months now and only yesterday had enough money saved to go to the post office and mail it. I arrived May 1st.

When I got off the plane it seemed the smell of the place rose up from the asphalt to greet me: tar, salt and sea, sweat and tropical flowers, or perhaps I only imagined the flowers. I took a taxi from the airport and booked into one of those small local hotels, slightly dreary and rundown but comfortable enough. I thought my business here would not take more than a month, but, my dear Jean, it takes an eternity here to accomplish all but the simplest tasks.

I took a shower when I came in and immediately set off to Mother's cottage. I found the place easily and it was just as I remembered it. Mother had never done renovations, so, as I walked down the long pitted driveway, I saw the cracked white paint and the garden overgrown with weeds. The house is quaint, set far back from the road with a mango tree shading the front porch and a large Poinciana tree near the gate. The shade gives the house an almost abandoned air, except for the birds—a cacophony of song overhead.

I knocked on the grilled gate, expecting Mrs. Smith, Mother's maid and companion, to open it. Instead, a young lady, not more than 30, came out. She was beautiful, with long black hair and wide brown eyes, almost innocent and childlike, but I looked closely into them and saw that they were hard and cruel. Perhaps I say this in retrospect, but I saw a change in her stance when I said I was Mother's son Errol, come to look at the house and the will. She appeared taken aback and folded her arms.

She said Mrs. Smith no longer worked there, and hadn't for some time. She, Jasmine Escobedo, had taken over from her and had been looking after my mother for the past two years. She didn't know where to find Mrs. Smith. Mother had been buried two days ago and the will had been read. I could enquire at the law offices of Burton, Burton and Anderson. I asked to come in and see Mother's possessions. I wanted her old photo albums and her furniture. Mother had had a beautiful china cabinet in mahogany and a dining room table with carved feet.

This Jasmine Escobedo would not let me in. She said she knew of no photo albums. The furniture, she said, came with the house, and the house belonged to her.

Naturally I was shocked. I was Mother's only child and her closest relative. I said, "We'll see about that, Ms. Escobedo," and I set off to find the offices of Burton, Burton and Anderson. It took me one week to accomplish this and another two weeks before I could get an appointment. I began to be concerned. This little island is more expensive than England and my money was running out.

Finally, I was able to hear the will read. Mother had left Jasmine Escobedo her property. She had had no money to speak of, and what little there was also went to Jasmine. I couldn't believe it, Jean, but there was Mother's signature, large and distinct and illegible as always. I asked about mother's personal belongings and was told to contact Ms. Escobedo.

I spent the next week hiring a lawyer. I decided to fight it. I do not for a moment believe that Mother would leave a stranger, and one whom I had never heard her mention, her property. But I could not get a lawyer to take the case. By then, the money was finished and I had to leave the hotel.

I took the soft black suitcase, the one I'd taken to Turkey a lifetime ago it seems, and walked out into the street. The heat descended on me; as I breathed, I pulled fire through my nostrils, and it was so hot the air couldn't reach my throat. I gasped and gasped and pulled at my shirt, undid my tie and clutched at my heart. I realized I was having a panic attack. Remember, I used to get them mildly when I felt stressed at the office? I sat under a tree in New Kingston (the place is completely built up with high rise buildings and fast food restaurants) with my suitcase at my feet and cried. No-one looked at me, Jean, except out of curiosity, and if I caught their eye, they looked away.

I sat there all day and thought many things. I thought that I wished I could tell you that I cannot call myself a Jamaican. I am nothing like these people here. It hit me as I sat under a tree I did not recognize, with the sun still managing to persecute me through the leaves, that I am indeed British. And although I mocked the British terribly, wanting to belong to a place that accepted me for my race, wanting to be understood, I am more like them than I will ever be Jamaican.

Jean, will you accept this black British fool's hand in marriage? I cried, Jean. You accused me of never showing emotion, but I sat under that tree and cried. I thought about our trip to Turkey, how I left you in the hotel room all day and went roaming the narrow alleyways, looking for a silk carpet. I should have just told you I needed to be alone, that I wanted to be a black man in a mud brown country and not British, strolling leisurely with a white English woman. I wanted to be recognized, somehow. I came back and found you crying, too afraid to go out, when you tried, a bus almost knocked you down. Jean, it hurts me to say that I feel Turkey is more civilized than here.

Before I continue, I must tell you how sorry I am for everything. I don't know why it took me so long to make up my mind. It seems I do love you, Jean, and when I think back I am appalled at how I treated you. I am sorry for criticizing your ankles. The women here, their ankles may be slender and their figures pleasing, but their beauty is all on the surface, like a mask which can be taken on or off at will. Their charm is like an act, a play, and, after the curtains are drawn, they resort to themselves, hard and cruel. Jean, I'd like to return to England to you. It appears that for the time being I am penniless. I should not have left my job in England, as you forewarned.

But enough of this wallowing in self-pity. I tracked down the old Mrs. Smith. She lives in a wooden shack, surrounded by many others like it with zinc roofs and rotten floors and garbage burning in the yard. She has lost her sight to diabetes; that is why she could no longer care for my mother. Mother, she said, was surely senile by the time Jasmine Escobedo came to care of her. No-one knows where Ms. Escobedo comes from or how she knew the job was available. That part is a gap. Mrs. Smith said that, from what she heard, Ms. Escobedo was a secretary to a wealthy man who owned a store in the downtown area. This wealthy man divorced his first wife of 30 years and married Jasmine. They have one child who is mentally handicapped.

Mrs. Smith said how unusual it was that Jasmine was in Mother's cottage because she lives in a large house in Stony Hill with her husband. Indeed, I later discovered Jasmine was there to paint the cottage, as she planned to rent it out. When I went next, a fat American widow was sitting on the porch reading, her bifocals low on her nose and her red hair tied back in a bun, and said she was the new tenant.

I was not particularly soiled that day, and she let me in, gave me lunch and listened to my story. Mother's furniture was gone, but I showed her my favourite spot outside, under the Julie mango tree where I climbed as a boy and picked the not yet ripe fruit and held it in both hands and bit into it, tearing the skin with my teeth. Or one would fall to the ground, soft and more orange, and I'd bite into its overripe sweetness. I hardly remembered, Jean, it only came back in smells and images. I was nine when my feet touched British soil and I only came back once—when I was 15, for a two-week holiday, in '68.

I am embarrassed to admit that I overstayed my visit. Evening had come and the sun had set, streaking the sky with oranges against a pink-grey background. The song of the cicadas encircled us, and I sat on the porch and watched a hummingbird waver for a moment, its wings flitting so fast that all I saw was a blur. It darted from one flower to another, then up to the mango tree and down again. I have never seen a bird fly so fast. The American lady—her name was Mel—gently took my arm and led me down the porch steps.

"You must leave now," she said softly. From then, I was on my own on the streets.

I don't like to remember this time, Jean. For the first time in my life, I begged. I tried to be gentlemanly at first, explaining my situation. One tall high-heeled lady turned to her friend and said, "Him talk nice, eeh?" Her orange-haired, overweight companion, in a skirt that was much too short, replied, "No give him nuttin." And they walked off laughing.

I tried again and a sympathetic brown-skinned young woman listened, then said, "I hope things work out for you. I don't have anything to give you. You should return to England." Then she shook her head sadly and walked to her car. I saw her look around and lock all the doors; then her car drove off into the night.

I looked up and saw the stars, and knew that I would sleep under them in the parking lot of a bank in New Kingston. I watched when people came out of the fast food restaurants; when they dumped their half-eaten food in the garbage, I retrieved it before the maggots could get to it.

There was one day in particular I will never forget. I walked a lonely road; the concrete bungalows stood close together, heavily grilled. Although some were painted bright blue and others yellow, most were a drab white. The area had the look of a rundown neighbourhood and the houses seemed like prison cells.

It was midday and the heat was dreadful. Sweat poured down my face and ran down my legs. I could no longer smell myself. A dead dog lay in the middle of the road and the stench coming from it was unbearable. But Jean, I didn't think about the smell. I thought that the dog looked like barbequed pork and how good it would be to eat. I looked at the dog for a while and walked through the neighbourhood, past the houses and came to a small, dirty beach. I imagined that, at one time, this had been a good neighbourhood, before people moved uptown.

I looked at the sea, muddy and dirty, with black plastic bags and juice boxes and prophylactics floating in the water near the sand, and knew it was time to come home.

So, Jean, I ask that you wire the money to The Bank of Nova Scotia so I may return as soon as possible. Thank you in advance.

I am,
Yours,
Errol

THE ARCHER BOY

Come in child. Come in out of the hot sun. You have such a pretty complexion. Don't let the sun spoil it. Come in. Put your school bag over there on the chair. What a way that purple tie look good on you. I have some chicken soup warming up. Go wash your hands. What? Oh, you mean the Archer boy next door. You knew him? Yes, he seemed normal to me too. But when you live next door to a family for as long as I have, you see a little more.

Let me see. They moved in a month after me. Townhouses were not as popular then. I bought this one; it has a slightly larger garden and they bought the one beside me, number 2. She was pregnant at the time. Boy, they made a pretty couple. She—her name was Sunny—tall and regal, always had her hair done, and she carried the pregnancy well. She never gained weight anywhere but her stomach. He, Mr. Archer, was tall and muscular, like them Olympic guys, and very quiet, but polite. He always nodded to me when we met in passing, but none of us knew him, really. He left shortly after the boy was born, about four months after. That was about the time Kay the hairdresser moved in to number 36 and we all went to her. Sunny told Kay that it was about another woman and that he has never helped her out with money or anything, not one day in his life. I remember a year later, and this I could swear on the Bible, I saw Mr. Archer in the supermarket with a young, long-haired Indian girl on his arm. He didn't recognize me but I glared at him. To think he had abandoned his pretty wife and newborn son.

Sunny named the baby Jeffrey. She told Kay she wasn't going to marry again. Everything now would be for the boy and her career. She did well, as well as any man, and she kept that house going herself. I would see her from time to time at Kay's or in the park with all the other young mothers, and you should have seen her. She was prouder than a peacock over Jeffrey. Her face lit up like a Christmas tree when the other mothers praised him. He stopped using a bottle at six months. He was potty trained by 18 months. He never crept, one day he just got up and walked. And, as he got older, they all said how well-mannered and polite Jeffrey was.

But let me tell you something. When the child was still a mere baby, around two years old, she brought him over and he had a little accident on my new pale peach carpet in the living room. Sunny acted like the child had committed murder. She beat him over and over again. She make him smell his urine like a dog. She shout and say, "Jeffrey, you know better. That's nasty and you've ruined Miss Mary's carpet."

"Never mind. Never mind," I said. "A little wee wee never hurt anybody. It's alright. He is just a child."

All the same, she just turned to me and said, "He has to learn."

They went home after that and from time to time I'd hear Sunny shouting at Jeffrey. These concrete walls are not thick as people like to believe. I would chuckle, hearing Sunny tell the young boy to tidy up his room and to fold his clothes. I remember she rebuked us when we cooed to him.

"Please don't baby talk to him," she said. "This child is going to be smart." And you know she never baby talked that child? She spoke to him from day one as if he were an adult. I'd see her pushing that pram and talking seriously to him, as if he understood every word.

Lord, he was a lovely child. He was always doing things to please his mother, and of course she never failed to tell us: how he drew pictures for her and said 'I love you, Mommy', and how he tried to help her wash the dishes and help with the housework. Sunny was always running over and telling me some smart, witty thing that Jeffery had said. I suppose we were her family, with her husband gone and her parents living in Canada, and she with no siblings I knew of.

And when the Common Entrance came around, what a big hullabaloo! From one whole year before, Jeffrey was taking extra lessons after school. The poor child never got a chance to play. He was at school all day and then extra lessons all evening. It's a sin what they do to these children. So when the day of the exam came, Sunny went to Kay and told her she was worried about Jeffrey. He was so nervous he couldn't eat his dinner and then he couldn't sleep. Then he wet his bed and she beat him. She told Kay that maybe she shouldn't have beat him, but he was 11 and for Christ sake, everybody has to learn to deal with life. Sunny told Kay that he went to the exam trembling and if a black boy could turn white, Jeffrey turned white that morning. It's a sin what they do to these children.

Anyway, he did well. He passed for Jamaica College, his second choice, but Sunny never stopped pulling strings till he got into Campion. I guess that's where you met him? Yes, he seemed like a happy boy to me too. But it was different. He would see me and his face would light up into a smile, and he was so polite; but when he turned away, it was like a shadow fell across the sun, and he would retreat into his own world. Sunny never knew that world.

As he got older, the teenage years, when Sunny started working long hours, I would pass by his window and smell the ganja coming from his window. How I know that smell? Well, you know I had a touch of the glaucoma and the doctor told me some ingredients in cannabis might be helpful. So it was only in these later years...

Anyway, child, I felt like Jeffrey was my own grandchild and I thought I should help out a bit. I started visiting in the evenings when Sunny wasn't home and bringing him dinner. It's hard to get conversation out of a teenager, but eventually, one evening when long shadows had fallen across the walls and the air was cool and the crickets and whistling toads were making a racket outside, he told me that he wanted to be a musician. When he finally got that out, Lord, the child did not stop talking about it. He said his mother refused to let him take music lessons. He wanted a guitar, but he felt he needed to learn the piano too.

One evening I went to his house and he had borrowed an old guitar from a friend. He made me sit in a large ruby-coloured easy chair and listen to him strum. I am tone deaf, so I never knew what was what, but you know that look when somebody loves what they're doing? It's a special look, child. It can transform the most hideous person into an angel. I saw a man once, short and squat and ugly, and he sat down to carve a piece of furniture. And I saw him put every ounce of passion and love into that piece of wood and it was like heaven opened up and light shone down on this man, and I saw his muscles taut and shiny with sweat, and all at once I saw that he was beautiful. And I've seen it again with a lady who came to sing at our church, and I saw it in the eyes of my gardener, Shorty, who looks at every flower he has planted with love and awe. And that's what I saw in the face of Jeffrey Archer when he pulled out a chair for me and got his friend's guitar and began to play. The late afternoon sun was coming in and shining on his face and tears rolled down from my eyes so that I had to turn away.

I heard Sunny's car a week later when she came in from work. I rushed out to greet her. I had been memorizing what to say about Jeffrey and the music. I forgot everything all at once and began blabbering like the old woman I am. I told her how talented I thought he was, but she was sharp.

"I can assure you that I am going to knock that nonsense from Jeffrey's head. This is real life. Look how hard I have to work, with no man to help me. Jeffrey has to forget this nonsense and be a man. The world is hard. You have to be the best to compete. I don't want no musician son who I have to be supporting for the rest of my life. I want Jeffrey to consider law or medicine. He needs a profession."

She said more. She talked for half an hour, but you get the gist of it. I felt sorry for Jeffrey but I thought, like the rest of us who missed our calling, he'd get by and maybe one day follow his dreams. You know, like Mr. Miller in number 40 who decided to go to university when he turned 50. Or the middle-aged woman in number 15 who just started taking singing lessons.

The extra lessons started again when the O'Levels came up. Oh yes, they are called CXC now. Yes, mi dear. I heard her shouting at him to study. It was a constant thing. I myself had gotten very busy with my woman's group so I didn't see them as often. It was quite a while later when I went to Kay for a colour, and she told me that Jeffrey had done badly in his exams. Apparently he had passed two out of eight subjects. I wondered if I should have gone over there and visited, but I really didn't know what to say.

Then, one evening I got this feeling that I had to do something. It just came over me while I was watching TV, and I got up and had a little something to eat. Then I walked around the house looking for things to do. It was such a strong feeling of unease. A picture of Sunny and Jeffrey floated into my mind, but when I opened the front door, her car was not there, and it had been so long since I visited Jeffrey that I felt foolish going over there now. I thought to myself that he probably wasn't even home. I remember now. That was a Friday evening. Sunny always came home late on Fridays.

I didn't sleep well that night. I tossed and turned and kept looking at the round alarm clock by my bed. At around 4 am I turned on the TV. I must have fallen asleep with the TV on, because when the screaming woke me up at 6 that morning, I thought it was the TV at first. I was groggy and tired and I turned it off. That's when that dreadful feeling of unease came back and I heard the screams of a wild animal. I dressed and rushed outside. Some of the neighbours came running too and we all went together to the sound. It led us to the back of Sunny's house.

I'll never forget it, child. I will never forget it. He used a rope. His body was ash grey, hanging from the mango tree. Sunny was trying to get the body down but she was a wreck, grabbing Jeffrey and then falling to the ground and beating the earth. To this day, Sunny just lets those lovely Julie mangoes fall and rot in her garden. She won't eat one.

We all went to the funeral. Then I visited a week after. Sunny and I hugged each other and bawled. She looked at me and said, "I want one more chance, Miss Mary. I beg Jesus to give me one more chance." By then, Sunny was probably too old to have children, but she said if it could happen in the Bible, it could happen to her too. She held a crucifix in her hand and she said she knew now it was all her fault. She had been too hard. She had not let him do what he wanted to do. She wanted him to be successful and smart, and not abandon her like his father had done. She said she pictured him every night, receiving an award and him saying, "I would not be here if it wasn't for my mother. Thank you Mom, for everything."

"Please Jesus," Sunny begged the crucifix in her hand. "I will do it right next time."

I visit her often these days. I bring her dinner, like I used to bring Jeffrey, and we talk about him. Nowadays she just sits and holds my hand. Two years is not so long, and her grief is still strong. Sunny pregnant again? I doubt it. She doesn't have a man friend that I know of. She spends her evenings alone, or with me or Kay.

She'll be alright. This is the way of life, my child. Sometimes we only get one chance. Anyway, child, eat your chicken soup. It's getting cold.

Of Mice or Men

On a hot, dry summer day–the kind when the wind whips up dry leaves and fine particles of dust and dirt to spit it everywhere and parch the throat–Cassandra Phillips stood on her balcony with her face to the sun, lamenting the state of her sofa.

The new sofa–it wasn't exactly new, she had bought it from an Indian man who owned an antique furniture store–had to be re-upholstered. Cass had been planning to fix it, anyway. One day, when things got better. One day when she had the money to spare. But now, squinting in the sun and holding back tears that threatened to block the hazy view of Kingston, she decided to go ahead and do it. The huge hole in its side meant mice had bitten through the fabric. It had to be re-upholstered.

This was for Cass just one more disaster on top of all the other minor disasters plaguing her, so that the mice in her sofa became a problem of monumental proportions. She didn't peer into the sofa to see if the mice were actually in there. She knew they were, because the helper Bea, who commented on everything, had seen one or two scuttling across the kitchen floor at night.

It wasn't a big deal, Cass' mother Margaret, tried to calm her. She knew a furniture man who did good work. Luckily for Cass, who became stressed at even minor issues, her mother and grandmother always knew such a man–a fridge fixer, a bent-over-in-the-sun gardener, a handy man, or a driver. The family, mostly women, had had to become resourceful and fend for themselves. Cass' grandfather had died young and her grandmother, then 45, had never remarried. Cass' parents had divorced amicably when she was three and her father had migrated to the States. Cass' own husband of late seemed a passive participant–if not a non-participant–in their marriage.

The women in Cass's family, stout, wide-hipped, and boxy-bottomed, would set their lips in a grimace, and mountains and ridges would appear between their brows; and, without complaining, they would accomplish what seemed to Cass, the most Herculean tasks. Cass was different: wispy, tall and slim, and feminine in her mannerisms. Having a baby and working made her feel overwhelmed and exhausted. Even before all of that, she was prone to complaining and sighing loudly and bitterly.

Margaret said she would take her to a place on Maresceaux Road to find material for the couch because she could get a discount there. The material they chose was not a bargain and Margaret, standing arms akimbo in the store, was annoyed. It had to be the most expensive, she muttered.

"This is Martha Stewart, mom. It must be a sign of better things to come. They are my two absolutely favourite colours, cobalt blue and bright yellow. This is no old-fashioned, ugly highlander plaid."

"And this fabric is thick and won't rip or tear," added Margaret, perspiration on her upper lip and getting caught up in Cass' excitement. "This will be a brand new sofa."

And because Cass was happy, Margaret was happy, and offered to buy it. Of late, it wasn't often that Cass was happy.

When Cass' husband Syd had first seen the sofa, he'd pouted with displeasure. He hadn't said much around Margaret but waited for the moment he and Cass were together and then said she'd be sitting on it alone. He liked new things and designer names that made him look rich. He would've been ashamed, he said, to tell his friends that the sofa was second-hand. Cass had almost begun to agree, because the sofa was ugly, old and beige and had mint green, wooden legs. Syd had said as much when he saw it, the corners of his mouth drawn down in a disapproving jowl. Cass could see how he had probably behaved as a boy, a spoilt rich boy. They were ugly, both the sofa and Syd's mouth. But she changed her mind when she thought that this sofa would really be theirs, not a gift from Syd's parents but something she had contributed to their home.

Cass' grandmother Hazel said: "It will be like brand new when we're finished with it." And later on, in private, she'd said to Cass: "Syd is that new breed, impatient and wanty-wanty, wants everything new and doesn't want to pay for it. He doesn't want to start small. Everything I have, your grandfather and I worked hard for. It didn't come overnight."

Hazel's lips were pursed and she clucked her tongue against the roof of her mouth. But Hazel was right. Cass had heard Syd in a jewellery store ask to see a Rolex watch and begin to bargain with the man, when he couldn't buy so much as a pack of diapers for the baby.

When the sofa came back it did look brand new. Gone were the hideous, mint green legs. Margaret had asked the upholsterer to replace them with modern large round wooden balls. The upholsterer dropped it off early Saturday morning and said to Cass, "Lady, you should have seen the chicken bones dat drop outta it!"

Cass had stuttered, "What?"

"Chicken bones lady. We had to clean out di whole inside. Rats tek over dis sofa."

Cass was horrified. She woke Syd in a temper.

"Chicken bones fell out of the sofa."

Syd was angry that she'd woken him. He'd gone to bed late, at least four in the morning, and he'd planned to sleep till noon and then head out to Lime Cay with the guys.

"I know where those chicken bones came from," Cass screamed. "You and your friends leave out the food till morning when I get up and throw it away. It's your fault. You and your friends' fault," she moaned, crying as she walked away and into the bathroom, where the stark whiteness of the walls imprisoned her.

From early on, right after they returned from their honeymoon, Syd's friends started to come over every night. Syd's house in Jack's Hill became their meeting point. Syd's parents had given the house to them as a wedding present. Syd's father had told them it would ease the strain of having to find rent or pay a mortgage. He didn't want them to suffer as he had suffered: sleeping on a mattress on the floor, saving every penny for a dresser, and living with his wife's nagging parents for five long years while they saved for a house. Money problems are the cause of many a marital break-up, Syd's mother had added. Having a place to call their own would solve that problem.

Cass had been grateful, but the house had never seemed like her own. She was already uncomfortable with Syd's parents, who had told her she could call them Mr. and Mrs. Reid and had never wavered from that formality. Syd's mother, the bossy Mrs. Reid, came over uninvited, which would not have been a problem, except she scrutinized everything and did the dishes in the sink, even when there was only one glass. She went into Syd's closet, took out his shirts and pants and ironed them. She opened the fridge and commented on the lack of food–what was Cass planning to feed her son? Cass, sitting on the sofa and breastfeeding the baby, and trying to control her large breasts which flopped out the baby's mouth every few seconds, had no answer.

Margaret said to Cass: "It's absurd how you are their daughter-in-law and they insist on Mr. and Mrs. Reid. I could never have my son-in-law call me Mrs. Phillips."

Hazel, who never failed to mention that she was a good and sound judge of character, sniffed at that.

"The Reids are the type of people who put on airs but they don't have a shred of common sense nor common courtesy. Imagine. You are a part of their family. Mr. and Mrs. Reid indeed. Mr. and Mrs. Reid my fat black ass."

And, every evening, Syd's friends came.

The core group never changed. There was Mark-the-loudmouth, Rolan-the-weed-provider, Julian who was chronically high, and Craig who dabbled in coke. Sometimes stragglers from other groups came for a loud domino or kalooki game. They drank cases of Red Stripe that didn't count as drinking, since Red Stripe was not hard liquor, and left the bottles on the floor.

At first, Cass fed them rice and peas and stew, or white rice and curry chicken. But she told Syd they couldn't afford to have impromptu dinner parties every night and she had better things to do than spend all her time cooking for his weed-head friends. So Syd bought the guys pizza, Chinese food, Kentucky or jerk chicken, and they'd eat and leave the bones and pizza boxes on the floor, or on the mahogany Ethan Allen coffee table, a Christmas gift from her in-laws. Cass woke every morning for work to a littered living room. She'd sweep it all in a large garbage bag before Bea came. Cass wouldn't have been able to face Bea had she left the mess there for her to clean up.

It was a pity, Cass told Margaret, that they didn't offer marriage classes in school. Margaret told Hazel that she thought Cass was having a difficult time.

"That's what happens when you marry spoiled rich boys," Hazel said, pursing her lips. "That's what happens when you have a house and a business handed to you on a silver platter. You don't learn the value of money."

"Maybe so," said Margaret, "but Cass has just had a baby and she is so stressed her milk is drying up. Besides, the money really belongs to Syd's father, not to Syd, and Mr. Reid is a tight-fisted old goat. He will never release the reins on the business to an incompetent like Syd, and the money only comes when he feels like Syd deserves it, which is almost never."

The baby was crying a lot and Cass, who once upon a time couldn't wait to leave Margaret's house, had been spending more and more time there. Margaret told Hazel about a conversation she'd had with Cass.

"I feel like this is really my home. You haven't changed my room a bit," Cass had said.

"You've only been gone two years. How much change do you expect?"

"It feels weird to be back here with a baby in my arms. It still feels strange that I'm a mother. Life is so weird and unpredictable. You never know how it's going to turn out. You swear it's going to turn out one way, but..."

Margaret, who could be a bit dramatic, took Cass' hands in hers and said, "Cass, if you're not happy and you truly don't think it's going to work out with Syd, you can move in. I'll help look after the baby."

"And then she just burst into tears," Margaret told Hazel. "And she wouldn't stop."

"So what did you do?"

"I hugged her and told her things always work out."

Hazel harrumphed in annoyance.

"Yes, but not always how you think they should. I always knew that boy had weakness in him. You can see from the weakness in his jaw line. Remember how your father's jaw was strong? Now, there was a man. You can see Syd has never known a hard day's work in his life. Spoiling children weakens their character. Did Cass ever tell you about the Rolex?"

"No," said Margaret, annoyed that she hadn't been told.

"Well, can you imagine the boy walk into store and ask 'bout Rolex, and Cass had to borrow diaper money from me? Imagine!"

Margaret called Cass.

"I spoke to the upholsterer. He told me about the chicken bones. How could that have happened?"

Cass shouted at her mother, "So now all of Kingston knows I have chicken bones in my sofa?"

"Oh, stop being so dramatic."

"It's Syd and his piggish friends. They're over all the time. He spends all our money on them. I can't stand it anymore. They eat and leave the food out all night. I've tried talking to them about it, but they're so stoned when they leave, they don't remember a thing. I've told Syd they can't come over every night, and it stops for a night or two and then they all come back again. They're loud and keep me up all night...

"He's leaving now and going to Lime Cay, to hang out with the same guys who left here at 4 o'clock this morning. It's like we're not even married. It's like the whole day is stretching before me and all I have to look forward to is hoping the baby doesn't cry."

Cass, feeling a headache coming on, massaged her temples and dabbed her eyes with her shirt.

"As if it's not hard enough living in Jamaica. As if I don't have other problems to deal with. Mom, is it supposed to be like this?"

Margaret focused on the sun coming through her kitchen window and how it lit up the oranges on the counter and made them bright orange and yellow. She stroked the edge of the counter and spoke in a soothing, husky voice.

"Don't worry, darling. I'm coming to pick you up for the day. We'll all spend the day together. I'll look after the baby while you get some rest. Grandma Hazel will be here and we'll have tea. Dry your tears, darling," she crooned.

But she had no answers. Hazel had said to her last week that you can't tell a woman to leave her man. She has to make those kinds of decisions by herself. As Hazel had said, you can't tell a woman with a new baby whose marriage is falling apart that her dreams will surely be shattered like broken glass in the road. That she will be the Alpha and Omega. She had to come upon that realization herself. She had to take the first step down what would surely be a difficult road.

Margaret had rolled her eyes.

Cass was not ready to go down any difficult road where she saw a dismal and skeletal future. Everyone she knew had problems. As Bea walked around saying, 'Everyone had their cross to carry. Everyone had a burden to bear.' In time, Syd would change, and there were so many things to look forward to. They were going to Miami for a week.

These things were running through Cass' mind as she carried the baby seat out to the car. She'd just told herself she was not going to let anything bother her, when Rolan-the-weed-provider, and Craig who dabbled in coke, drove into the driveway and stepped out of the car, pulling a large and battered black suitcase on wheels behind them.

"What are you doing here?" asked Cass.

Syd interjected: "I told them they could stay here the week. They have nowhere else to go. I'll tell you in the car. This is serious stuff, man." And he urged Cass into the car.

"Keep the doors locked," he shouted and waved at the guys, then turned to Cass.

"Cassandra, before you carry on,"—Syd whispered urgently, though Cass could hardly carry on in the backseat while Syd's father, the stern Mr. Reid, was driving them to the airport—"just listen. They are watching the house for the week and they promised to be tidy. Rohan's father kicked him out because he searched his room and found his stash. He's using the week to find somewhere else to stay. I promise it's going to work out. Stop worrying about them and let's enjoy this vacation."

He reached over and stroked her cheek and held her hand—something he hadn't done for a long time.

Syd Reid could always sweet-talk her, Cass thought. He'd sweet-talked her into having sex the first time, sweet-talked her into marriage, and, although she had been ready, she suspected he was far from it. He'd insisted he was, and he sweet-talked her every time he suspected she was ready to quarrel. Could this be, thought Cass, an untimely marriage, where she and Syd were perfect for each other but it wasn't the right time? Maybe if she'd met him later, when he was in his thirties and more mature. Was she staying with him because everyone said they made a good couple? Syd, too, was tall and thin and extremely good-looking.

Now he leaned back and closed his almond eyes—eyes that slanted and were seductive: dark brown, fringed with short, thick lashes, and, in truth, really belonged on a woman—and Cass watched him. Syd's wide mouth and full, soft lips seemed to smirk. When he didn't get his own way, those lips would curl into a pout and he'd sulk for hours—once, even for days.

Now he was confident he'd quelled her anger.

But Cass felt a rising rage grip her. It felt as though it came at her from outside the car, from the people on the road. She imagined they hated her; all their hatred seemed to come at her from nowhere. The hot, stuffy car vibrated with anger; Cass wondered how Syd's father was unaware of it. The heat of the noonday sun threatened to suffocate her and she coughed. She felt a sharp pain on her thigh and imagined a knife's point was ripping out her skin, but looking down and seeing her hands, she realized it was her own nails digging into her there. She shouldn't be unhappy, she thought, looking at an old woman in tattered dirty clothes limping slowly on the broken concrete sidewalk. Wasn't this an area of town that had been a 'good area' once, before her time? Now graffiti-splattered walls and makeshift stalls had been constructed in unlikely places. She had everything compared to some people. Yet her life was empty.

Cass' eyes glittered in the Miami shops. She didn't ask Syd where the money came from (his father, of course. Syd hardly showed up at work), but he doled it out and she comforted the emptiness in her heart by shopping. She shopped in a frenzy, rushing from store to store, trying on outfits carelessly. Yet when she got back to the apartment and laid out her purchases, the old familiar despair returned. Cass hid it by matching costume jewelry with outfits and shoes.

"You should get into fashion," said Syd, watching her.

She smiled at him and thought, "You should drop dead."

It was becoming a habit, this way she had of answering people one way while saying something quite different in her mind.

That night in the apartment in Miami, with the air conditioner blowing stale chilled air across her face, Cass dreamt she was climbing a path on a mountain. As she walked, it became darker, and she worried she'd have nowhere to sleep for the night. She searched the landscape and saw it was covered with rocks and moss. But tall trees lined the path and she was almost at the top. Would it make sense to turn back? The sun was setting and Cass felt cold. A cold wind blew and she struggled on, trying to make it to the top. Ahead of her, an unknown figure shouted, "Go down, go down, run! It's going to blow." She looked up and saw thousands of mice running down the mountain. They filled the path, and it seemed they would run over her. Terrified, she stepped aside and ran alongside them down the mountain. The figure of a slender man ran, some way behind her, urging her on.

"Hurry, hurry..." he said, and Cass woke in a sweat as she stepped on a mouse and heard the crunch of its cartilage under her bare feet and saw the blood ooze and stain the pale arch of her delicate, dark brown foot.

Pizza boxes were piled high on the kitchen counter, a soda cup was on its side, and purple soda was still dripping from the coffee table to the floor when Cass and Syd walked through the door. Cass was tired from the travel and nauseated. The hot reek of days' old garbage assaulted her. She sat down wearily on the sofa. The baby's face was still red from crying all the way from Miami to Kingston. Syd, who said he was embarrassed and disturbed by the racket, had gone and sat at the back of the plane.

Rolan and Craig were not there, but they had not vacated the house: their suitcase lay open on the bedroom floor and their clothes hung from doorknobs, over door tops and were strewn on the floor.

"What pigs!" Syd said, in an attempt to pacify Cass.

In her mind she answered, "When I leave you, you'll have your friends to thank. You can all live together like this." She shrugged at him and called her mother.

Syd stooped to clean up the soda, aware that he was treading on perilous ground. That night Cass saw a dark shape hovering in the corner. It was the size of a dog, but she recognized the head of a rat and saw the twitching nose as it sniffed at her at her end of the bed. She trembled and willed herself to wake, but when she reached down to pinch herself, she realized she was awake. Syd snored softly beside her. She tried to shake him but her hand reached into viscous liquid. She saw the digital clock on the nightstand change from 3:37 to 3:38, and she opened her mouth to scream, but a garbled, strangled sound came from her throat.

After that, night after night, the rat shadow came. Cass felt herself unraveling. She wondered if Syd's drugs had somehow rubbed off him and into her while they slept, and she'd somehow become dysfunctional and hallucinatory.

One Saturday morning, she woke up late and heard Bea whispering, 'Miss Cass, Miss Cass, wake up, Miss Cass, and come look pon di sofa."

Groggily, Cass walked into the living room. There was a huge hole in the new fabric.

"Is the rat dem do it, Miss Cass. I don' know how I never notice it before. I don' tink dem tek time do it. Is like overnight, Miss Cass."

Cass was shaking when she woke Syd. She heard herself speaking calmly, but the voice didn't sound like hers. She heard someone say, "Syd, the mice have eaten a hole in the new sofa. Syd, this is your fault. Fix it, Syd."

Syd got up and went downstairs. He peered in with a flashlight and with a gloved hand removed five baby mice, the fur not yet formed on them, the skin whitish pink. Cass shuddered as he put them in a bag and crushed them outside. She tried to wipe their image from her mind. She'd wanted them dead, but now when she thought of them, so vulnerable, so like a baby fetus and defenseless, she sobbed with her head in her hands. Their mother was sure to return. Cass pictured it clearly in her head; the mother mouse searching in vain and despair, and maybe even seeking revenge by attacking Cass' baby upstairs.

Bea suggested getting a cat. She had one that lived in her area, a cat called Goldie that she would bring to work Monday morning.

"Is it a stray, Bea? Because I don't want a stray," Cass said.

"No, Miss Cass. It's not a stray. It's a cat in my district, but you know how black people don' like cat. Goldie need a home."

The cat spent the first two days hiding and, on the third day, got her foot caught in a mouse trap. She ran around the house shrieking and mewing with the rat trap behind her. When Cass finally caught her and pulled it off, Goldie ran out of the house and into the next door neighbour's yard, and was attacked and killed by their large German Shepherd.

"It's a good thing, too," said Hazel in what she thought was a comforting way, while Cass cried on her shoulder. "Because the cat would have eventually sat on the baby's face and suffocated her."

The upholsterer said there was nothing that he could do. He could patch the spot with a piece of the fabric he had left over. Other than that, he'd have to redo the entire thing. But it wasn't possible. Syd's father had cut his salary unless he started to work a regular work week, like everyone else. But Syd preferred to party late into the night.

One day, after another sleepless night where the rat shadow had danced in the corners of her bedroom, its eyes glowing red and seeming to take physical form, Cass looked in the mirror and saw herself truthfully. She was still young at 27. But laugh lines were drawing her mouth down, and she saw herself as growing old, a baby on her hip, a shapeless brown dress hiding the weight she'd gained over the last few months. She saw herself looking resentful and unattractive. Her mouth was always dry, and the little things she'd done to make herself feel good had long been abandoned.

She called her mother. "I'm coming home, mom. The baby and I are coming home."

Syd sat on the patched sofa and watched the movers cart away half of their furniture. At first he'd gotten angry and thrown a glass against the wall. He insisted he was keeping the TV, stereo and, funnily enough, the patchwork sofa.

"Keep them," Cass had said simply.

But his face was ashen when Cass handed him a typewritten list of all the reasons why she was leaving. It was three pages long and had dates of things she'd said to him and he to her.

"Just so you won't question my decision," she'd said, so calmly that he didn't recognize the woman he'd married.

He looked at her warily.

"Is this for a lawyer?"

"No. It's for you."

"Cass, don't leave. If you leave this house, I'm not obligated to look after you or the baby. I mean it. My father has already said as much. Cass! Cass! Awright, den. G'wan. G'wan."

The shadowed rat had stopped coming once she'd begun writing the list. The list was like a confession where, with each word she wrote, she became clean and felt curiously at peace. The rat stopped hovering over her, it seemed, once she knew what she was going to do. Her grandmother had said the life of a single mother would not be easy, but as they'd always done, the women stepped in and performed.

Cass continued to work full time. Her grandmother looked after the baby in the day. As the child grew and her grandmother got too old, the task fell to Margaret, who enjoyed almost every minute of it.

One year to the day after Cass left Syd, Mr. and Mrs. Reid decided to get in touch and meet their grandchild. They made it very clear that Cass should not come to them for money, but that they would pay their granddaughter's school fees and had set up a fund for when the time came for her to go to college.

Syd remarried Rolan-the-weed-provider's sister, and had two more children. He did become a better father with age and made sure to call his daughter almost every night before she went to bed.

Once, when Syd saw Cass at a party, he told her how much he loved his beautiful and caring wife. But as he drank more and his speech became slurred, he lurched into Cass in a sloppy embrace and claimed he'd love her forever, no matter who he married. It was even rumored (according to Hazel's friend's granddaughter, who'd heard it from Mark-the-loudmouth's girlfriend, who had heard it from Mark, who had heard it from Julian, who had heard it from Syd's new wife herself) that when Syd got drunk, he'd say hurtful things to his new wife like, "I don't love you, I love Cassandra Phillips. You think Cassandra Phillips is letting her batty spread like you? You can't cook to save your life. You know who can cook? Cassandra can cook. That's who!"

Years later, Cass ran into Craig who dabbled in coke. She still had this residual anger at seeing him and she was tempted to turn away but he ran to her and hugged her close.

"Wow, Cass. You look great. It's been so long."

He had an hour to kill before he picked up his daughter from ballet, he said, and he knew a great little place around the corner where they could grab some coffee or some fruit juice. Mark-the-loudmouth was happily married and now living in Fort Lauderdale. Rolan-the-weed-provider had two kids and lived in Miami with his girlfriend. Julian was still chronically high and living the party life of a teenaged boy. Craig himself was separated and about to get a divorce. He'd been addicted to cocaine for years and it finally had taken over his life. His wife had left him after two years of marriage. He still loved her.

He was so open that Cass said, "I hated you guys, you know. I really hated you. For years I blamed you for things not working out with Syd and me."

Craig nodded sympathetically.

"I guess none of us were married then. We still thought of Syd as a single guy. We weren't thinking of you at all."

He reached across the table and took her hand tentatively.

"I'm sorry, Cass. We were immature, I guess."

They both shook their heads in silence, and Cass felt a warm feeling inside her. The anger she'd felt all these years melted away. His words were like a treasure she'd had all along, but had only just found, and she smiled.

"Thank you," she told him.

Moments lapsed. Cass looked up into the distance. The mountains seemed far away, blue and softly jagged against the darkening sky. The sun had shifted behind a cloud. When, as suddenly as it had disappeared, it came out again, it lit up their table, and blossoms from a large tree sparkled in the sunlight. Cass heard a car horn as if from far away and for a moment felt ethereal, suspended in time. A golden cat asleep in the sun, stretched out on the hot concrete, yawned, then suddenly rose and darted towards a movement in the bushes.

THE MULE

Mango season is here. I know because two months ago when I was on the outside I saw the delicate white blossoms and the first young green mangoes, hard and clustered together, hanging low against the bright blue sky. I'd give anything for a mango now, a Julie or a Bombay. I imagine cutting the Bombay all around and meeting in the middle, hearing the suction sound as I twist both halves off and seeing the juices running onto my plate. I eat the half without the seed with a small fruit spoon. It's sweet. I suck the pulp from the seed until it is white and the sweet has gone and the mango is tangy.

I'd give anything for some decent food and not this stuff that constipates me.

I'm surprised I'm coherent enough to write. Usually I lie here, silent, unable to speak because a million thoughts are running through my head and my stomach is knotted and I realize my life is over. But last night I begged God for peace. I begged Him to let me sleep and to forget that I'm lying on a lice-infested mattress with cockroaches and rats crawling all over my room. Then it happened, an unbelievable feeling of tranquility, and then I was able to sleep. It was the first time I slept deeply in here.

The judge gave me a light sentence, or so she said. One year and four months. She said I'm lucky because if I was caught in America, the judge would've given me five years. When my father came to visit, he said I'm lucky considering how stupid I am. I didn't answer him. What was there to say? When I looked him in the eye and gave him the full screw-face, he said, "Not only are you incredibly stupid, you're dumb too." I didn't try and defend myself. He flashed a newspaper at me and said, "Your name is in print. Deh calling you a mule, a damn pack horse."

My family is a lost cause. Whatever I say they're going to throw me down anyways; that's why I totally lost myself in my friends. Not that it did me any good.

The thing is, this wasn't even my idea. For real. It was my boyfriend Sean who said, "Yow, Chantal. You want to make some easy money?" When I heard I was shocked so he said, "Yow, babe. Where you think your friend Valerie get that new car? And where you think she get the money to move out on her own? Babe, the people that get caught is a rare thing. Most people get through. Is only the few who get caught wind up in the newspaper."

I should have said they also wind up in jail but I didn't think of that then. I thought how much I wanted to move out of my parents' house and how much I wanted a new car. It's hell to come home after four years of university when you've had all this freedom, and your mother is asking where you are going and what time you'll be home. Sean and I talked about moving in together but when we started looking and heard the price of rent, we gave up. Then Sean came up with an idea. He said he knew nuff stewardess who carry the stuff in their hand luggage and never get searched. He was telling me I should swallow some of it but I would never do that. And what? Have it burst in my stomach and die there on the spot? I don't think so. Sean said strapping it to my leg would be fine and I put some in a package in my underwear as well. I don't malice Sean. I know he can't deal with this. That's why he hasn't come to visit, not even once. Now I realize I can't expect anything from anybody. You just have to take people for what they are. Whatever they show you, that's it.

My mother and grandmother came earlier today. They had on the tight-lipped, pissed off look. When I saw them I broke down and cried but they said they were disappointed and ashamed nuff time. It was like the more I cried, the more disappointed they became. For real. So I stopped and got angry. I said what's done is done and I could use a little more support. That argument was squashed. I could see that my mother wanted to cry. Her face was puffy and her makeup streaked. She was staring at me, her eyes piercing into mine, her hands clenched into fists and her square jaw set. It was a look that demanded answers. Then visiting hours were over and I was relieved.

I still don't understand how I got caught. It's like they saw me and zoomed in. I wore a thick, long BCBG black skirt with pantyhose, so no one could have seen the packets taped tightly to my legs with duct tape. When I lie here and analyze everything, I wonder if it was at the check-in counter. The plastic package in my underwear made my crotch itch. I remembered Sean warning me not to fidget or walk funny but I had to scratch my crotch. It was early afternoon, hot, and I was sweating. I scratched again and shifted the package close to my ass. That felt a little better. That was the only time, I swear. I was calm and cool when the lady at the glass doors took my ticket. I was friendly to everybody. I wonder now if I talked too much. Then my bags were on the X-ray machine and suddenly two thick-bodied women asked me to come with them. It was like, they knew. I can't think what I did to give myself away.

I wish I was a fly on the wall but I know what everyone is saying. Sean would be like, "Yow. Cyah believe it myself." My brother in Miami, "How Chantal so fool?" Major emphasis on the 'fool.' My aunts and grandaunts all talking amongst themselves, saying how I embarrass the family, how I've ruined my life, how I know better because I come from a good family. That one is a joke. Grandma was saying how people who have things, work many years for them and how young people today just want things handed to them on a platter. No-one sees I'm the victim here, that no matter how long and hard I worked, I couldn't move out of my parents' house, I couldn't afford a car, much less pay the rent and utility bills. I'm the victim!

I can see my uncle and his wife, him stern and judgmental, she, soft and pitying. But I don't need her pity or yours. I don't want your pity. I made a mistake, but the fucked thing is that if I knew I could do it and not get caught, I would do it again. Four thousand US dollars for one trip. Yeah. If I knew for sure that I absolutely would not get caught, I would do it again. But I can't go back. When I get out of here, I'm going far away. I can't stay and live with these faces around me. The curiosity. The pity. The shame. The disappointment. The anger. The self-satisfied, moralistic, judgmental mask on everyone's face.

I guess that's why I had this weird dream the other night. I went home and every room was empty. I walked into my bedroom and the bed was gone, the desk and the computer were gone, even the curtains and my photographs, just like we'd moved house and cleared out, except I didn't know it. I woke up frightened. I can't go back, ever.

When I get out of here, I'm going far, somewhere like Europe or Australia. I should fit in well in Australia; that's a country where criminals can start over. I hear they have mangoes in Australia. I hear there's a place that's a lot like Jamaica all the way north, tropical. I'm going to get there. I have 13 months, six days, 17 hours and 55 seconds to go.

MERMAID ON A ROCK

He sent the girls photos of himself and his cousin posing by the mermaid in Copenhagen. There were five photos in all. In one of them he was holding the mermaid's breast and smiling lewdly. I wondered why he'd sent that one to his young daughters. They hadn't heard from him in months.

He'd gotten fat. Strange how someone you married when he was young changed so much with age. His face had filled out, all the lean hard lines were gone. Gone were the hard, steely grey eyes, confident in youth and inexperience. No baggage yet – none that you knew of, anyway.

In our twenties we glossed over childhood baggage as something that happened a long time ago and won't affect us and something that doesn't really matter anyway. In our thirties and forties it comes back–childhood baggage–like acid reflux, and we think it's what's holding us back, blocking us from getting to that great place, the right path to success, from which there will be no coming down until retirement. He had had more childhood baggage than he could handle.

His eyes were watery in the photo–but couldn't that be from the cold?–but there was no mistaking the disillusionment, the disappointment. It was even more pronounced than when I was with him. Before I left him.

The mermaid's body was glossy and smaller than I remembered. I had seen her once and I had been disappointed. I'd hitchhiked from north of Denmark just to see her, and there she was, petite and sad, perched on a rock. Not what I had expected.

But all these things were not my first thoughts on seeing his photo. My first thought was: Fancy that, him off to Denmark, travelling and spending money and not sending much for the girls.

Fancy that. Off to Denmark. His face, with its leonine features was covered with stubble, partly covered by his lank dirty blond hair.

I had liked his hair once. He'd worn it short and square, a type of crew cut, and peroxided it so I thought at first glance it was grey. He had worn a gold earring in his ear. I had first seen him at the airport in Bangkok and fell instantly in love. He was Danish but lived at the time in Oslo; he was a photographer and he travelled all the time, he said. His jaw was square and strong, there were faint laugh lines etched around his mouth and eyes, and he had a long, straight nose. He was young then, younger than I thought. I loved his strength.

Loved it. Past tense. How could I have known a few hard knocks in life would send him to the bottle? These are things you never know. The beginning of a romance is always rosy.

It was overcast in Copenhagen the day the photo was taken. The water is pewter. The mermaid looks dusted in spots with bright green and she seems different depending on the angle of the camera. From the side where you can't see her face, she is graceful and demure, lost in thought. From the front, she is unhappy, staring off into the distance at something unattainable. Was it a sailor she pined for? She is only a mermaid from her knees down, not like all the mermaids in cartoons and movies where the tail begins at the torso. She's got thighs and knees and ankles and the tail starts at her shin, fins attached to bone. She sits with her legs tucked under her.

I don't keep the photos. I run out and buy albums for the girls and give the photos to them. Whenever you miss daddy, I say, you can look at your albums. I say it joyfully, as if it isn't a pathetic substitute.

Long before things between us had turned sour we'd talked about what we'd do if we ever divorced, which, of course, we never would because we were so in love: I hope you won't be a distant father and not care about your children... No, I know it will never happen, but I'd hope if it did you'd love them and support them and keep in touch with them, unlike so many other fathers... Yes, I know you're not like that, but I always wonder why fathers never seem to care as much... Well, if they do, why do they stay away... because of the pain?... Are you kidding? All the more reason... I know you'd be different... I'm just saying, you know... I said I know you are different... that's why I married you... You're sweet...Come here, baby...

The time I went to Copenhagen it was cold and grey, too. It was a last stab at freedom before I was to marry the following summer. He and his camera had gone to Amsterdam and I was alone and lonely in the flat, sanding down a wooden chair I'd bought in an antique shop.

"We should take the ferry to Denmark and hitchhike to Copenhagen," I said to Katrina.

Katrina at 18 was 10 years younger than me. She was taller and wider, a stark contrast to my light brown wraithlike appearance, with a broad happy face and long blonde hair. She was a Nordic nymph, buxom and fair, no freckles on her creamy complexion, with light blue eyes and long brown lashes flecked with blonde at the tips. She laughed and smiled at everything. Many years later, when she told me she'd miscarried her first two babies, her wide mouth and pink lips still appeared to smile. Come to think of it, I've never seen her sad, even when, jealous of her youth, suspicious of her boundless and perplexing optimism, I treated her badly. Didn't she understand homesickness, heartbreak, want, the desolation of not belonging, and the despair that long, cold, dark winters brought? She spoke softly and giggled at things I said.

"I love you, Vanessa," she'd say pronouncing it Wanessa, and then I'd feel bad at my cynicism. But still Katrina said she loved me. I didn't know why. We lived in the same building, a run-down white wooden building on a hill in the middle of town with a cobblestoned road running past it, where the Sunday morning church bell rang early and woke us up. To me, I had no choice but to befriend her. She wasn't embarrassed to speak English or to show her feelings. She sought me out and made me feel exotic. I pretended not to be grateful, and since she made me feel old, I acted the part of a wise know-it-all and rolled my eyes at her obvious immaturity.

"When you get to my age you'll know better," I'd sniff importantly.

Katrina would giggle.

"Oh, Wanessa, you're not that old. You're only 28."

She'd giggle again, and I'd be furious, partly because she was right, partly because I couldn't stand her happiness.

Looking back, this bitterness of mine was at my impending loss of freedom. I had got sucked in and lost in all the 'shoulds' of life: should settle down, should get married, should have a child, should not be gallivanting around like that. But here was I having met him while gallivanting and we got into this relationship thing, and every settled day told me I should not be doing this thing, that I should be gallivanting still and, oh God, what would I be doing now if I had followed that inner voice?

"We should hitchhike to Copenhagen."

"Kobenhaven." (Giggle) "Ja, ja, let's do it, Wanessa. Can't we?"

Like I'm her mother and she's asking me to go for ice cream.

I said brusquely: "Of course not. I have to finish sanding this chair. I'm painting it tangerine."

"I'll help you. We'll do it when we get back. We'll take the ferry–it's not so expensive–to Hirtshals, hitch to Aalberg, stay the night and hitch to Kobenhaven."

I said frowning: "I don't know." This was unlike the impulsive and adventurous person I wanted to be. "Maybe we could. I've always wanted to see the little mermaid."

"Yes, yes. Lille Havfruen."

"What?"

"Lille Havfruen. The Little Mermaid. Me, too. I want to see." She jumped up and down and clapped her hands.

So we did it. We endured rude Danish truck drivers, sleazy Lebanese men who almost drove us the wrong way because they knew of a great party, and spoke to each other in their own harsh ugly language, and I was so scared we'd be raped and killed, that I had reached around to pinch Katrina to say I thought we'd gotten ourselves into a bind but instead pinched the man sitting between us so that he thought I liked him and grinned at me and I thought what a pity if we died this way, a bald middle-aged, gnome-like, bespectacled man, who said he really shouldn't pick us up because he could be fined and what were two nice girls doing hitchhiking because it really wasn't safe and how did Denmark compare to Norway?

There's a photo of me standing by The Little Mermaid. The wind is blowing my curly brown hair in my face, and my hands are tucked deeply into the yellow satin-lined pockets of my black leather jacket. I am wearing a burgundy wool turtleneck; my eyes are small and my cheeks are red. The water is steel grey and across the harbour there are tall, white, thin smokestacks and a crane. I was irritated as hell because I was freezing but still smiled for the camera.

Two photos taken with the mermaid on the rock. That one with Katrina and this one with him cupping the mermaid's breast. What a lifetime in between. The intervening years—those failed years that are painful to write about. The denial that you've made a mistake but that the show must go on, for the children's sake. Your yo-yo love, the onslaught of unkind words, the quarrels where making up isn't passionate but only leads to loathing and disgust, the hypercritical eyes, the small irritations that turn into an issue, major big-time I-can't-stand-it-no-more issues, the futile attempts to change him, giving way to lack of interest, the yearning for change and freedom, and all the ridiculous, totally useless what ifs... What if I had not felt pressured by those shoulds...

"This is not going to work."

Silence.

"I'm unhappy all the time. When are you going to start working again?"

Silence.

"We can't go on like this. We keep having this same conversation week after week."

"Well, you're such a negative person, so I'm not surprised. You keep talking about it. Why don't you leave, then?" His head was bobbing and weaving.

"I wasn't negative before. You made me this way. You need to find a real job. We need to live apart. I can't live with you anymore."

"Whatever, Vanessa." It came out sounding, "Whathheva, Vaneth."

"I can't talk to you when you've been drinking. It's not even 11 o'clock."

Silence.

"Couldn't even wait for lunchtime, could you."

He waved me away, his mouth agape, tongue thick and coated, head hung low, sitting on a closed toilet seat, his head in his hands.

"You're pathetic. I'm leaving, you know. This time I'm really leaving."

"Are you still drinking?"

"No."

"Good. Good for you. How's the work?"

Angrily: "I'm freelance, you know. No severance pay for me."

Don't take it on. Let it slide.

"I have something to tell you," I say, and pause. Then: "I've started seeing someone."

"You don't waste time, do you? Well, I guess he can support the kids, then."

"How can you say that? They're your kids."

"Are they?" He laughs bitterly.

Just ignore him. He's still hurt.

"They miss you. Why don't you call them sometimes?"

"I miss them. You can't imagine the pain."

"What about my pain?" I try not to shout. "I'm here with all the burden, all the headache and worry."

"I wish it were me," he says wearily. "I wish I was the one with my girls, with all of you. I still love you... I know you don't still love me... you can't possibly imagine the pain."

"Mommy, tell us a story."

It was night and they should've been in bed, but we were out in the garden. The moon directly overhead was full and bright and surrounded by a soft hazy red glow. The sky, midnight blue above and deep violet in front of us, was studded with stars and a thin web of cirrus. Laughter came from a house across the street. A chorus from the crickets and toads filled the night air.

"You hear that sound?" I tell them. "I used to think it was the stars twinkling because of 'Twinkle twinkle little star.' Don't the crickets and whistling toads twinkle?"

"Mommy, please tell us a story like you used to long ago."

Once upon a time there was a little girl who lived in Denmark. Her name was Katrina and she wanted to be a mermaid. She lived in a beautiful city called Copenhagen, and every day after school she visited the mermaid carved in bronze (is it really bronze?) perched on a rock by the harbour. A boy her age called Lars (Lars? That's Swedish. Oh, never mind. Just continue) would also come and sit by the mermaid. One day, he told Katrina a story.

"Once there was a handsome sailor. A beautiful mermaid fell in love with him and he with her. Every day he woke up early and went up on deck and there she'd be, following the ship, all the way through the deep blue sea into the Danish harbour. There, they had to say goodbye. They looked sadly at each other and cried. Then she dived underwater and never saw him again. He was heartbroken and carved her image in bronze, perched on a rock. (What's the real story anyway?) He came to the mermaid on the rock every day. He got older and got married and had a son. His son grew up and told his own son about the little mermaid. It was his great-grandfather who'd carved the mermaid," Lars said.

Lars and Katrina grew up, fell in love and got married. They had a son named Thomas. Thomas grew up and had a son called Thor. (How old is this mermaid, anyway? Am I going back too many generations?) One day Thor and Thomas were sitting by the little mermaid. Suddenly, up from the deep grey water, came a beautiful maiden. She saw Thor and smiled. How he looked like her beloved sailor from so long ago! Mermaids stay young for much longer than humans, you know. She smiled at him, blew a kiss and dived under the water like a dolphin except that she had two slightly scaly feet with fins on them.

Thomas and Thor were so excited. They rushed to Lars' house. He was an old man by now and very sick. They told him they had seen the little mermaid and how beautiful she was, how much she resembled the mermaid on the rock. Lars took Thomas' hand and said, "I knew she was real and that she would come back." Then he drew his last breath.

"I knew it, mommy. I knew mermaids were real. Cool. Now I can go to school and tell everyone that they really do exist."

"Hmm. And you know what? One day I'm going to take you and your sister to see the mermaid on the rock in Copenhagen. Just the three of us."

"Can we visit daddy in Denmark too, and we can all visit the little mermaid together?"

"Maybe," I say softly, tenderly, and stroke her cheek.

"Why do you lie to your children," this new one says, "making excuses for their father? It will only hurt them in the long run."

"Because I want them to know he loves them and always will, no matter what."

"What a way to show it, not calling. If it was me, I would call and visit my children."

"All men say that."

"No. I know myself. I would be different. You think it's good telling them all that nonsense about fairies and mermaids and all that? Not that I want to interfere or anything."

"It's no different from the tooth fairy or Santa Claus. I just take it a step further, I guess."

"But you have them walking around looking into flowers for fairies and the older one stares out to sea looking for a mermaid she'll never see."

"How do you know? Anything is possible."

He looked at me oddly, like he thought I might have a defect he'd only just come to see and that somehow that made everything different.

"You know that is not possible."

"If there is one thing I do know, it's that you can't know everything. You can't know what lies ahead."

His eyes have narrowed and he is frowning. Yet I stand my ground and look him straight in the eye.

"I will teach my girls to believe in themselves," I said with a confidence that I didn't know I had. "And I will teach them to take charge of their own lives and dreams."

ARE YOU DOING ANY WRITING?

Lillian used to be a poet. She's not anymore, not because she gave it up but because she's dead. Or 'expired' as my Punjabi friend says—expired—as if she were a plastic tub of yoghurt that has passed its 'best before' date and is all curdled and runny. All that I have left of Lillian are two of her books of poetry and a vague memory of the one time I went to visit her to tell her how much I liked her poetry.

I had visited because I also wanted to see what her house was like. It was in a gated-community and I knew her son-in-law was wealthy. I can't remember much of her place but that's because I'm not a sensor, the type who remembers details of things around you. I'm a perceiver. I notice relationships—how they work or don't work. K.E. had told me that was the problem with my writing. That I don't notice the natural world around me, like how the sunlight coming through a window can cast a glow on someone's face.

Now I always include the sunlight in my writing.

Thinking back to my visit with Lillian, I remember that her life and house seemed idyllic to me. She had an aura of calm and contentment, though I knew she'd been married four times and divorced and outlived all her husbands. She was sitting on the verandah with a cup of tea in her hand, with the shadow of a maid in the background busy at house chores. It was a scene from plantation life, almost. Lillian wore a long, loose flowing dress and even though she was hunched over, she still managed to look quite the diva, her thinning black hair cut short, her body slim and her eyes bright blue. Back then, she was at least eighty-five.

"Welcome, my dear, do sit down. Would you like a cup of tea?"

I felt the charm of old world comfort and luxury envelop me. She called to the maid who came and brought me a cup of tea and the maid smiled at me in a friendly way, as if there was nothing more she'd like to do than to bring me a cup of tea. So unlike these insolent young girls nowadays who come from the city begging work, their eyes shifty and hard, their dark skin blotchy with black spots, signs of hard ghetto living. If you ask them to bring you something they practically throw it at you, their downturned mouths and angry eyes unable to hide the resentment that oozes out of them. This anger at being poor and black. They mix up colour in all this, never seeing that being black doesn't mean you're poor and being white doesn't make you automatically rich. They hate me and I hate them.

I can't tell you that the sunlight dappled on anything or that it cast a beautiful glow on Lillian but I can tell you it was a sunny day. It usually is in Kingston and I wouldn't have gone out if it had been raining. I would have lain on my father's king-sized bed with the remote in my hand channel surfing, or I'd fall asleep with the sound of the heavy raindrops splattering on the pavement outside.

So it was sunny and I had nothing to say so I said what I had come to say.

"I really love your poetry," I said. It was true. I didn't like poetry before but Lillian's poetry had 'fuck' and 'bitch' in it and I could see that she hated her mother until she, Lillian, had turned forty, but then it was too late because her mother had died.

"Thank you, my dear," she said.

What courage, I thought, to write a poem with the word 'fuck' in it but still manage to make it beautiful and deep and thought-provoking so that I kept reading it over and over again and when I went to bed the words still haunted me so I couldn't sleep. The poem was about a failed marriage, a fiery, passionate, jealous, angry relationship.

"And you, my dear, are a very gifted writer. I'm your fan."

I couldn't believe it. Lillian liked my writing. Lillian said she was a fan of my writing. I felt my spirit soar. I felt lightheaded.

"Really?" I gushed. "Oh, thank you. That means so much to me to hear you say that."

I vowed I would go home and write story after story in the hope that Lillian would read them.

Then I went away to another land. I asked our club leader K. E. about Lillian.

"I took her out for her birthday," he said. "She is fine, feisty as ever and as much a diva as always."

I wanted to ask what that meant. I didn't know Lillian so well to know what that meant.

"Like how?" I asked.

"Like a woman. You have to compliment them or they get cranky."

I wanted to attend Lillian's funeral but of course, I couldn't. I was thousands of miles away and separated by sea and credit card debt. I was a limb severed from the body that nourished my creativity, cast off and apart from where I should have been. Club leader K.E. had said this would happen to me.

"A lot of writers go abroad and find they can't write. They don't know the lay of the land. It's not in their blood. Then they try to write about home and there's no depth, or they write about a home that existed twenty years ago."

"I will never be that type of writer," I insisted. "Never!"

But I became an even worse type of writer, the type who isn't writing at all and who uses every excuse to blame it on someone or something else.

Glenn used to be a writer. Club leader K.E. said he would probably be one of the best new young Caribbean writers. The new batch, K.E. called them. Glenn's stories were rich in detail, like a colourful tapestry. I read with envy, devoured the words. Glenn was the cliché, tall, dark and handsome, but I wasn't interested in him that way, even though my marriage was floundering. We just connected as artists connect. We had some conversations, some moments of mild flirtation and he sent me the occasional email. So when I received a mass email one day that requested that none of the writers of the club contact Glenn and that he would no longer be attending club meetings, it was quite a shock. How could someone so talented give up writing? I thought Glenn felt like me, that life without writing wouldn't be a life at all.

"What happened to Glenn?" I asked K.E.

"Glenn found religion." K.E. waved his hand impatiently like he had no time for nonsense and I knew he didn't. If K.E. found your writing wanting and he knew you could do better, he'd shake your paper like he was shaking you, and maybe even throw it on the floor. He had once said make sure no one ever said, 'so what' about your writing.

"Promise me you won't find religion," K.E. said.

I personally didn't see how religion and writing were connected.

"It's not likely," I said. "It's not likely at all. I can't believe Glenn has given up writing. I'm so shocked."

"I'm more shocked he gave up sex," smirked K.E. and I remembered how Glenn's writing could send a tingle down my back and have me squirming uncomfortably in my seat.

"He didn't!" I was incredulous, eager for more gossip.

"He did. Don't find religion, kid. Don't get saved. It ruins the writing."

"I won't. Do you think Glenn had AIDS? From his writing I think he slept around." It had to be something drastic, I thought, for someone to give up a promising writing career.

"I always thought he was gay," said K.E. "but I don't think he had AIDS."

I tried to contact Glenn after that, to show that no matter what, we could be friends and I wanted to find out why he would write off a whole set of people he'd been close to at the writing club. We shared so much. He wrote back saying he was going away for a while and that he was severing contact with the writing club. He didn't say it right out but he kind of asked me not to write him because he would be unable to keep in touch. So I didn't. I simply deleted his name from my contact list as if he didn't exist anymore. That's one bonus of living in this electronic age. No ratty tatty address books with names and numbers crossed out.

I kept in touch with K.E. for a long time after I moved abroad. After all, I told people, he is my mentor, he's brilliant and if he wasn't so much older than I, I would've shared much more with him than my writing. And K.E. was way older than me, older than my father even. I imagine sex with him would have been like the scene in Sex and the City where Samantha sees her new lover walking to the bathroom and she sees how old he is, the way his muscles have given way to flab, the way his bottom jiggled as he walked and it turned her off. She had rushed out of the bedroom. I don't think I would have been so shallow as that, but I kept my fantasies about K.E. strictly in my head.

It didn't help that my husband at the time wasn't working with a full deck of cards. There was zero communication between us on levels that mattered to me. I wanted to talk Hemingway, whom I'd just discovered thanks to K.E., and Updike and Jean Rhys and plenty others. He, that is the ex, was listening to a new dance hall song that consisted of someone farting and the singer rapping about how bad it smelled. He would laugh uproariously and I would be torn. Should I smile and go along with the show, wipe the disdain from my face? Should I draw down the corners of my mouth, deepen those cross creases between my eyebrows and call him a jackass? Should I tell him how K.E. is twice the man he is, that I love K.E. for his mind, and that every minute I have to spend with him, the husband, was torture, and was made more torturous knowing there were other people I could be spending time with, not just K.E., but Lillian and Glenn, of course Glenn before he had found religion and lost all common sense.

It always bothers me when older couples get divorced. I think what a waste to have travelled so far for nothing. But with my ex, I knew we would never walk that journey. It was doomed from the minute I stepped into the tall presence of K.E., from the moment I heard his booming voice of authority and when he said my name, he said it like I should know more than I do, be more than who I was, and if I didn't, he would notice and call me up on it. He called me kid. He always said, "You're talented, kid. But you have a lot to learn." I felt excited in his presence, like I was going places.

I felt awed around him, like a kid around a movie star.

Living 'abroad' was more than a different way of life, but what some people don't know is how hard it can be to pursue your dreams for yourself. My Punjabi friend said she is a 'nothing' here but a 'someone' over there, she has everything over there and nothing here. "Why did you come then?" I asked. She tells me she came for a job and she uses her hand and her head nods side to side. She complains that there is no one here to do her housework.

K.E. emailed me asking if I'm doing any writing. I say I'm working on something and I say it's hard what with the laundry and the cooking and the working. I'm not sure he understands because he tells me to remember that I'm a writer and if I don't write, it's a waste of my talent.

"What you need," he tells me, "is someone who can mind you, a rich husband who understands your need to write and then lets you do it. That's all that matters, you know, the writing."

I do know.

K.E. came to see me. Actually he didn't come to see me specifically. He happened to be lecturing in the city where I live so he took me to lunch. That was two years ago. He still did the writing club 'back home' and he told me there were so many new writers, good writers. I was jealous.

"You don't think of yourself as a writer," he said matter-of-factly.

One morning, soon after that meeting, I got out of bed, the wrong side some would say, had my morning cup of coffee and then, like an oxygen tank with too much pressure building up, I exploded. I threw laundry about, yelled, burst into tears.

What do you need? asked my new husband with our baby in his arms.

"I'm a writer. I need to write."

"I'll take the children," he said, and he did.

He took them for three hours. I sat at the computer and I checked my email. I went on Facebook and called a couple of people I hadn't spoken to in a while. I sat back at the computer and the urge to get a load of laundry in overtook me. The urge to wipe the floor became stronger and stronger as I sat there staring at some black spots on grey and blue tile. There was no sun. The day was grey and gloomy signaling the start of another winter. It was imperative to change over the clothes – put away the shorts, summer dresses and short sleeves and pull out the sweaters, the cords, the scarves and the hats. This process can be arduous and one cannot procrastinate, I reasoned with myself. One day will be sunny and the next day you'll walk outside and see your breath.

When my husband walked in three hours later, the house was spotless.

Even small handprints that had smeared the walls for weeks were finally gone. Because the fact is, I explained, if your house is not 'company ready' and someone happens to stop by and see that mountain of paper or the laundry strewn over the sofa because you didn't have time to fold it, and the dishes piled in the sink because you didn't clear the dishwasher, well, every woman knows that's a failure of another kind.

I took the baby with me when I went to lunch with K.E. She slept through it all, her tiny head full of dark curls was tilted to the side and her profile, her button nose was adorable.

"She's lovely," said K.E. "You are still full of the maternal glow. Maybe you should concentrate on being a mother, for now. You know when women are new mothers they turn inward."

Was this the same man I knew from ten years ago? I didn't want to hear about maternal instinct. But as usual, K.E. was right. I came home and tried to write but the baby kept crying and in response, my breasts filled with milk, my nipples grew hard and erect, and I leaked down my shirt. I wanted to hold her and throw her away at the same time. If I didn't think of K.E. and how I felt I was letting him down, I would hold her to me tightly and never let her go.

K.E. used to be a writer and a writer's club leader and my mentor. I guess he also used to be a lecturer too. 'Used to be' is not because he's given up any of those things. It's because he's dead. I kept meaning to call him but I was waiting for inspiration. When he asked, "Are you doing any writing?" I wanted to have an answer and I wanted that answer to be 'yes.'

They say pancreatic cancer takes people fast. K.E. didn't tell me he was sick and I couldn't make it to his funeral. I'd like to think that after all the judgment, Lillian would welcome K.E. and then they would sit down for the business of tea and some poetry in the world hereafter. That's how I'll remember them.

I still hear him from time to time in the back of my head. Like a guilty conscience. "Are you doing any writing?"

LETTER FROM INDIA

So I shouldn't have opened someone else's mail, you say. Perhaps you're right. But it was a lonely Sunday morning and I was angry.

The letter had arrived Friday afternoon and sat on the kitchen counter all weekend. The envelope was paper-thin and had red typing. I'd glanced at it when I came home from work on Friday and seen that it was addressed to Lorna Browne, who had probably lived in my rented townhouse before me. I had been there seven months now. The letter came from India; I tossed it aside.

I watched TV Friday night until it put me to sleep at 4 o'clock in the morning. I spent Saturday looking at the phone, walking by it, willing Hardev to call. Whenever I had the urge to call him, I ran to the kitchen and ate the pastries I'd bought on my way home from work. I watched TV and made a list of all the things I would do with my life but would never do, because I was not whole and did not have the will.

I met Hardev seven years ago. He was Indian, a Sikh, and he had come to Jamaica from Toronto. He had relatives here. I was 28, he was 30. I gave him everything. I overlooked everything. He was disgusted with the bathing suits Jamaican women wore, so I traded all my bikinis for a plain black one-piece and hardly went to the beach. I did not mention marriage for the first four years, and then only after the probing questions and hints from my family. They wanted me to be sure that the relationship was going somewhere after all the time I'd invested in it. They liked Hardev. He was fun, charming, ambitious, and doing very well with his store downtown.

You say I should have seen the signs when his mother visited and ignored me, giving me hostile stares when Hardev wasn't looking? Maybe, but it was a three-week visit and I was busy at work. She didn't have time to get to know me, I rationalized, and she would be returning to Toronto, and I would have Hardev here alone.

One cool December evening when we walked in his garden and the poinsettias were in bloom, the air was crisp and the Hawaiian-like scent of the night-blooming Cereus wafted past us on the breeze, I mentioned marriage. I didn't ask Hardev to marry me. I only mentioned that I was not getting younger, and that all my friends were getting married. I said how everyone said our relationship was amazing. We never fought, we didn't always agree, but we were good friends. Hardev agreed and pulled me closer. I took it as a positive sign. After a year, I assumed he wasn't ready for marriage, the way most men are not ready when they are young. I assumed I was there with him and I would be the one.

Then, seven years later, he informed me quite politely that his family was sending him to India to find a wife. He was dry-eyed and unemotional. What did I expect, he asked when I screamed, and cried and felt ashamed. But then I screamed and cried again. I had given him so much: myself, my years, my time. It was a betrayal. Why hadn't he told me this from the very beginning?

Don't say I should have known. Hardev never led me to believe he was one for arranged marriages. I admit there was one conversation when we discussed it and argued. "I would never want someone choosing for me. I want to marry for love," I'd insisted.

In the end he agreed and said, 'Yes,' he would want to choose, too.

"And what if I were white," I screeched into his ear. "Would you have married me then?"

No, he insisted. It wouldn't have mattered. I wasn't Indian. I wasn't Sikh.

And so it was over. Hardev left, and there was a large gaping hole in my life. Where were the friends who should've been there? What beach did people go to now, and how would my body fit into bikinis I hadn't worn for seven years? My life was over. I had been betrayed. I wanted to see Hardev fitted just right on a guillotine, only his head and hands visible to me as I stood in the crowd and watched the blade come down.

I always thought that he would call; but he never called. It seemed odd to me that you could spend seven years with a person and then never call—not even to say I miss you, or how are you?

So I opened the letter from India. I opened it to see if I could figure out what I'd done wrong, to perhaps glean something of the Indian psyche. I opened it because I was lonely and it was something with a human connection, something I could touch. I opened it because it felt good to rip open the envelope.

A picture fell out. It was of a couple at a wedding banquet. I noticed her first: young chubby, round face and a beautiful blue and gold flower stuck between her brows. Her sari was gold, the material appeared to be spun from magical pixie dust that one only reads about in fairy tales. She wore thick gold jewelry around her neck and arms, and she smiled slightly, not so much self-assured as hopeful and naive.

He was handsome: black wavy hair and light brown skin. His name was Asha; the letter was from him. He was young, but not as young as she, and his large dark eyes were soulful. His full lips appeared to want to smile for the camera; they were parted slightly and turned up at the corners, but they did not make it into a smile.

The letter began, 'My dear Lorna,' and I heard in that a longing and I said the name Lorna and dragged it out a long time, my mouth shaped in an 'O.' *Lohhhrrrnna.*

He wrote, 'How is my beloved Jamaica?' And I saw him here, living and enjoying a new exotic land, and then returning to India and yearning for his beloved Jamaica. There are lots of job vacancy advertisements in the papers in India for Jamaica, he said, but he could not return after the bad experience he had here.

I wonder what that experience was. Did they fire him because they saw he was bright and ambitious and would one day compete with them? Did he argue with management and not get along with one person who ate away at his self-esteem, day after hot tropical day? Had he been held up at gun point and robbed of his money? He never said, but Lorna must know.

'Why haven't you written in so long,' he wrote, and 'what is happening in your life? Are you married?'

He said his wife and new baby are fine, but he thinks of Lorna often and, as he writes, her photo sits before him. 'Please send me copies of the photos we took together,' he asks her, and I see them on the beach and at parties and maybe even on a trip to the mountains, where he holds her hand and she looks up at him and smiles.

But Lorna is smarter than me. She knows that one day he will go back, and when she smiles she knows that, for her, there is someone of her own culture waiting in the wings. She laughs with him and enjoys that moment because she knows one day he will be married to someone of his own culture, sitting at a wedding banquet just like the one in the picture he has sent.

He implores her to reply soon, and to send her email address so they can communicate often, because he remembers her so very much. I hear all his longing for something that will never be and I feel guilty that Lorna will never get this letter. He envies her opportunity to travel, 'So lucky you are, Lorna,' and I feel that he respects his new wife and loves his child, but is trapped, as I am trapped. He is not free, as I am not free.

'What took you so long to reply, Lorna,' he asks and again he requests that she write soon.

Wake up Asha. Stop pining for something you gave up. Lorna is busy with her own life. Maybe she is married now. She doesn't care the way you do. Hardev doesn't care the way I do. That's the way love goes.

Late at night, when the TV fails to put me to sleep and I lie awake in the darkness, the ceiling fan swirling above my head, the soft whine of a mosquito in my ear, and the faraway barking of the neighbourhood dogs in the distance, I close my eyes and think of Asha in India. The image of his face appears before me and it seems to me that his pain and mine are entwined, like a long rope, his bitterness and mine, his longing and mine come together swirling across the oceans to meet and wrap around each other, making a dark, hazy mist of anguish that goes upward, upward, never reaching the sky. I hold Asha's image for as long as I can. Then I fall asleep and dream strange dreams that I don't remember in the morning.

A GOOD MAN IS HARD TO FIND

I'm not in love with Carl and haven't been in years so even that hormonal infused time of the month when I'm ovulating, that time when it must be like living in the body of a sex-starved teenager, I had no desire for Carl. I'd run out of excuses to not fuck him. There's a limit to the amount of headaches I can fake and I can't have my period three weeks out of four. The last time I told him no, I'm on my period, he said, "Again?" He said it with such quiet disbelief that I pulled down my underwear and said aggressively, "Do you want to see the blood?" He turned away and said no, he didn't, and good thing too because there wasn't any blood to see. Another man would've had the guts to check. Not Carl. He's an ostrich, his head buried in the sand not wanting to face life. If I even slapped Carl with a used pad from my menstrual cycle, he might flinch a little but then he'd forgive me. He'd take it, not wanting to see that I didn't, couldn't love him. That kind of love is sickening.

Carl gave me permission to verbally abuse him, so I did. Not that he told me I could call him names like idiot, dumb ass and moron, but he never stood up for himself. Didn't dispute it or tell me he wouldn't tolerate such vile behaviour. When I spoke to him, my voice was tinged with hostility and disdain. When I woke up beside him, still sleepy with vivid technicolour dreams of Paris at dusk or dreams of me, unbelievably taking flight, soaring above the ground in wonder, I'd see Carl sleeping beside me and I wouldn't feel numb or empty. I'd feel irritation. It would come upon me suddenly like a thief in the night and hit me. My skin would itch like I had a case of severe eczema and tingle as if insects were crawling under my skin, eating me alive from the inside and I would wonder what I would do to escape his placid gaze that day. I would wash my face and brush my teeth as if I were in a war with my own body, brushing my hair with such unnecessary strength that I pulled half of it out my head.

I won't make Carl out to be worse than he really is, not even I would stoop that low. I'll tell it like it was. He never helped with anything even though I worked and he didn't, he claiming he couldn't find a job. I would come in the door to find the house the same way I'd left it: laundry undone, the kitchen sink piled with dishes and Carl watching TV. This shit builds up over time. Then Carl started using my money to buy beer. I'd come home to find he'd downed a six-pack and was in a kind of stupor, smelly and rheumy-eyed like some old man, when we were only in our thirties. 'What lay down the road,' I asked myself, 'if it's like this now?'

"One day I'm going to leave you. There's no future in this. I don't know when or how, but I will," I told him so regularly so that he came to ignore me. Of course, at first, he begged me not to leave, told me he'd change. Then over time, when I didn't leave, he stopped believing me. The day he lost our rent money, eighteen hundred dollars, was the day I decided I'd leave him. I'd tried everything before, to get him to stop throwing away our money and find a job. I cajoled, lectured, I hugged and said we'd get through it all together. I suggested counselling, wept, screamed, I lunged for his neck. I told the women at work I couldn't stand him anymore and I told Dwight who sits beside me, that I hated myself for thinking it, but wouldn't it make life easier if Carl just disappeared one day, just disappeared and never came back? It would be simpler than a divorce. "Why doesn't he just leave me?" I complained. "He knows I can't stand the sight of him. Why doesn't he have an affair like other guys would and then that would give us both a reason to break it off?"

Dwight smiled and said in Jamaican patois, "Him don't want to lose a nice ting like you. You pretty and you educated." Then Dwight would give me a look that told me he was available. I made sure to crush his hopes immediately. Dwight was not my type and even in my crazed horny state, Dwight, with his small dark eyes too close together and his oddly-shaped shaved head, was not attractive to me.

"Even though I can't stand Carl, I would never cheat on him. I took a vow. I'm not that kind of person," I said to Dwight in a voice that I hoped sounded sincere and virginal. Naturally this was a big lie as the guy in Accounting can testify because I fucked *him* good and proper in the male washroom at some nightclub in the city. It must have been my ovulation time, eggs were ready to drop because the dress I chose was skin tight sans underwear. Men who I wouldn't look at twice were suddenly more attractive and I looked them all directly in the eye as I sauntered by, my hips swinging twice as wide, my breasts pushed right up with one of those Victoria Secret push-up bras. It could've been anybody really but Anthony from Accounting was there and he bought me a drink and then another. His eyes lingered on mine and travelled down my body and it was good to feel that tingle of lust again, to feel my lips swelling with readiness and aching with desire. He put his fingers inside me right there at the bar and felt my wetness, and when he realized I wasn't wearing underwear, I saw his arousal ready to burst through his pants.

"I could make it happen," said Dwight.

"What?" I wasn't sure what he was talking about. I was still thinking about Anthony holding my breasts and banging away while his balls bounced on my thighs.

"I could make it happen that Carl just disappears."

I couldn't tell if Dwight was joking. We joked all the time, both of us having a penchant for saying the most inappropriate things in the workplace. Dwight would say things like, "Get ready to bust out of this place. That bredda over there in the turban and the beard looks like he's working for Al Quaida." I'd laugh gleefully. Dwight always said one day the world would be all brown with the mixing of people and then people would have to find something else to be prejudiced about. Now I thought that Dwight had to be telling one of his jokes, so I decided to play along with it.

"Oh really, Dwight. And just how would you make Carl disappear?"

"Brown Girl, I have my ways. I still have links to my posse. But you see how you tell all the women how you having troubles, you has to stop that. You has to go on like everything good between you and Carl. You has to stop talk 'bout you troubles from today."

"Dwight, what are you talking about?"

"Simone, I'm talking about giving you freedom. Freedom to date whoever you want to date and get that *bloodclat* out of your life."

"No, I wouldn't want him to actually disappear. I'd feel terrible. I'd feel so guilty. How would I live my life after that? I just want him to fall in love with someone else. You're so evil, Dwight, so bad." I laughed.

"I can make that happen too. What kind of girl him like? White? Black? Brown? Chiney? Coolie?"

"You can't make a person fall in love with someone else. That's ridiculous. Geez Dwight, get back to work."

"You want to put money on it?"

"Well, if you're serious, I suppose he looks at blondes with big breasts but not the sleazy type, the wholesome athletic girl next door type."

Dwight gave a knowing nod and grinned. "Yeah man. I know just what type you mean. Give me three weeks and Carl will be packing his bags, telling you that him is sorry but him find someone new."

"Whatever you say, Dwight. You crazy *rass*." I smiled at him and gave him a playful squeeze on his arm.

For three weeks, every time the women at work asked me how things were going at home, nosy Dwight looked over and gave me a warning glare. I didn't even know why I lied. "Fine, everything is fine," I said. "Peachy." My voice had an edge of sarcasm. Dwight rushed over. "Sistah, you can do better than that. Where are your acting skills? Come man, you have to make it real."

So I said to everyone, "I can't believe Carl and I are actually getting along. I hope it lasts. Knock on wood," and everyone knocked on their desks. Shawna, who is religious and quotes the Bible, looked up to the ceiling and said, "Praise God. He can perform miracles." Patricia, who is cynical and hates men, said, "Yeah, until the asshole fucks up again. Just give him time."

At the end of three weeks, Carl came in the house with his hang dog look, carefully putting bags of groceries on the counter.

"Simone, I have to tell you something," he said standing at the grey marble topped counter with a hand on his hip looking slightly effeminate to me. Unwashed dishes were in the sink that I had to get to before nightfall. I hadn't cleared the dishwasher for two weeks.

"Now? I'm a little busy." I was on Facebook, posting a picture of myself in a skin tight red dress, awaiting the likes that popped up almost immediately.

"Yes, now." He took a dramatically deep breath. I didn't put the computer down, just glanced over at him.

"Simone, I met someone recently but I promise you I've done nothing. Not even kissed her."

I stared at a spot between his eyes, my mouth tightly closed.

"She pursued me but I told her I was married and in love with my wife."

I didn't say anything so he continued.

"I met her at the grocery store. Her bag busted open in front of me and her groceries spilled all over the floor so I stopped to help her. Then she gave me her number and I gave her mine. I'm sorry. I don't know why I did that. Anyway, she called me. Just to say hi. I don't know why I even called her back after that. I'm so sorry. We started texting but when it got sexual, I drew the line. I mean, she's a nice girl. Very young. Twenty-two. But I'm not interested. I deleted her number. I can show you my phone."

Carl was quite pleased with himself that he thought he snagged a twenty-two year old. He knew I'd been upset when I turned thirty. Asshole. His passive aggressiveness was easy to read. The question remained, was this girl the bait? I glared at him for a moment and returned to the computer. He walked over to my chair and stroked my hair. I could see Carl finally feeling useful and needed as he picked up the groceries, then driving home planning what he would say to me, how he would phrase the words that would allow me to appreciate and hang on to him.

"I know you're angry, Simone, but I would never do anything to hurt you. I promise." I shook his hand off my head. It was the first time in my life that I couldn't wait to get to work. Had to find out if Dwight had a hand in this.

Fucking Dwight had to be off sick the next day. I texted him a million times but he didn't reply. I didn't know how to act around Carl because I was too pissed off that he was still in my face. I couldn't even act like I was hurt that he'd met someone else. I wanted to scream, 'why didn't you bang the bitch in the supermarket parking lot, you fucking loser?'

The next day Dwight walked in as pleased as punch. "What're you smiling for? I asked him. "Your plan didn't work at all. It was you who set up the girl in the supermarket, right?"

"She was the wrong gal, sistah. The wrong girl. I have to find a next girl and it goin' to work this time."

"Don't bother. Carl will begin to wonder how come women are coming on to him all of a sudden. Anyway, I don't think he's going to cheat on me."

"If you don't think that plan will work, we'll come up with another plan." Dwight looked at me pointedly but as he said that, his phone rang and he took it. I slumped over to my desk and put my head in my hands. If I left Carl, the employment insurance money would dry up, not that it was much but it helped. I'd be on my own with the measly little money my sales job brought in. Anthony from Accounting had a wife, plus Canadian men didn't know how to be supportive to a woman, as if a fuck came for free.

Day after that, Dwight and I went on the road to visit clients. I genuinely liked Dwight as a friend because he made me laugh and we had a birthplace in common. I was careful of Dwight because our backgrounds were very different.

"Tell me, Dwight, do you really have a posse? A gang?" I leaned over seductively and stroked his arm.

"Yeah. I grew up with those guys. We started a gang way back, in the nineties but I got out. I wanted to be legit, get a job, for real. But if I need a favour, those guys have my back."

"I thought a person could never leave a gang."

"The gang leader can leave the gang and put someone else in charge." Dwight turned to me and grinned. This time, I didn't notice his close-knit eyes. I noticed how his pants bulged at the crotch and that his arms were well muscled. I shivered, catching myself. I refused to stoop that low, because ridding myself of Carl was one thing. How would I ever rid myself of Dwight? I shifted slightly in the seat and self-consciously tugged at my skirt hem to fit it over my knees.

"Have you ever killed a man?" I asked.

"I've killed someone. But girl, don't ask me those questions."

"I just want to know how it feels."

"It feels terrible."

I looked out the window at the rush of road flashing by and big nondescript office buildings spread out from each other. Once in a while I'd glimpse the backs of suburban home developments so close together that I imagined neighbours could watch each other going to the toilet. It was early spring and there was the awakening of life again. Patches of green were visible on the otherwise brown and barren landscape and the sky was a dull hazy blue. There was a sameness to the barren land. It was sickening, this sameness of North America, which curdled my enthusiasm for life but at least I was out of the city and felt calmer than I'd felt in months.

"Since we're driving so far out of town, we should stay over in Niagara Falls. That way we can see a few more clients tomorrow," said Dwight. He glanced at me expectantly.

Who did he think he was fooling. I looked at him with my eyebrows raised. "Stay where, may I ask?"

"The company will pay for a hotel if it's for business? Separate rooms, girl, chill out."

"And what do I tell Carl?"

"Tell Carl whatever you want. It's not like you have *pickney* to go home and feed. Business is business. When are we going to come out this way again? I ain't making this trip during the summer. I'm thinking money."

"Maybe," I shrugged looking out the window at the rare patches of green and the dreary landscape again.

We got two rooms at the Marriot. I showered and met Dwight for dinner. After dinner we sat in the hotel lounge and had a drink. Dwight sat across from me with his arms crossed and his legs open wide. He had a sleepy look on his face.

"You look like you smoked some weed," I laughed.

"I have some in the room. Want a draw?"

"Sure, why not. I haven't smoked up in years."

We went back to his room and I sat on his bed. He lit up the spliff and handed it to me. I felt nothing at all but lightheaded with a dry scratchy feeling in my throat. I inhaled again, drawing the smoke deep into my throat and held it there for a moment. Dwight was standing over by the window looking out, his back to me, posing, showing me his rhomboids rippling through the cotton shirt clinging to his back. He's waiting for me to approach him and run my hands along his back, I thought, but I won't. Never.

"Let's go back to the lounge," I suggested, but didn't move.

Dwight lit up again. We smoked for a while then became suddenly quiet. I turned to ask him something and found he was staring at me. "Simone, girl, you are hot," he groaned and I collapsed against him, his tongue searching for mine. I heard myself moan in pleasure through the haze that filled my head. I had no intention of this happening. A part of me was thoroughly disgusted and another part just relaxed into the moment.

Dwight was pretty good about keeping our trysts on the down low. He practically ignored me at work saying it was part of a greater plan.

"What greater plan? Don't do anything stupid, Dwight." It was after my period. I'd lost amorous feelings in general and certainly all feeling for Dwight. He was back to being an over-muscled dude I worked with and nothing else. He kept calling me after work to meet him at out of the way places.

"No, I can't," I'd say. "It's part of a greater plan." He was such an idiot that he didn't sense the sarcasm and replied, "true ting, true ting." What a moron.

One evening I walked in after work and sensed something had changed. After I walked around, made myself a sandwich since I'd long stopped cooking for Carl, it hit me that what was different was the absence of Carl. His clothes and shit were all there, his cell was on the dining room table, his wallet was on the dresser upstairs, nothing was missing but Carl. The indentation in the sofa where his wrinkled rump sat all day wasn't there and the house felt unnaturally empty. I called his parents and pretended to care where Carl was. "I thought he might have gone to visit you," I said to his mother Andrea, filling my voice with worry. Andrea got all maternal, asking me a million questions, keeping me on the line, asking when I'd seen him last and asking why I hadn't gone to the police. "Why would I go to the police, Andrea? He's probably visiting a friend. Don't worry." I heard her take a sharp, agonized breath. She wanted to scream at me and tell me Carl was her baby. I wanted to say, if you hadn't over-mothered the big lump, he wouldn't have turned out to be so useless. I hung up the phone feeling irritated that I'd called her. I shouldn't have, especially since I rarely called her.

When Carl didn't come back during the night, I called Dwight and asked him if he knew why my husband was missing.

"No, why would I know anything about your husband?" Then he hung up the phone.

I drove to work with a sickened feeling in my stomach and walked straight to Dwight's desk.

"Carl's gone," I hissed at him. "I have to report it to the police today. Now in fact. It's going to look bad if I don't go now. Tell me what to say. I hope you didn't do anything stupid, Dwight. If you know where he is, tell me."

"I have no idea what you're talking about."

"Just so you know, Dwight, I'm not involved in any of this shit. Whatever you've done, I'm not involved. I didn't ask for this. I didn't want this."

Dwight looked hard at me and got up, and ushered me over to my desk.

"Have a seat," he said slowly and firmly, his broad hand on my shoulder and pushing down hard so I had no choice but to bend my knees and sink into the chair. "I have work to do," he said coldly and strode away.

"What a stinking bastard," I thought unable to work. "I'm not going to jail for Dwight."

On the way to the police station, I debated whether I should mention Dwight or keep him out of it. If I mentioned I slept with someone else, I'd be an accomplice. No-one would be convinced that I'd been joking. The whole office knew I couldn't stand Carl. I'd be arrested for sure. On the other hand, I could keep Dwight out of it and pretend I knew absolutely nothing. I could deny I'd fucked Dwight or hire a really good lawyer. Someone Jewish.

The police asked me if Carl had disappeared before. "Not for so long," I said, but he goes for long walks sometimes. It was a lie. Carl rarely got his flabby ass off the sofa. They took all the information and said they'd have to come to my house for the investigation. I had to sign a paper allowing them in. When they came a few hours later, I had such an attack of anxiety when I saw them at the door but I figured the frown on my face could be mistaken for worry. I sat on the sofa and wrung my hands, spoke in a trembling voice and squeezed my knees together to keep from shaking. Another officer, a harsh, bitter-looking blonde woman went upstairs to look around. After they left, I called Andrea to let her know the police were investigating. She started crying on the phone and said she was coming over. I was pissed. I had to rush and clean up the place, shove laundry into a room and close the door, clean the kitchen and just as I was getting going, I heard a knock on the glass sliding door that led to the garden. I jumped. There was no-one there until I looked down and there was Dwight on the ground, wearing black.

"What the hell are you doing?" I asked opening the door. He looked around and then crawled in. "Are you crazy? Get up. Why are you here?"

"A black man is the first person the police are coming for, guilty or not," he said. "I just want to clear up a few things."

"Did you do something to Carl? Is he alive? Because if you killed him, you're really stupid."

"Whether I did or didn't, you got what you want. The guy is gone," he said closing all my curtains. He spoke in a whisper, in case, he said, the police bugged the place. We went outside to talk and I was annoyed because it was cold and I could see our breath. I shivered and Dwight went to put his arm around me.

"No. Don't," I commanded. "Not here. Especially since you will be a suspect."

"No-one can find out about us," he said. "I'm not going to jail because of some stupid ass white man."

"But you killed him," I said.

"Didn't say I did. Didn't say I didn't. Just saying I'm not going to jail for some fool."

"Don't call Carl a fool," I said. "Now I'm alone. Do you realize that? Do you know that I can't be alone? I've never been alone in my life. I can't live alone." I started to shout and wave my hands around to make my point.

"Hush up. You want the neighbours to hear you? I will check on you from time to time. Just come to work as usual. We'll talk there. Act like we're getting closer. When Carl doesn't come back, I'll move in. It's going to look natural. Like I was comforting you in your grief and then tings just happened."

I smiled but I was thinking that I'd rather have a cockroach move in than Dwight. I shuddered and he mistook it for weakness so he pulled me into his arms. I hid my scowling disgust in his sleeve. Dwight wore way too much cologne. It made my nose itch. I pulled away and put several feet between us. "I'm allergic to cologne," I said.

Someone calling my name made me jump and Dwight froze and hit the ground like he was in a shootout. Shit. It was Andrea.

"Simone," she called over the gate dividing the driveway from the garden. "Are you there?"

"Yes, I'm here. Go to the front door. I'm coming in." I hissed to Dwight. "It's Carl's mother. Lie low."

Andrea didn't move. "I've been at the front door for ages ringing the doorbell and knocking." Her voice had a grating nasal whine.

"I've been outside. I couldn't stay in the house a moment longer without Carl," I said.

"Is anyone with you? I heard voices."

"No. Course not. I'm thinking out loud. It's a bad habit. Go around to the front door, Andrea. I'll let you in."

Andrea coming over didn't help. She walked around looking at everything. "I haven't had time to clean," I said. "I've been very busy driving around the neighbourhood doing my own investigation. Who knows how hard the police are trying."

"That's exactly what I want to talk to you about. I want us to mobilize ourselves and do a concentrated search, get the community to help us. Give me your most recent photo of Carl." We can drive around posting pictures everywhere. Neighbourhoods near and far."

"Geez, Andrea. Isn't that interfering with the police investigation? Should we be doing our own thing without consulting them?"

She stared at me in disbelief. "Do you want to find him or not? I'm not relying on the police. I know what I'm going to do. You can do what you want to do."

"No, of course I want to find him. I'm going to help. I just want to make sure it's okay with the police."

Andrea got up and walked to the screen door and opened it. "You really shouldn't sit outside in the dark. Besides it's so cold tonight. Why would you want to be out there?"

"I couldn't breathe in here," I said and she nodded in understanding and closed the door again.

I was glad when she left. At work, that horrible twat Patricia insinuated that it must be somewhat of a relief that Carl had disappeared.

"How could you say something like that?" I asked her. "I would never wish Carl's death, no matter what."

"I didn't say he was dead. I said he'd disappeared. Why? Do you know something the police don't?" She looked at me smirking with her head cocked to one side.

"I said that because of the odds. That's what the police told me, that the longer a person is missing, the less chance they are alive." I looked at her with hostility. She didn't censor a thing that came out of her droopy, dried up mouth. I didn't talk to Patricia after that.

By this time, Carl's disappearance was all over the news. I had reporters outside my house but I wasn't a prime suspect. Carl had disappeared during the day when I was at work and so was Dwight. Patricia and the other women betrayed me by telling the police that Carl and I didn't get along. I no longer ate lunch with them and I asked to be transferred to another department.

How could a man just disappear in this age of cell phones and satellites and cameras everywhere? Dwight wasn't that smart. I thought about fucking him again so he could tell me where he hid the body but the thought was repulsive. He was harassing me all the time, wanting to come over, wanting to make it known that we were an item.

"It's too soon for us to be together," I told him, though six months had passed and there was no sign of Carl. "It's a well-known and accepted fact that a year is the length of time for a widow to mourn," I said.

"I never hear of that in my life," said Dwight bitterly.

Like all news, the publicity waned. The police had investigated me and I was clean as a whistle. Around this time, I realized I hadn't heard a peep from that annoying Andrea so I called her. Her voice was as cold as a witch's tit. "What do you want?" she asked. It put me completely off guard.

"Well, hello to you too," I said.

"What do you want, Simone?"

"Just wanted to know if you had any news about Carl. I haven't heard from you in so long."

"Carl is gone because of you, Simone. You should know that."

"Excuse me? You better watch how you run your mouth making accusations. I would never do anything to hurt Carl."

"Oh yes you would and you did. You're just lucky I haven't gone to the police."

My head swirled with confusion. If Carl was dead and she knew it, why wouldn't she have gone to the police? She wouldn't protect me. I decided to play dumb.

"Andrea, I have no idea what you're talking about. I miss Carl too. He was everything to me."

"Really? Then why..."

"Go on. Why what?" There was silence.

"I'm not supposed to tell you anything, but I'm going to send you something Carl saw before he left. And by the way, he doesn't want to be found."

"He's alive? You've heard from him? Where is he?"

"As I said, I'll send you what he saw before he left. Don't go to the police. He doesn't want to be found."

Three days later, a small package came in the mail. It was a single USB. I stuck it into my computer, clicked on it and there was Anthony and I in the washroom. I was oblivious in my lust, my eyes closed, my hands clutching the door, my head swirling side to side, my back arched and my haunches raised to meet Anthony, oblivious to the fact that Anthony, that scumbag, was holding his phone and recording it.

I sat there with my computer on my lap for hours, my mind detached from my body. I couldn't move yet images of myself and Anthony, then Dwight, roiled around in my head. I replayed images of a year ago, trying to recall if Carl had changed at all in the weeks or days before his disappearance. I couldn't think of anything. I searched the house. I pulled every book out of our bookcase. There were two books on Australia I hadn't seen before. As far as I knew, Carl had never expressed any interest in traveling. I bet the bastard was there, hiding from me. He didn't even have the guts to stand up to me, to confront me about Anthony.

I drove to Andrea's house. She opened the door and I said, "Carl's in Australia alive and well, Andrea. Don't try to hide it." Her flinch and the way her eyes blinked rapidly twice, told me I'd hit the jackpot.

"You knew he was alive all this time and you let the police investigate me, ruin my life and my reputation?"

"You ruined your own reputation," she said. "Now leave us alone and don't try to find Carl."

Dwight came over that night. "I can't be with you, Dwight. You're a murderer. You killed my husband and that's not what I wanted."

"That *is* what you wanted. Girl, I did it for you."

I looked at Dwight long and hard. He probably never belonged in a gang, never killed a fly in his life.

"Get out Dwight. You disgust me." He didn't argue. He left.

I went back to work and resigned (who knew how many people had seen that video) but not before making sure I got Anthony's home address. I drove to his house early one morning and waited until he left for work. I knocked on his door. His lovely wife opened it. She was a beauty with golden tresses, large innocent brown eyes and a pouty pink mouth. I told her I was Anthony's co-worker, could I come in as I had some important information for her. I watched those large, innocent eyes watching the video. I was waiting for the tears I knew would flow. Yes, it was spiteful, but my marriage was wrecked so why not. Miss Blonde cocked her head to the side. No tears came. She turned to me.

"You know, I can't fuck Anthony without this video playing in my head. Notice the way he's mostly into himself? Grinning into the camera like he thinks he's John Holmes pre-Aids."

I was utterly confused. "John who?"

"You don't know John Holmes, the porno star with the enormous dick?"

"Oh yes, I know who you mean," I had no clue what she was talking about. Why wasn't she bawling her eyes out like a wailing banshee? Why was I still sitting in her house like we were having a frigging tea party in an English garden?

"You don't know shit." She got up and went to the fridge and poured herself a glass of milk and downed it like a teenage boy. "Ah, that was good," she said. "Want some?"

"No. I don't drink milk." I sat there uncomfortably. Maybe this woman wanted a piece of pussy action. I wasn't adverse to the idea but the whole thing was so unexpected.

"When I first looked through Anthony's phone and saw that vile recording, I was perturbed but I wasn't about to react rashly," she said after staring at me for what seemed like a long time. "I figured you were just another one of his crotches. Then I was in the parking lot of your office one day and who do I see walk out?"

I shrugged.

"You! I saw you and realized that you thought you were hot shit. Your husband was sitting in the car waiting for you. He picked you up that day and you started to shout at him for eating in your car. He looked like a puppy dog who'd been scolded. I was so sad for him. It was so humiliating. You can't do that to a man, you know. Then I came to visit Anthony one day and walked by your desk. I heard you talking with some women and heard you say you wished your husband would just... let me get the exact words... would just fucking disappear and leave you alone. So, are you here to thank me?"

"What? *You* sent that video to Carl?"

"'Course I did. I see myself as saving Carl from you and fulfilling your dreams, all in one shot. I'm glad you came today. If you'd have come tomorrow, you'd have missed me." She smiled a dazzling smile with brilliant white teeth. "I'm taking a little trip to the other side of the world. Australia, in fact. I leave later tonight."

She kept smiling at me. "It's so hard to find a good man, isn't it? Someone who doesn't cheat or gamble. If you find a good man, you got to hang on for dear life."

THE WALL

The cockroach crawled out of a hole onto the deck where the wind battered it about, lifting its wings so that it seemed it would fly off into the great blue abyss. It struggled to remain on its legs, the dark brown wings turning pale yellow as the wind went under them and they fluttered like butterflies in the breeze. Francine wanted to throw it in the sea, but she would never have touched it, to see how it would fare. Would it succumb, or would it beat its wings in vain against the heavy salt water until it died from fatigue? It seemed strange to her that a cockroach was in the boat where it didn't belong.

She ran her fingers through her short, brown hair and stared at the deck, old and rusty from neglect. The boat was old and belonged to her brother's friend. It had taken them 15 minutes to start it; the two boys had had to use a car battery. Her brother Adam had said he hoped she would not be too disappointed if it didn't start and they couldn't dive that day.

Francine had shrugged. "It'll start."

Adam wanted to please her. She had been so sick recently, but now she was well and even though she shouldn't dive they were not going deep, only down to 50 feet, so that couldn't hurt her lungs. She was so strong, anyway, to have recovered from the pneumonia yet again.

The wind lifted the cockroach so that it was airborne and came towards Francine and dropped at her feet. She curled her toes and stared at it, her reaction to it dulled, as it was to all things around her.

They drove the boat out to open sea along the rugged shoreline. The rocks were sharp and dark. Three fishermen sat at a cove fishing. A pelican flew low, close to the shore, circled high in the air again, then swooped down steeply and dove in for its meal. They passed a brightly coloured wooden boat, the red and green paint peeling. Four men stood in it examining a large wire cage in which several lobsters fought to escape. Francine closed her eyes and breathed deeply, inhaling the strong smell of the salt sea and gasoline. When she looked around her again, the water had changed from bright blue to deep turquoise.

Adam's friend Lee was driving the boat. "We're in deep waters now," he said. They reached the dive site and circled so Adam could grab the buoy and tie the boat to its rope. Francine stared at Lee but she was hardly aware of his presence. He was dark and muscular, with fine features. Lee had been Adam's friend since kindergarten. Francine had had a crush on him once. He had returned her eye contact and flirtatious smiles, and then there had been long phone talks with promises to go out on a real date, but somehow nothing happened. Then Francine had gone away and when she returned, Lee was at university and thank God for that, otherwise he too might be sick and not here right now and not her friend.

Lee stopped the boat and turned off the engine. "This is it," he said. "Ready?'

Adam and Francine nodded and put on their equipment.

"Why are you using so much weight?" Adam said to Francine.

"I usually use ten pounds."

"You usually use six."

"No, ten and two more in my pocket, just in case."

"Remember," Lee interrupted, "everyone stick together."

It had been 18 months since Francine's last dive but today she was calm. It was a hot day, slightly overcast and a little windy, but the sea was tranquil. They went under and as usual Adam was overprotective, asking her constantly with dive signals if she was okay, and reaching over to check her pressure gauge.

Francine remembered a dive two years ago when she ran out of air. That time she had not been diving for a while and she had forgotten to check the pressure gauge. When Adam realized, his eyes had widened and he had pointed to his secondary regulator, so she could breathe through it. Francine had been confused. She had forgotten what to do: breathe in and take the regulator, or breathe out. She breathed out, took his regulator and swallowed a mouthful of salt water. She had choked and panicked, and clawed her way to the surface. Adam had stayed beside her, trying to slow her ascent and keep her calm. Francine blinked hard to block out that memory. She would not think of that now.

The wall began 40 feet below sea level, a coral reef with a drop-off plunging 400 feet then coming to a plateau, plunging again, and continuing like this to the depths of the ocean floor. The wall supported a variety of marine life. Lobsters, crabs and moray eels hid in the small crevices jutting from the rock and small sharks lurked at night in the caves. All types of coral spread out over the surface and groups of fish darted here and there, feeding on the algae. Lee pointed to a spotted moray eel darting from one hole in the wall to another. Small bright purple and yellow fish avoided the divers and turned quickly and swam in the opposite direction.

Francine had to be careful. If she swam too far behind, Adam and Lee would wait for her. If she timed it perfectly, they would get involved in lobster-watching and not notice she had gone. Visibility was perfect though, she thought, at least 100 feet. Francine swam and turned her head to the right. The wall was beautiful. Purple fan coral dotted the rock and silver fish swam around orange tube coral. She turned her head to the left. There was nothing there. That was the unknown, a blue expanse of ocean. Adam and Lee had swum ahead. Francine turned and swam away from them, toward the blue expanse, kicking her fins hard. Then she breathed out, pressed the deflate button and felt herself sinking.

Francine had thought she would not be afraid. She had thought it would be better this way. Her family would say she died in a diving accident. They wouldn't have to be embarrassed and say she died from complications or 'cancer.' That's what she had overheard her father say to her mother, that he would tell people 'the cancer' had come back.

"What cancer?" Her mother had said annoyed. "Everyone knows Francine never had no cancer."

But they lived on a small island and people would talk, insisted Francine's father. People would not understand.

It was not so long ago, when she was a girl, Francine's mother reminded her husband, that people called cancer 'the big C' and did not talk about it. Besides, Francine thought, Adam and Lee always said this would be the best way to go. Past 150 feet, everything was so funny, you wouldn't even realize you were dying.

But nothing was funny now and it seemed to Francine that her life and now this sudden end were both a mistake. The knowledge that her life would not include the good 'ole college days, marriage, children and grandchildren had been too great a burden for her. The stream of thoughts in her head, the regret, the guilt, the anger and the fear, made her more tired than the illness, and she had wanted to tell her friends, to warn everyone about the dangers. She had made one mistake. It could have happened to anyone. It could not end like this. And now she started to feel powerful and strong, and she knew she could handle people and their talk.

Her eyes widened and she searched for Adam. Francine had reached 150 ft., then 190. She tried to inflate but it seemed rather funny and futile all at once. In a small place somewhere in the back of her head, there was a nagging feeling of fear and doubt, a small knot in her stomach. Francine giggled. There was something she was supposed to do. What was she supposed to do? Oh, yes, get rid of some weight. She fumbled with her weight belt but it was jammed beneath her jacket. She was not concerned. If she had not eaten the spice bun for breakfast she would be lighter, she mused, but oh God, how many things had she done that she wasn't supposed to do and most of it had never gotten her into trouble except for that one time and it made her sick and she could never have known, would never have known it was a real *faux pas* or was it a *parlez vous francais* and she had not gotten a chance to go to Europe, but she still could, because Adam would find her. Adam, Adam, she loved Adam more than anyone in the world, and her parents, and she wanted to wake up in her bed to the smell of eggs and bacon even if bacon was rather fatty and fresh orange juice with all the pulp tomorrow morning, oh how funny everything was.

Francine saw the large grey fish coming towards her. She knew it was male because of the large penis hanging down. The fish told her it wanted to waltz with her and she suddenly realized there was an orchestra nearby. She giggled and asked, "Are you sure? Most men would not want to dance with me, not now with the illness."

The fish smiled and Francine knew it was okay and she laughed aloud and stretched out her arms wide to embrace the fish and the sea and the music.

Retribution

I have seen it all, heard it all. Even when people don't see me and I'm standing right there, I see them, I hear them. That is my role. To be there but not be there. To see but not to see and not to talk what I see. That is the role of a helper. Some people call us maids, servants, housekeepers but here, we are helpers, although why, I don't know because sometimes, we don't merely help. Sometimes we do everything.

Here, on this small island, is not like there, North America, Europe or Australia, where maids drive around in small, pretty cars, offering their services and charging big dollars to clean a house. There, where they arrive in those cars and hop out with their cleaning products and hop back in and drive away. No. Here, we arrive early and leave late, catching unreliable buses to a home vastly different from the one we've left. Here, we are not treated as equals, never mind that it's the twenty-first century and there is Black History Month and a black president in the United States. Here, not much has changed since slavery, except the master. The master can be black, brown, white, Chinese, Indian, good, bad, or indifferent. The old colonial ways still exist and that is the way it is.

My daughter lives in Toronto and every year she begs me to come. Not just come to visit but to come and live. I make excuses, that I don't like the cold, that I can't be uprooted at the ripe old age of sixty-two but the truth is, I, Valsie Bogle, cannot leave Ms. Dawn. I could never leave Ms. Dawn, even now as she is getting married again, fourth time around, and I know she couldn't live without me. My own people tell me I'm stupid to trust uptown people and that they are not loyal to anyone, only to their money. But not Ms. Dawn. She trusts me with her life even though I've failed her once. I trust her with mine.

I'm scrubbing and cleaning and I'm down on my old hands and knees making this big old house shine. After the church ceremony, everybody is coming here and tomorrow morning early, the caterers will arrive with the food, and the wedding cake lady who lives in Barbican will come with the round three-tiered cake with delicate pink roses. Ms. Dawn will be fussing and preening and hugging me and screaming at me and for me, her moods up and down like a toilet seat. For a big fifty-year-old woman, Ms. Dawn sure can act like a fifteen-year-old gal.

Ms. Dawn is really Mrs. Dawn, but seeing that I knew her since she was a young girl, before she ever married Paul Ferguson, I still call her Ms. Dawn. I started working for her mother, and then after Ms. Dawn got married and needed reliable help, I went to her. At first, they shared me. Ms. Dawn got me Mondays, Wednesdays and Saturdays and her mother had me Tuesdays, Thursdays and Fridays, but Ms. Dawn kept complaining to her mother and to me that she needed me more often and her mother gave in, like she'd always given in. It's not that Ms. Dawn isn't a sweet lady with her heart in the right place, but she has a little spoilt way about her. Her mother could never say no to her and maybe that was part of the problem. Who is to say?

The first house she lived in as a married woman was in Havendale. It was a small house with a nice garden with mango tree, lemon tree, breadfruit tree, and the bougainvillea hanging over the fence like a bridal bouquet, and it was back when times were good, before the big migrations and the political upheavals, riots and crime. People walked the streets easily after nightfall and neighbours chatted to each other over the fence. That is how Ms. Dawn got to know her neighbours so well. But in the way of a small island, she knew Patrick Lane before. I remember when she told me that her brother had gone to school with Patrick Lane and that he'd come to her house once when she was a shy teenager. She saw this handsome boy in her brother's bedroom and she made excuses to go in and look at him. Then she never saw him again until now, when he ended up being her neighbour. Not just him of course, him and his pretty young wife, Carolyn and their new baby daughter, Tracey. Ms. Dawn and Mr. Ferguson were trying themselves to have a baby and from the sounds I heard at night, they were trying a little too hard. I had to tell her myself. "Ms. Dawn," I said one morning when she asked me to bring her breakfast in bed. "You can't try every night you know, Ma'am. It will thin out the sperm and wear out the man. You have to give the man a little time to recuperate. Every three days will do."

She must have taken my advice because she got pregnant shortly after with Robert. Well, we didn't know he was Robert then, but we found out nine months and some weeks later when he came out wide-eyed and screaming as if the world bewildered him already. What a handful he was, always demanding attention. If he wasn't crying, he was shouting or running or jumping all over the furniture.

Anyway, Ms. Dawn and Ms. Carolyn became good friends. They both had young children, they were both young and beautiful and they both had handsome husbands. Which leads me to ask the question, 'Why people who have everything want more?' You ever notice how the richest people still want to be richer? It's like nothing is good enough for mankind, or womankind for that matter. Ms. Dawn and Ms. Carolyn had dinner parties at each other's houses, they had teas where they only invited other ladies and Ms. Dawn would have me make those annoying cucumber sandwiches and she, breathing down my neck to cut the crusts off the bread and to place them just so on the tray. Now I know the word to describe Ms. Dawn. It's 'controlling.' I learned that from my daughter in Toronto. One day when she was visiting, she said, "Mamma, why are you so controlling?" I'd never heard that one before, but I knew exactly what she meant, and all because I said, "We're not stopping here for jerk chicken because I don't like that jerk man, we are going to the jerk man I always buy from." What was wrong with that?

So back and forth between each other's houses day and night and I can't pinpoint the moment I knew something was going on, but one time, I went outside and I saw Mr. Lane chatting with Ms. Dawn at the garden fence. It seemed innocent enough, but when Ms. Dawn turned to walk inside, Mr. Lane gave her backside a long, lingering look and it didn't help that she was wearing those jeans shorts that were too short and a top that bared her belly. And was it my imagination that I felt Ms. Dawn could feel Mr. Lane's eyes on her because I swear I saw her hips sway side to side more than usual? Now I know people can get into a heat like dogs and I know Ms. Dawn and Ms. Carolyn and the two misters weren't more than twenty-five years at the time, but people have to learn to keep their hands to themselves.

There was one dinner party where Ms. Dawn was in the kitchen and Mr. Lane came in pretending to ask for a glass of water and I saw him rub Ms. Dawn's behind and quickly kiss her neck when he thought no-one was watching. But I'm always watching. And poor Mr. Ferguson and Ms. Carolyn sitting in the living room talking and suspecting nothing. It's not my business so I couldn't say anything and I wasn't supposed to know, at first, but then the chances they started taking! Ms. Carolyn went back to work at the airlines as a ticket clerk so she wasn't home and Mr. Lane would come home early and walk over. Ms. Dawn would hand Robert to me and tell me to take him for a walk, and she and Mr. Lane would carry on in the master bedroom like two animals, and I could smell the sex on them when they walked out. He couldn't even look me in the eye and she acted like she was doing nothing wrong, just went into the kitchen and started dinner while I bathed and fed Robert. What a trial and tribulation. Of course, I knew that nothing like that could go on forever and I knew she was vex like hell when Ms. Carolyn became pregnant again. Then as if in retaliation, Ms. Dawn got pregnant again and they both had two girl babies born four months apart. Luckily for them, Ms. Dawn's baby girl looked like Mr. Ferguson and Ms. Carolyn's baby girl favoured her own husband. Although if you ask me, brown-skinned pickney all look alike.

Now, I don't know what it is about uptown people but they don't seem to like raising their own children. Irma (Ms. Carolyn's helper) and I talked about it all the time. We would go to the back fence after we fed the children lunch and while they played in the garden, we talked about all the goings on with the two families. It was worse when Ms. Dawn found out I had a bit of education and could help with homework. My education is a bit of a long story, suffice to say that my father was an English man who came to Jamaica and worked the land. He wasn't any old uneducated peasant as he liked to call people. He had an education and he schooled me at home. Not only that but after he died and I went to Kingston, one very 'more-British-than-the-Queen-Mrs. Ellis' made sure that not one word of patois came out of my mouth while I was working for her and she corrected me until I swore she was an English teacher in another life. I'm not showing off but I've always picked up things quickly and I have a memory like an elephant. I wanted to work in an office, wear starched suits and fine leather shoes, but when my father died, my mother had to work so we left the country, my schooling ended and she brought me to town to learn the highly demanding trade of being a 'good helper.' So there I was, not only cooking and cleaning, but helping the children with their homework too.

Ms. Dawn would come home from the hairdresser and the manicurist and say she needed to lie down. Irma and I fed those children, cooked for them, cleaned up after them, bathed them, helped them with homework while their parents worked, had parties, went to parties and whatever else they did. In this way five years passed, so that in September of that year, Robert was nine and the little girl, Rebecca was five. I myself, am so surprised that the shenanigans of Ms. Dawn and Mr. Lane went unnoticed for so long. I began to wonder if Mr. Ferguson was simple-minded or simply downright stupid. Even I could see right through the lies Ms. Dawn told, how she was going to get her nails done, but after five hours, she would come back with some ridiculous excuse about running into friends and stopping to chat. I don't know how she and Ms. Carolyn remained friends but it all came to an end the weekend I left for my own home.

When I came back the Monday morning, it was as if I walked into a different household. The windows were locked up tight, the house was dark, the children were crying and Ms. Dawn was in bed with the pillow over her head. When she got up, her face was drawn and puffy like she'd been crying all night. I couldn't wait to run to the back fence to find out from Irma what had happened over the weekend. She didn't come out at our usual time and I stood there calling for ages and then Ms. Carolyn came out and said in an angry voice, "Irma is busy and doesn't have time to come out here and gossip. What do you want, Valsie?"

"Nothing, Ms. Carolyn." I thought quickly. "Irma had a bad headache before I left on the weekend and I just wanted to make sure she was better."

"Irma is quite fine," she said and disappeared into her house.

"Something must be wrong with Ms. Carolyn," I commented to Ms. Dawn as I peeled potatoes for dinner. I was making mashed potatoes and pork chops with apple sauce. That's when I knew something was terribly wrong because Ms. Dawn, who likes a piece of gossip, didn't comment. She looked at me with watery eyes and retreated to her bedroom again where she stayed the rest of the night.

Eventually, I got the story from Irma. Ms. Carolyn had gone off to the country that weekend with her parents, the girls and Irma. The girls, Tracey and Donna, came down with a bad stomach flu so they left one day early, came back into town, drove right home, walked inside and went straight to the bedroom. They saw a sight none of them are likely to forget. Ms. Dawn's back was arched and she and Mr. Lane were... well I don't need to repeat everything Irma told me. Those older Havendale houses are one-storey so even if Mr. Lane had heard the car, there was no time to hide Ms. Dawn or get her out of the house. Anyway from what Irma told me, they didn't hear anything at all because they were quite oblivious. Ms. Carolyn started throwing all kinds of things at the naked couple, screaming that Ms. Dawn was a lying two-faced bitch, Mr. Lane was a lying, two-timing son-of-a-bitch and so on. Irma said she didn't know Ms. Carolyn knew such language and she didn't care that her daughters were right there, both of them standing wide-eyed seeing all that adultery and fornication. Ms. Carolyn must have broken every plate in the house. Ms. Dawn ran out of the house naked like a dog was at her heels, one hand clutching her clothes to her chest and the other hand trying to hide her behind, but everybody on the street know the story and that's why she lock up in her room now because she shame. She can't face me and she can't face her own children. And to make matters worse, Mr. Ferguson had to drive in at that moment that Ms. Dawn was running from Mr. Lane's house naked as the day she was born. My daughter in Toronto says it's called Murphy's Law but I call it God Watching From Above. I don't know who Murphy is, but I don't think Mr. Ferguson expected to see his wife running out of Mr. Lane's house naked. Irma said his mouth opened and closed like a fish and then she saw him leave after an hour with three suitcases. One suitcase says you might come back but three suitcases say you're never coming back.

Everything changed. For a few days, I had to coax Ms. Dawn from her bedroom and practically spoon-feed her. Then the next thing I knew, Mr. Lane moved into that house in Havendale. Can you imagine such a thing? Him living right next door to Ms. Carolyn? Yes! He moved in and he tried to see his children next door but Ms. Carolyn refused to let him enter the house and his children didn't act like they wanted to see him anyway. Things eventually settled down but not before Ms. Carolyn and Mr. Ferguson decided to try a thing and get together but I think it was only revenge or loneliness. Mr. Ferguson moved into Ms. Carolyn's house for a while. Can you imagine the rampant gossip about this couple swap? But it didn't work out. I hear Mr. Ferguson is quite happy nowadays, married to a nice woman and he has other children. Ms. Carolyn took off to foreign, left for Canada never to be seen in Jamaica again, left her pickney dem, Tracey and Donna, with Mr. Lane and Ms. Dawn.

Ms. Dawn and Mr. Lane got married in the dusk of day. It wasn't the big, elaborate affair that her first wedding was. It seemed rather subdued. Ms. Dawn was happy enough but it was her guests that seemed to be quiet and watchful, as if still considering this turn of events. It wasn't a church wedding this time. It was in the garden of some rich person's Great House up in the mountains. It had a magnificent garden with orchids and bougainvillea, crotons and hibiscus, and the white chairs that stood in rows had big beautiful pink bows tied on them. I heard one woman say that the decorations were stunning but when the ceremony got under way and the priest asked, "Patrick, do you take Dawn to be your lawful wedded wife?", a piece of thunder came out of nowhere and a flash of lightning pierced the evening sky. Everybody looked up because the day had been bright and sunny with a bit of cool mountain breeze. The sky darkened to an indigo blue and a piece of torrential rain came down, drenching the bride and groom, the guests, the chairs and even the priest. Everybody ran for cover and there was much toweling off and murmuring, and when everybody settled again in the hall of the Great House, the priest started again and Ms. Dawn and Mr. Lane said their vows. Then Ms. Dawn started to laugh like a crazy person and she said, "What a rain!" in a voice that was loud and unnatural.

The Havendale home became a crowded house. Remember now that there were four children for me to look after. Two for him and two for her and then before I blink my eyes, she got pregnant and they had their first child together. It was a boy and they named him Damian. He looked just like Mr. Lane, with dark curly hair and long limbs, a straight nose and fine features. What a handsome boy and two years after that, they had another son, who they named David. That house on Havendale got even smaller and since Mr. Lane had started his own business and was doing well, they moved into a spacious house in Cherry Gardens with six bedrooms and two living rooms, a large sunny kitchen where I could wash and cut and chop and look out into the garden, and a swimming pool.

All this happened over five years so the older children had become teenagers but what I remember most was that Ms. Dawn was always jealous when Mr. Lane went out. I think she was scared that the same way he cheated on Ms. Carolyn, he could very well cheat on her. That's what I think because she wasn't the jealous type before. Before she was like a peacock, strutting around town with her pretty hair and freshly painted nails and new clothes. I know a peacock is male but that's how Ms. Dawn looked to me, like a person that nothing could touch, pretty and perfect. Now she became a pigeon, worrying about everything, her hair, her figure, her clothes and which woman was flirting with Mr. Lane. Don't think I didn't hear her on the phone chatting to her friends, gossiping, sizing up people as if that was all life was about.

Isn't it funny how you can wake up one morning and be going along as usual, washing your face, brushing your teeth, eating, drinking, talking like every other day that passed before that and then by nightfall, a change so drastic can shatter your world and you wonder how you can ever go on again? If you don't understand what I mean, you've never had tragedy strike.

I got up that morning, August 15, 1980 and washed my face, brushed my teeth, got breakfast ready for Mr. Lane who was going out. I started on my morning cleaning routine. The older children, Tracey and Donna, Robert and Rebecca were fast asleep and I knew they wouldn't wake until noon. Around eleven, I was taking care of Damian and David and trying to cook at the same time. Ms. Dawn told me that people were coming to dinner and the house had to be cleaned and the food cooked by seven. As I said before, I don't usually speak patois but patois came out of my mouth that time. "Me one cyah look after so much pickney and clean and cook, Ms. Dawn. I only 'ave two hand and two foot." David was tugging on my skirt and Damian was crying for breakfast.

"It just has to be done, Valsie," said Ms. Dawn in that high and mighty tone uptown people use and the truth is, that tone makes my skin crawl.

"It cyah be done just so, Ms. Dawn."

"Well, Valsie, I have to go to the supermarket so I can't be of much help right now." She was turning to go but I stopped her.

"Ms. Dawn, wake up the older children and ask them to help." I muttered under my breath, "Lazy, wutless, useless pickney sleeping till noon and things have to get done. It would never be my pickney."

"That's a wonderful idea, Valsie. I'll wake them up." Ms. Dawn went upstairs and after a while, the four of them came down bleary-eyed and resentful, asking me what it was they were to do.

I told them that they could clean the entire house or look after Damian and David. Grudgingly they took the young boys upstairs and I could hear all of them romping as I prepared and cooked what was to be the main courses that evening: roast lamb and roast chicken. Then I set about cleaning that house. It was big and I dusted, I polished, I swept, I vacuumed. I wasn't surprised that Ms. Dawn's quick trip to the supermarket had turned into all day. I walked upstairs to tell everyone lunch was ready. It was quiet. Robert was sitting in his bedroom playing one of those stupid video games. Rebecca and Donna were watching TV.

"Where are Damian and David?" I asked them.

"With Tracey." They barely looked up.

I walked into Tracey's room and saw that she was lying in bed on her stomach turning the pages of Cosmopolitan magazine.

"Where are the babies?" I asked, even though Damian was five and David, two.

"Playing video games with Robert."

"No," I answered and my heart gave a warning thud. "No, they're not."

She looked up then and saw my face. I ran out of her room and started calling for them. "Damian, David," I shouted, running from room to room. "Put down the stupid game and help me look," I shouted to Robert. "Turn off the TV and check downstairs," I shouted to the girls.

We checked every room upstairs and then we raced downstairs, checking the kitchen, the dining room, under the table, the living room, even my bedroom and bathroom, the area Ms. Dawn called the maid's quarters. There was no sign of the boys and then everyone froze when Rebecca said, "the pool."

My heart was pounding and my mouth was dryer than an old coconut. It was as if none of us wanted to be the first to go outside. We stared at each other not wanting to move, then Robert was the first to run out. I was right behind him but he was the first to see the two dark shapes in the pool. My world stopped spinning and everything I did was in slow motion. I saw Robert dive into the pool and pull out little David and Tracey jumped in and lifted Damian to the surface. Robert helped her push him out of the pool. I can't swim so I rushed to David and dropped to my knees, hugging him to my chest.

"Don't do that," shouted Robert. He pushed me aside and put his mouth on David's mouth, pinched his nose and breathed into it but anyone could see that it was too late. Tracey was doing the same with Damian and Rebecca and Donna were sobbing and holding on to each other. I became detached and felt as if my soul was leaving my body. I rose out of my body to see the scene from above, the square shaped pool with dark blue tiles, the water innocently sparkling in the sun, the lifeless bodies of two sweet little children who could've been sleeping in the sun, and finally, the guilt, fear, shock and horror on all our faces like a mask. My arms held David and rocked him. Donna walked into the living room and came back out with blankets to put over the babies and Robert called the ambulance which we knew mightn't come because that was how it was. It was too late anyway. No, it wasn't really happening. It was a dream. I was still in my bed sleeping and I would soon awake. I knew it wasn't a dream when I heard Ms. Dawn come back, shouting, "Valsie, where are you? I need help with the groceries. Robert, Rebecca, girls? Where is everybody?"

No-one moved. No-one rushed to her side but my spirit came rushing back down into my body where I could feel the awful fear and lump in my belly and the fear spread to my every limb. I was holding David in my arms, sobbing and kissing his face. Ms. Dawn came through the sliding door ready to wage war on us because no one had come to her aid but as she stepped outside into the bright sunlight, she stopped and looked at us sharply and then at the babies. Her face drained of colour and she slumped down to the concrete floor. She didn't faint but she crawled towards the bodies, her voice a low, scratchy whisper, "What have you all done?" She repeated it louder. "What have you all done?" She grabbed David from me and felt for his heart. She put him down and felt for Damian's pulse. Then she screamed a sound so loud and piercing, so full of anguish and it didn't stop. I don't know how she got the breath to scream so loudly. I tried to hold her but she clawed at my face and she pushed us all away, screaming hysterically so that the neighbours on both sides came over to see what was happening.

Well, you know the teenage pickney tried to blame me, said I was supposed to be looking after Damian and David. I could only shake my head at the unfairness of it all. In the end Ms. Dawn couldn't get a straight answer from any of them because they all had a different story. Robert said he told Tracey it was her turn to watch them. She said no, he never said that and so on. I cursed myself that I had even suggested that those wutless pickney could be trusted with the babies. Every night I asked myself why I didn't watch them and forget about the blasted house and the food. I still ask myself that to this day.

Ms. Dawn was vex with the world after that but more so with the teenagers than with me because they had not done their duty. I myself couldn't look at any of them without feeling angry so you can imagine how Ms. Dawn felt. She was angry with the teenagers and she was angry with God, she was angry with herself, but most of all, she was angry at Mr. Lane's children, Tracey and Donna. It was like she couldn't look at them for long before her mouth twisted like she was eating poison. As for Mr. Lane, he took to going out more often and Ms. Dawn lost the light in her eyes. Her movements became slow and lethargic as if it drained her to even put a spoon of soup to her mouth. Her hair was unwashed and bushy and sometimes in the evening, I sat her down in front of her dressing table and brushed it to get out the knots.

It couldn't have been easy for those children. Ms. Dawn had no interest in any of them and neither did Mr. Lane. "Ms. Dawn," I said to her one evening as she sat alone for dinner. "All those children need you, you know, ma'am. Remember they have all lost two little brothers. You have to live for the children you have."

Why did I open my mouth? "Valsie, don't talk to me about it. All of you killed my babies."

"Hush, ma'am. Don't say that so loud. The children will hear you and take it to heart."

"I don't care if they hear me. It's their fault. God must really hate me to take away my children like that."

It got so bad that Tracey and Donna had to leave the residence. Ms. Dawn treated them so badly that Mr. Lane got in touch with his ex-wife, Ms. Carolyn and told her that Tracey and Donna were coming to live with her in Canada. It was a sad day when Mr. Lane dropped them at the airport. Ms. Dawn didn't even hug them goodbye but Robert and Rebecca cried and begged them to stay, as if they had a choice. Mr. Lane must have felt angry because when he came home from the airport, he moved into the guest room and I saw him cast some seriously resentful glances at Ms. Dawn. I suppose Tracey and Donna would be big women now with children of their own but I don't really know because I've never seen nor heard from them again.

It was some months after the tragedy that I first heard talk of retribution. The helper next door asked me, "You think it's retribution what happened to Ms. Dawn's babies?"

"What you a talk 'bout?" I said lapsing into patois.

"My mistress say she know the whole story, how Ms. Dawn mash up Mr. Lane's marriage and then tek away the woman pickney dem and dat's why she lose her two pickney."

"No such thing happened," I said defensively. "Ms. Carolyn left her children here and moved to Canada."

"I hear a lot of people say it's retribution," said the helper sniffing and turning away, leaving me to ponder her words. "It's not me who say it, it's my mistress friend dem. I listen when they talk and that's what they say."

"Accidents happen," I said but she was long out of earshot. "Pastor say God is a forgiving God," I shouted at her retreating figure. But that night I lay awake long into the night wondering why such a terrible fate should befall Ms. Dawn and then I had to wonder if somebody *obeah* her. Now I don't usually believe in *obeah* and superstition but I really had to wonder if somebody put a curse on her because how come I never saw the babies come downstairs. They would've had to pass me in the kitchen to go into the living room, open the door, and go out onto the verandah. I never heard a splash but then the radio was on and it was Mutty Perkins' talk show that I was listening to so intently. It's something I've thought about a lot of the time, that somebody *obeah* Ms. Dawn because no one person can have that much bad luck and how come I never saw those babies pass me while I was cleaning?

Some people are judgmental and act like they are all high and mighty but you have to walk in a man's shoes to really understand him. For instance, during that time, you might have asked me, "Why are you working for a crazy, drunken woman?" Yes, Ms. Dawn took to the bottle like a baby to the breast. Even Mr. Lane started to drink heavily and one evening, he came home stinking of white rum and he started to grab up my backside. I picked up a pot to hit him but he passed out at my feet and I had to clean up his vomit in the morning. He left shortly after that and Ms. Dawn was alone again. The big house in Cherry Gardens was sold and we had to move. It took a long time to find a new place because Ms. Dawn needed something cheap and in a good area of town. The place also had to have helper's quarters for me because I was a live-in. I suggested to Ms. Dawn that I find a place myself and come to work in the mornings but she wouldn't have it. After all, who would make sure the older children were fed, that they did their homework (by then the children were doing CXC examinations and I couldn't help them at all) and rouse Ms. Dawn when she drank herself to sleep.

We moved into a small townhouse in the Norbrook area but it's a miracle that Ms. Dawn's liver is still working after the drinking she did in those times. I know because even when I was supposed to be sleeping, I heard her calling her friends and weeping into the phone, bawling and cursing. I don't know how her friends put up with it. Sometimes she would knock on my door, come into my room and sit at the foot of my bed and bawl, asking me to tell her why God hated her so much. Then the carousing started with men who were much too young for her. By then she would've been in her early forties and some of the young boys who left the house in the morning with a stupid grin on their faces, weren't more than twenty.

Robert went off to college in Miami. He had gotten closer to Mr. Ferguson after the tragedy and Mr. Ferguson was paying for the education. Ms. Dawn was living off her investments as she put it and the inheritance from her father but it wasn't enough to send Robert to school. From time to time, I would hear her screaming at Mr. Ferguson, that she needed more money for school fees for Rebecca but usually they stayed clear of each other. Then Rebecca went off to school and Ms. Dawn and I were alone in the house. She was still carrying on with her drinking and the partying but when she met this one white man, she became quite calm. He was a foreigner and he called himself a fruit. I couldn't understand why anybody would call themselves a fruit. What fruit was it now? I remember. He called himself a Kiwi and he spoke in a nice soothing way. Ms. Dawn stopped all that carousing out at night and we all settled down again in a new house. I thought it was a bit too soon to go get herself married again but she did. Now her last name at that time was Warren.

I know Ms. Dawn still grieved, especially when the babies' birthdays rolled around and on the anniversary of their death. I know she grieved as the years passed when she looked at other people's boy children, looked at them with a haunting expression that bordered on desire. Sometimes when we were shopping, she would stop in the aisle and whisper, "Valsie, doesn't that boy look like Damian?" I would look and the boy would look nothing like Damian at all. "Not really," I would say, but that wouldn't stop her from running up to the boy and his mother and she would, ooh and aah over this boy child, pinching his cheek and ruffling his hair. She's lucky she didn't live in North America because my daughter in Toronto tells me a person can get arrested for approaching and touching somebody else's pickney even if it's all innocent. But you and me both know what life is like. The calm is only the calm before the storm. That brief period of happiness with Mr. Warren was the calm. The storm was Robert.

Rebecca called one weekend morning while Ms. Dawn was in bed and told her that she didn't think Robert was going to school. Mr. Ferguson was paying for school but every time Rebecca called Robert, he was in New York, or in California on trips as he called them, with his friends. Then the phone calls started and it became a circus. Ms. Dawn called Mr. Ferguson and cussed him off, told him he needed to be a better father, more attentive to what was happening with his son. Then he cussed her off and told her she was a poor mother, so wrapped up in her new husband that she had no time for her children. That shattered her because only when we believe something is true, do we fall apart. Then Ms. Dawn had to leave her honeymoon bed and go to Miami to see what was happening with Robert. What she saw was a sorry sight.

She didn't tell Robert she was arriving and she didn't even stop at her hotel. She took a taxi straight to Robert's apartment. She said when she knocked at the door unexpectedly, a boy who was stoned out of his mind, opened the door. She said the smell of stale cigarettes and beer, of dirty laundry and mold, hit her. All around were empty beer bottles, rolling paper, weed, wet towels, a sink piled high with dirty plates, and on the couch, a naked girl. She said it was a pigsty. She asked for Robert and the stoned boy pointed to a bedroom. Robert was sleeping in the middle of the afternoon with a needle and syringe by his bedside. There were no books or schoolbag or anything to indicate he was going to school—just more beer bottles and ashtrays full of cigarettes. Ms. Dawn shook Robert awake and asked him what the hell was going on.

I sometimes wonder if the outcome would've been different if Ms. Dawn and Mr. Ferguson would've been civil to each other. Some people might say its fate and even more say its retribution, but common sense tells me that if they could've just worked together, it might have all fallen into place. But no use regretting because they couldn't get along. Ms. Dawn called Mr. Ferguson to Miami because Robert had a serious drug addiction. They stayed there for three weeks to organize him into rehab. When Ms. Dawn came home all happy and optimistic about Robert, I knew she was putting on a happy face for Mr. Warren, and trying to make out like her life wasn't so chaotic. I knew it was all bullshit, pardon me, because Robert called about three times from rehab, telling me how all his parents did was fight, call each other names, and worse, Mr. Ferguson blamed Robert's drug addiction on Ms. Dawn. He said Robert was fucked up because she blamed him for Damian and David. He said Robert was a mess because of her drinking and her young men. Poor Ms. Dawn. Of course, she started drinking again and who could blame her. I knew she called her friends because I heard them talking about it one time, how she called them at 3 am drunk or stoned out of her mind, sobbing about her babies, about

Robert, about wanting to end her life.

Poor Mr. Warren was baffled and bewildered because instead of staying by Ms. Dawn's side as a strong Christian man would, he folded like a bad hand of cards. One early morning at the beginning of the Christmas season when the air was chilly and pure and the fresh Christmas breeze cooled down the place, when the poinsettias started to bloom in the garden, he just picked up and quietly left the house with five suitcases. So you know he really wasn't coming back. Ms. Dawn couldn't even scream or beg him to stay because she was passed out drunk. What a trial and a tribulation! When she woke up, she went into shock because she just looked around, asked me if I had seen Mr. Warren and when I told her he took his skinny white foreign ass out with five suitcases, she just fainted. When she woke up, she went straight to the bottle and stayed in some strange kind of drunkenness for days on end.

One day I heard her in the toilet. She vomited until there was nothing to vomit. I stood by her and held her long, black bushy hair while she retched and heaved until I got scared that she was going to bring up all her insides into the toilet. I undressed her and put her into the bath and soaped up her body the way I soaped up the children when they were babies. I held her head and made her sip water. She lay in bed for days until one morning, I got up as usual and she was up before me, watering the plants. I knew she had come back. She gave me a wan smile and said, "Good morning, Valsie. Thank you," and my heart filled with a painful kind of happiness and I felt water come to my eyes.

When Robert came out of rehab two months later, Ms. Dawn felt he should come home, leave Miami and return to the island where we could all keep an eye on him. And after all, who knows a person better than the people of his home? There would be comfort and understanding. Mr. Ferguson, however, felt he should continue his education, pick up where he left off so he could make something of himself. He thought there was no place for Robert on a small island with its small people and island mentality where time was spent gossiping about each other. He harboured hopes of Robert becoming a lawyer, or so Ms. Dawn told me. As much as she loved Robert, she said she would be happy if he got a job in the bank as a teller or even better, on the north coast in a hotel. He would love that, she told me with enthusiasm, working near the beach with the tourists. "He's great with people, isn't he?" she asked me, wanting confirmation of her hopes and dreams. "I'm going to talk to some of my friends in the tourist industry and ask them to set up interviews for Robert," she said with renewed vigour that summer.

None of this was to happen because on August 15, 1985, five years to the day of the babies' deaths, Robert picked up a hand gun and put it to his head. He pulled the trigger and was no more. He left no note. It seemed telling to us all that it was August 15th. Perhaps he felt he was being kind so that there would be only one day of mourning for Ms. Dawn. Perhaps he wanted to make some kind of statement. Ms. Dawn said the doctor told her that with all the drugs in his body, it was unlikely he knew what day it was and that it had to be purely coincidence that it was on August 15. As God is my witness, that cannot be coincidence.

Ms. Dawn became a born again Christian. This means she stopped going to her Catholic Church on Shortwood Road (which she never attended anyway except on Easter Sunday or for funerals) and she attended a church on Oakland Road where she invited me and a few friends to a ceremony where she was immersed in water. She practically forced me to join too but I can tell you with surety, that I felt no different after coming up out of that water. She stopped drinking and carousing, she shunned her former friends, and all that manicuring and pedicuring that she did before, became secondary.

It might have seemed that this period of life was better but the house became eerily quiet. Gone were the days of the rambunctious teenagers and me constantly cleaning after them. I felt useless. I cooked for the two of us and the house was kept clean apart from the little bit of dusting and laundry. Once I politely suggested that she didn't really need me anymore and she became frantic, looked at me wide-eyed and said she was planning a dinner party the next weekend and she needed me more than ever. So once again, there I was peeling and chopping and dicing, frying and steaming and roasting. All for naught. Not one person except the pastor showed up and he gorged himself on those lamb chops like gluttony wasn't one of the seven deadly sins.

Those were the quiet years. I fervently believe that Ms. Dawn felt that God had punished her, that there was indeed retribution on her life, because the amount of praying and asking for forgiveness she did, would send all of Kingston to heaven. One day when she was lambasting me for some foolishness, telling me how I'm lazy and how God sees what she can't see, I said to her, "Ms. Dawn. Look at nature. Everything survives in nature with balance. Too much water, the plants die. Too much sun, the plants die. The right balance, everything all right. I'm not saying you can't believe in God and go to Church. But all this preaching in my ears is too much. Even the good Lord would get tired of it."

She said to me, "Valsie, are you wearing my red lipstick?"

"Yes, ma'am."

"You took my red lipstick out of the garbage?"

"Yes, ma'am. I see no reason to throw out good lipstick and makeup just because the pastor says a woman shouldn't wear makeup. I don't think God concerns Himself with red lipstick."

"Valsie, that's disgusting. You took my makeup out of the garbage."

"I surely did, ma'am. Waste not, want not."

After that, Ms. Dawn went and bought a new red lipstick. Thank God she started wearing makeup again and going to get her manicures. It signaled to me that the worse was over, especially when Rebecca started coming over more often and bringing her boyfriend. Ms. Dawn finally stopped giving her money away to the born again church and she put some aside to help with Rebecca's wedding. Now I didn't help at that wedding seeing that it was catered and held in the country at some fancy resort but I can tell you what happened just by listening to Ms. Dawn's conversations when she returned.

"Your father seems quite happy with his wife," she said to Rebecca one evening.

"Yes, he is."

"She seems like a nice woman. What's her name, again?"

"Mom, you know her name is Catherine."

"Are you close to her? You seem close to her."

"She's a nice person. I love you, though."

That Rebecca always knew what to say to make her mother smile.

"Even your stepfather, that weakling, is married again to some young girl. I wonder if I'll ever marry again, not that I want to. I mean, I'm quite fine as I am. Just me and Valsie. Valsie," she called out. "I know you're listening to every word."

"Sorry, ma'am. I couldn't hear what you said. Please repeat." Then they both practically fell off their chairs laughing. I couldn't help but chuckle in the kitchen myself.

Ms. Dawn met Russell Wright at an art show at Devon House. She said she didn't find him attractive at first. There was hair in his nose and ears and he had a paunch. She told Rebecca he looked pompous but that she read him all wrong. He was staring at the artwork like he was some important art curator but he turned to her, smiled and said, "Art is so peaceful, isn't it?"

She nodded because she wasn't about to engage a strange man in conversation. Then she looked at him and pointed to another piece. "That one is done by my daughter," she said.

"It's beautiful. I'm going to buy it."

"Really?" Suddenly she became suspicious. "Do you really like it?"

"I think she's incredibly good. I noticed it before but since I have some connection to the artist seeing that I'm standing here chatting with the artist's mother, then, of course, I will add it to my art collection."

Ms. Dawn had laughed with glee. Her daughter had just made over a thousand U.S. dollars. Then he said the words that drew them together like butterflies to flowers. He said, "My daughter was an artist, a budding artist anyway, before she passed away. She had just finished her portfolio to apply to art school."

"Your daughter passed away? I'm so very sorry," said Ms. Dawn. Apparently her eyes had filled with tears. "It's okay," he said. "I've learned to accept and deal with the pain."

"I haven't," said Ms. Dawn. "My three sons, my babies passed away too."

Russell Wright led her to a quiet spot where they sat under a large tree. The art fair went on around them, the bustle of traffic in the distance, the songs of the birds, all were faint because Ms. Dawn only heard the soothing voice of Russell Wright who was a returning resident and hadn't lived in Jamaica for years. He'd come back to the country of his birth to heal from the loss of his daughter and his wife who were killed instantly in a car accident in Boston. Meeting Russell wasn't at all romantic at first, she told Rebecca, it was soothing, like a balm had been spread on her deep, deep wound, like someone had wrapped her in a warm cozy blanket and protected her from the severity of the world. That's how he made her feel and after ten minutes on the bench, she no longer saw his hairy nose and ears. It was as if the physical completely vanished and they saw each other's souls, two souls sitting on a bench sharing a lifetime of sorrow, pain and regret. She told him everything, how she drank, about Robert, Damian and David and even the past that she never spoke about, that time so long ago when she took Ms. Carolyn's husband. When she asked him if he thought God had punished her, he had taken her hand and kissed it, and had shaken his head. Good and terrible things happen to good and terrible people. He couldn't say if it was part of a plan but at this stage of his life, he was going to enjoy what was left of it, for if it's one thing he knew with certainty, it was that he wasn't going to be here forever.

When Rebecca packed up her paintings and found her mother sitting beside the man who had bought her painting, she smiled. Her mother's face wore an expression she'd never seen before and she told me later she realized it was tranquility.

Ms. Dawn was oddly serene. Everybody was buzzing around her, fixing her hair, the makeup artist was applying more makeup I don't know for what reason, the house was alive with chatter and laughter. Ms. Dawn really surprised me by sitting quiet and smiling through it all. Not once did she order anybody around to do her bidding. Everything was already done but I was re-arranging the flowers on the table where nothing needed to be rearranged. She caught my eye. I came over to her.

"Is everything alright, Ms. Dawn? You should be getting dressed soon."

Everything is fine, Valsie. I believe I am happy."

"Mr. Wright is a nice man, such a nice warm man. No airs about him at all."

She nodded. "He's a good man. I just hope..." Her voice trailed off.

"Ma'am?"

"Valsie, you know I never meant to hurt anybody."

"I know, ma'am."

"I realize the pain will never go away completely but I feel much better."

She sighed as if she'd just come through a long illness. I sighed along with her and she patted my hand and got up and walked up the staircase to put on her wedding gown. I heard someone whisper: 'why is a fifty-year-old woman wearing a wedding gown on her fourth marriage like some young virgin girl?' I wish I could've cussed two bad words to the woman but you know these uptown people, judgmental bitches, all of them. I had to shut my mouth and pretend I didn't hear her badmouthing Ms. Dawn.

But to me, the wedding gown signaled a new beginning. As Ms. Dawn walked down the aisle of the Anglican Church in Stony Hill with the gown stretching out behind her toward Mr. Wright who was standing quietly and smiling, she was like a new bride. Her skin was glowing and she was genuinely happy. Rebecca was her matron of honor, standing pretty with a bouquet of orchids in her hands. When the service was over and everyone left the church in a lively procession, Ms. Dawn and Mr. Wright hugged each and every person. In the midst of all that laughter and friendship, I saw a familiar face in the crowd. I had to look twice, then three times and I almost strained my eyes looking because it wasn't my imagination. There was Robert holding Damian and David's hands, all of them smiling at Ms. Dawn. I couldn't believe my eyes. I walked slowly towards them and I wanted to shout, Ms. Dawn, your babies are here, all of them are here, but when I blinked and looked again, Ms. Dawn was kissing Mr. Wright and the babies were gone.

Reviews for *I Too Hear the Drums*

With a powerfully engaging style of narrative, Peta-Gaye Nash draws the reader into the lives of her characters, exploring with their innermost voices, the tensions of personal relationships and racial identity, set in the dual, conflicting worlds of North America and the Caribbean.

– *Fred W. Kennedy, educator, author of historical fiction,* Daddy Sharpe *(2008)*

Clever, fresh, and compelling. Peta-Gaye Nash's stories grip the reader with an intense and realistic desire to grab on for the wild up and down ride. The mix of Creole and standard English is done with professionalism and style. This collection is a first in many ways.

– *Mary Hanna, literary critic*

In this new collection of short stories, Peta-Gaye Nash reveals her power and grace as a writer, exploring important topics with an unflinching eye.

– *Sarah Pekkanen, author of* The Opposite of Me *(2010)*

www.ingramcontent.com/pod-product-compliance
Ingram Content Group UK Ltd.
Pitfield, Milton Keynes, MK11 3LW, UK
UKHW020142250726
13967UKWH00002B/804

9 781926 926445